Paul Birch was a modern detective. He worked in an office, never carried a gun, was on good terms with the police, and worked on cases involving embezzlement, missing person, and security plans. Murder was the last thing he wanted to get involved in despite his girlfriend's romantic ideas about what his job should be. So when he reluctantly agrees to look into what appears to be suicide, Dusty decides she should be involved a well, and that's when things start to get out of control.

Managansett Press

Don D'Ammassa is the author of:

Horror
Blood Beast
Servant of Chaos*
Caverns of Chaos*
Wings over Manhattan
The Gargoyle
That Way Madness Lies*
Little Evils*
Passing Death*
Date with the Dark*
The Devil Is in the Details

Science Fiction
Scarab
Haven
Narcissus
Translation Station
The Sinking Island*

Mysteries
Murder in Silverplate
Dead of Winter*
Death at the Art Gallery*

Fantasy
The Kaleidoscope*
Elaborate Lies*

Nonfiction
The Encyclopedia of Science Fiction
The Encyclopedia of Fantasy and Horror
The Encyclopedia of Adventure Fiction
Masters of Detection Vol I*
Masters of Detection Vol II*

*published by Managansett Press

DEATH AT THE ART GALLERY

Don D'Ammassa

Managansett Press

Managansett Press Edition 2015

DEATH AT
THE ART
GALLERY

CHAPTER ONE

Dusty and I had been seeing each other for a couple of months before she finally talked me into letting her visit my office. Her very first comment was that I needed to change the sign on my door, and that has been the refrain of our relationship ever since. It read then, and does now for that matter, "Birch Investigations," which is simple and accurate, but she has grander ideas thanks to an endearing but occasionally irritating excess of imagination. A valuable asset to her career as a writer but not always conducive to domestic peace and quiet.

"Paul Birch, Private Detective, sounds much better, don't you think?"

"Why not Private Eye?" I had responded lightly, the first time. "And with the silhouette of a Maltese falcon above crossed pistols. I could shave less often, buy myself a trench coat and keep a bottle of cheap scotch in the desk drawer. Of course that means I'd have to drink a lot and hang around with a lot of unsavory characters. Oh, and every once in a while I could let myself be knocked unconscious or get framed for a murder I didn't commit."

"I'm serious, Paul. Add a hint of intrigue to your image and your customers will remember and mention you to their friends."

"The last thing my customers want is intrigue. They want discretion and results, for which I charge them fees that fall slightly short of exorbitant. I've never carried a weapon on a job, I've never been shot at or assaulted or arrested, and I'm happy to say I don't have a running feud with the police. I'd rather keep things that way."

"Oh, you're no fun."

"This isn't supposed to be fun. This is supposed to be work."

I had introduced her to my staff. Steve was temping as my receptionist at the time, but I hired him a couple of weeks later when it was clear that Adrienne was not coming back. Tina Kirk has been with me almost from the start, a very good data analyst when she's not running from one office to the next, keeping our network functioning. Tina isn't antisocial and she usually isn't interested in relating to casual acquaintances, but she actually smiled and nodded before turning back to her screen, which was tantamount to a testimonial in Dusty's favor. Tina's focus on the job is extraordinary, sometimes obsessive, and I couldn't count the number of times I'd been forced to shoo her out of the office so we could lock up for the day. Barry Shaw, who joined the firm a couple of years after Tina, is my financial and accounting expert. He also wants me to change the sign on the door, but his is a more personal preference. He'd like it to be "Birch and Shaw." I've discovered that the best tactical response to his sorties on the subject is to ignore him; they've devolved into a kind of ritual but at the core Barry is serious, and ambitious.

Then we went upstairs to Merrilee's domain. Merrilee Brubaker is probably the most petite woman I've ever met, just barely five feet tall with bones so delicate that I took exaggerated care shaking her hand the first time we met. Unnecessarily, of course. Merrilee was tough minded and tough bodied. Her tongue was sharp enough to cut through steel and she had no trouble keeping the "kids" in line. The kids were my interns, part timers, and underachievers, varying between eight and twelve at any given time. The big cases we handled downstairs had nice fat fees, but they came at unpredictable intervals. The meat and potatoes of the operation were upstairs.

Remember those exciting movies about skip tracing, detectives tracking down missing witnesses or delinquent dads or people named in wills? Forget it. It was never that glamorous to start with, and in the age of the internet, it's mindlessly prosaic. Each of Merrilee's charges sits at a desk with a phone and a computer, processing requests from law firms, businesses, collection agencies, and private individuals. Most of the time it takes less than thirty minutes to come up with a current address, or an obituary. We handle about five hundred a week and our success rate is well over ninety percent. Dusty and Merrilee acted like old friends almost from the start, but I could tell that Dusty was disappointed by the banality of it all. Most people are; that's one reason we keep Merrilee's kids out of sight.

Dusty pretended to be impressed with our offices, but I could tell she was disappointed. I'm not sure what she expected—perhaps a weapons room, a rogues' gallery of villains we'd brought to heel, seedy furniture and an ashtray full of lipstick stained cigarette butts. What she saw instead was neatly kept work stations—except for Tina's—with a wireless network, a sophisticated interoffice intercom system, a server room, and a reception area that looks like it belongs in a medical clinic.

She was favorably impressed with my staff despite her disappointment that they weren't more colorful. Barry fancies himself something of a ladies' man and he flirted a little even though I was standing right there. None of us took it very seriously and I soon disengaged her and took her to the very last stop on her tour. My office.

"Now this is more like it."

I had to admit that I had made some minor concessions to the romantic. My framed license to practice was displayed prominently, but the rest of the walls were mostly decorated with posters from old movies—Humphrey Bogart as Sam Slade, Robert Mitchum and Powers Boothe, both in the role of Philip Marlowe, and William Powell and Myrna Loy as Nick and Nora Charles. Interspersed with the posters was a selection of black and white stills from similar films, Charlie Chan, the Saint, and Mr. Moto. I have a large collection of movie memorabilia and this had seemed the most appropriate place to display these particular items. In fact, Dusty and I had first met at a noir film festival, during a break in the marathon Lone Wolf program.

"Dusty, the most exciting and dangerous work we get is the occasional divorce case, and I don't even take those unless things are unusually slow. Most of our time is spent going through financial statements, decoding computer files, tracing titles, preparing depositions for court battles, and sifting through paperwork. Once in a while we do a little clandestine surveillance, but most of that is static—hidden cameras or recorders. I doubt very much that I could follow anyone without being spotted and I've never once called all the suspects together to reveal the identity of the villain."

"You make it sound so dull."

"It is dull. I like it that way." And I do. But you can't always have what you want.

It was about six months after Dusty's first visit that Kari Spencer walked into my office. Dusty and I had been living together for less than two weeks at that point and we were still bumping into each other's corners, gradually wearing them smooth. She was still after me to change the company name—it had become a running joke between us—and she and Tina occasionally met for lunch, which I found astonishing. Tina's lunch box almost seemed like part of her office decor. When she ran into Barry, he pretended to be hitting on her. At least, I think he was pretending, since he wasn't bothered if I happened to be within earshot. On that particular morning she'd finished off the milk before I had my coffee and the line at the donut shop was so long that I'd driven away in disgust. I was not in a good mood.

Steve had properly gauged my frame of mind within seconds of my arrival, possibly because my normally cheery "Good morning!" had been replaced by a peremptory demand for coffee. I was fuming in my office when he brought it in, the cup precariously balanced in his lap as he steered his wheelchair through the doorway. Steve lost both of his legs in Afghanistan.

The prospect of coffee was soothing and I felt a twinge of guilt for my earlier surliness. "Thanks. What's on this morning's schedule?" I tried to sound more pleasant but the sound that emerged was still rough.

Steve set the coffee on the corner of my desk and I resisted the urge to lunge for it and gulp it down. "Three more boxes of paperwork arrived from the Gideon estate. Barry is going to drop them off at Carson's so she can start cataloguing them. Tina is still working on those spreadsheets from the Merrivale case but with the date stamps all questionable, she's not sure she can prove anything even though we know it was fraud. Zoe Clark called to tell you she's not having much luck finding the Bencolin kid but she's still looking. And you have an appointment at ten. Potential new client."

"Representing who?"

Steve shook his head. "Herself, apparently. Name's Kari Spencer. She said it was a personal matter."

I grimaced. "Probably another wandering husband. That makes five this month." And I had turned down the first four. So far I'd managed to avoid having a gun pointed in my direction, but I'd been verbally threatened three times in my career, and in each instance it had been a divorce case. I charged much more for divorce work than my competition, deliberately. It was obviously very profitable and I'd done a lot of it when I was younger, but now that I could afford to be finicky, I tried to stay away from anything sordid. It was dangerous, tedious, and depressing. We had an adequate if not comfortable workload at the moment and I expected to recommend that Mrs. Spencer try one of the agencies which were more comfortable with that sort of work.

"She corrected me when I called her Mrs. Spencer. She's not married."

Which still left a philandering boyfriend as a possibility. Or girlfriend, for that matter. Steve handed me the monthly financials and I took a deep breath and plunged in. We'd closed a couple of big cases the previous month, both for well known local companies. Unfortunately, our biggest clients were almost always our slowest payers. Factor in our receivables and the bottom line was pretty good. Our cash situation was less enviable; big law firms will slap a whopping interest charge if you're late with a check, but they'll let an invoice sit unpaid for six months or more. I'd reinvested most of last year's profits and in retrospect I should probably have held back a larger cushion. Unlike Philip Marlowe, we wouldn't be falling behind in the office rent—I owned the building—but I wouldn't be buying myself a company car any time soon.

The intercom buzzed a while later, just as I was finishing a second cup of coffee. "Miss Spencer is here, Mr. Birch."

"I'll be right out."

There was a mirror near the office door. Just a mirror, not one way glass. I adjusted my tie and glanced up at Bogart. Dusty says I look a little like him but I don't see it. I think I'm better looking. I wiggled my upper lip. Definitely better looking.

Kari Spencer was sitting in the lobby, legs crossed, staring absently to one side. She stood up immediately when she saw me, her expression serious but calm. I estimated that she was somewhere in her early to mid-twenties, mildly attractive but nothing out of the ordinary. She was tastefully and, I suspected, expensively dressed, blouse, sweater, skirt, with an oversized shoulder bag that looked like genuine leather.

"Good morning, Miss Spencer. I'm Paul Birch." We shook hands. Her grip was firm, confident. "Can we get you something? Coffee? Tea?"

"No, nothing for me thanks." There was a hint of agitation in her voice but I couldn't tell if it was nervousness or impatience.

"Let's go into my office then."

I took my time getting settled behind the desk, surreptitiously studying my prospective client. Sometimes you can get a good feel for a situation by paying attention to how someone acts when they first arrive. If they sit too far back in the seat, then they're on the defensive, or they're frightened, or they don't really want to be there. If they sit too far forward, it usually means that they're angry or aggressive, used to being in control of a situation, poised to make demands. One of my business clients routinely pulls his chair close enough that he can lay his hands on my desk, a perhaps unconscious effort to assert his own authority. Sometimes their reaction to the film posters was suggestive as well.

Kari Spencer ignored the posters, or perhaps didn't even notice them. She appeared to be relaxed and alert but not impatient or upset. Probably not a cheating boyfriend, then.

"How can we help you, Miss Spencer?"

I'm not sure what I was expecting. There was no wedding ring, but she might be divorced. Delinquent alimony was more common than you might think. Or she might want a missing person found, a friend or relative who'd gone missing, but not in such a way that the police would be interested. She was attractive, so another possibility was sexual harassment, on the job or elsewhere. A year earlier we'd helped a slightly older woman prove her case against her employer. In a moment of partial prescience, I wondered if possibly she'd been adopted as a child and wanted to find her biological parents. There'd been a rash of such inquiries during the past year, but I'd only accepted one case where there was a physiological problem that justified having the records opened. It's almost impossible otherwise. What she said next caught me completely by surprise.

"I want you to find out who murdered my uncle."

For a second or two, I wondered if this young woman was a friend of Dusty's, someone she'd talked into helping her with a practical joke. I had only once been approached to investigate a suspicious death, and it had been obvious from the outset that Evan Mallory had died of natural causes and that his widow lacked a firm grip on reality. But there was no hint of amusement in Kari Spencer's face. She was deadly serious and, I sensed, fiercely angry.

I cleared my throat. "Miss Spencer, murder investigations are conducted by the police or the FBI. Despite what you might see on television or in the movies, private investigators rarely get involved in criminal cases, at least those involving violence. The police don't want us muddying the waters and, frankly, we aren't equipped with the necessary resources or forensic capabilities."

"I understand that perfectly, Mr. Birch. But it doesn't apply in this situation."

I blinked and I think my professional smile slipped a bit. "And why is that?"

"Because there is no police investigation, at least not any more. The medical examiner declared it a suicide and the police are no longer interested."

"But you think it was murder."

She shook her head. "I know it was murder, Mr. Birch. My uncle would never have killed himself."

I suppressed the urge to sigh. This already sounded like a no-win situation. Relatives never believed that their loved ones would have taken their own lives. If Kari Spencer was determined to believe that her uncle hadn't killed himself, then it was unlikely that she would accept any information I uncovered that didn't corroborate her opinion. And if the medical examiner's verdict was correct, as it almost certainly was, there was very little chance that I would find any contrary evidence sufficient to satisfy her or move the authorities into reopening the case.

"With all due respect to your feelings, Miss Spencer, the police usually aren't wrong in cases like this."

"I expected you to be skeptical, Mr. Birch. You don't have to waltz around the issue. I'm not asking you to accept my opinion rather than the medical examiner's. What I am asking is that you investigate and draw your own conclusions."

I settled back into my seat. "Tell me a little more about the circumstances of your uncle's death."

She seemed to relax slightly as she launched into what was almost certainly a prepared summation. "My uncle was Walter Spencer, the sculptor. You might have heard of him." She paused until I shook my head. "He was quite well known at one time, but he hasn't been able to work much these past few years. He had arthritis in his hands among other things. The doctors were able to eliminate some of the pain, but they couldn't do anything about the trembling."

I made a mental note that she'd just suggested a perfectly good motive for suicide. "How old was your uncle?"

"Seventy-two. Uncle Walter was one of the partners in a very successful art gallery in Providence, the Tontine." That name rang a bell. I'd driven past it a few times although I'd never been inside. "There were five partners when he died, but originally there were two more. Both of them passed away some years back."

"Who inherits your uncle's share of the business?'

Her eyes flashed. "That's the interesting part. His share gets divided equally among the surviving partners, just as they all divided up the shares of the two who died earlier. That's how the studio got its name. A tontine is a kind of shared will."

"Actually it's more like a game," I contradicted her. "They were popular in the 19th Century in various forms. The most common was as you just described it. A group of people pooled part or all of their wealth so that whoever lived the longest ended up with everything invested in the tontine. Another variation was for each member to choose an outside party as his playing piece, and the sponsor of the last survivor won the pool. The incitement to mischief in such cases should be obvious."

She leaned forward, her face showing considerable animation. "Exactly, Mr. Birch. The four surviving owners each had an excellent motive for killing him."

I shook my head. "The fact that someone had something to gain from your uncle's death doesn't mean that he was murdered. What about the rest of his estate, for example? Who inherited that?"

"As a matter of fact, I did." She met my eyes steadily. "We were very close, Mr. Birch. My uncle raised me after my mother died."

"What about your father?"

"He was otherwise preoccupied." There was more than a hint of resentment, and I quickly changed the subject.

"Where and how did your uncle die?"

"He was at the Tontine. He had an office there, and a small studio, although I don't suppose he used that any more. Uncle Walt referred to himself as a 'retired artist'. He enjoyed talking to the customers and making suggestions about how the galleries should be arranged although Avery, that's Avery Carr, made most of the routine decisions."

"Is Carr another of the partners?"

She nodded. "He's more or less the manager as well. He was never as successful as the others and some time ago, at least ten years, they appointed him manager and gave him a relatively free hand. Earl Garner only comes in once a year for the annual board meeting now, and I don't think Kristina Kwan is actively involved any more either. Michelle—that's Michelle Bernstein - has a studio in the back."

I had heard of Kristina Kwan, but the other names rang no bells. "Doesn't Kwan design jewelry?" Dusty sometimes wore a pendant with a fancy double "K" inscribed on the back. She wasn't into gaudy very much and the anomaly had made this item memorable.

"Yes, among other things. She's gone very commercial. Uncle Walter made fun of her sometimes, but I think he was a little bit jealous."

We'd strayed from the point, but I was just being polite. I had no intention of taking this case and planned only to ask a few questions so that Miss Spencer didn't feel as though I was dismissing her out of hand, even if I was. "So your uncle was in his office when he died?"

"Yes. It happened some time on a Sunday night between 11:00 PM and 1:00 in the morning. The gallery was closed on the following Monday so he wasn't found until Tuesday when the cleaning service came in."

"And the date?"

She told me. Almost six weeks had passed.

"Was he missed at all on Monday?"

She shook her head. "No, he lives by himself. I moved out when I left for college and when I came back to Providence I wanted a place of my own."

"All right, how exactly was he killed?"

"He was shot through the head." For the first time, I heard just the faintest hint of a quaver in her voice. "The gun was lying on the floor beside him and it had his fingerprints on it. No one else's. But that doesn't prove anything. It could all have been faked."

She was right, but it wasn't as easy as she implied. The fingerprints had to be where they would have been if the decedent had actually gripped the weapon, and the angle of the bullet would raise eyebrows if it didn't conform to a very specific pattern.

Suicides don't shoot themselves between the eyes, for example. Try holding a toy gun in that position and you'll understand why.

"Was there a suicide note?"

She shook her head. "No, and that's another reason why I'm convinced it was murder. Uncle Walter was a very good man, Mr. Birch, but like most artists, he had an oversized ego. He loved being the center of attention and I can't imagine him giving the last performance of his life without providing liner notes." She dropped her eyes. "Sorry, that sounds facetious, but it's the kind of thing Uncle Walter would have said."

"It might be that he felt no explanation was necessary, Miss Spencer. Your uncle was in at least occasional pain, lived alone, could no longer work in the profession he loved. There may well have been other problems that you aren't aware of. It's entirely possible that he decided to take his own life."

Kari abruptly turned to her shoulder bag and opened it. I waited patiently as she fished around inside, then drew out a small plastic prescription bottle and set it on my desk.

"What's that?"

"I took that from my uncle's medicine cabinet. It was his escape route."

"Escape route?" But I already suspected what she was about to tell me.

"His arthritis was treatable but not curable, and the doctor told him it would get worse, not better. He was pretty stoic about it but I visited him on one of his really bad days last year. He was wearing his slippers because he couldn't manage his shoes and he'd already taken the limit on his medication. My uncle was a vibrant, active man all his life. Seeing him like that was a shock. I'm afraid I wasn't very good about it; I started to cry because I knew he wasn't ever going to get better and I didn't see how he could stand to be in so much pain. He ended up soothing me, Mr. Birch, and told me that he was too stubborn to be stopped by a little discomfort. And then he let me in on his little secret. If the arthritis ever got too bad and went on too long, he had an escape route. This was it." She pointed to the plastic bottle. "I don't know exactly what they are. Some kind of sleeping pills, I imagine. But if Uncle Walter had wanted to go, this is the way he would have done it. He would never have blown his brains all over the 17th Century oriental carpet that he was so fond of showing off to visitors."

"I assume you've said all of this to the police?"

She sighed. "Detective Harris appreciated the fact that I was reluctant to accept that my uncle killed himself, but without any evidence to the contrary, he was unable, not to say unwilling, to disregard the medical examiner's conclusions."

"Let's say just for the sake of argument that I agree with you that some of the circumstances of his death are at least open to question if not actively suspicious. I still don't see that there's anything we can do to help you. As I've already pointed out, the police are far better equipped to evaluate the physical evidence and they apparently found nothing to warrant a closer look. I can have my staff review the police reports if you want, but it would probably be just a waste of our time and your money."

She shook her head. "That's not what I'm looking for. I was referred to you, Mr. Birch, by Robert Osterville. You remember him, don't you?'

"Yes, of course." Bob Osterville had hired us shortly after inheriting his father's business. Although a routine audit of the books had uncovered no irregularities, he was certain that there should have been more assets. He was right. The managing director and the CFO had found an almost undetectable way to reclassify some inventory as obsolete or damaged and sell it to themselves at a discounted rate, only to resell it to Osterville Inc again at full cost as a subcontractor.

"Bob said you had good instincts and that if there was any irregularity at the Tontine, you would be able to find out."

Normally I welcome referrals, but only when they're viable. "Do you have any reason to believe that's the case?"

For the first time, she seemed uncertain of her ground. "Not exactly. But there was a lot of tension there, infighting. It's been going on for at least a few years now and it's been getting steadily worse. Uncle Walter wouldn't tell me much, but I know that he was more and more upset about it. Toward the end he even hinted that the gallery might have to shut down."

I sat back in my chair, trying to look more interested than I actually was. "If I understand you correctly, your uncle's interest in the Tontine went to his partners."

"That's right. The surviving partners only, of course."

"I'm sorry, but if you have no financial interest, then you have no leverage. The remaining owners would be perfectly justified in refusing to even allow me an interview, let alone an audit. Without access to their financial records, there's very little chance of discovering any misfeasance."

She leaned forward, her face suddenly animated. "What if one of them did agree?"

I felt as though I'd just stepped into a trap. "I suppose that would depend upon the nature of their partnership agreement. If he or she had sufficient authority..." I let the sentence hang.

"I've spoken to Avery Carr and he's willing to cooperate. He hasn't said he agrees with me but he wants to clear the air, and I think he also suspects that Uncle didn't kill himself. He just won't admit it."

"That still doesn't mean the other partners will cooperate."

"Maybe not, but Avery's the managing director. None of them wants the job so they won't fight him, not too hard anyway. And since I'm paying you, not the Tontine, there really shouldn't be any objection from the others."

That didn't mean they wouldn't object, of course. I still wasn't crazy about it. The odds were pretty good that Kari Spencer was wrong, that her uncle really had killed himself, that I wouldn't find anything suspicious in the operation of the art gallery, and that I would be forced to charge her a hefty sum for essentially no return. My services don't come cheap and I like to provide good value for the money. This wasn't my kind of case.

"I'll be completely frank with you, Miss Spencer. I think you'd be wasting your money to pursue this further."

"That seems to be everyone's opinion, Mr. Birch. But it's my money and I'll waste it if I want to. All I'm asking is that you speak to each of the partners and anyone else you think necessary and draw your own conclusions. Will you take the case or shall I try elsewhere?"

I hesitated. Sooner or later, probably sooner, she would find an agency willing to accept her money. They might even conduct a cursory investigation. On the other hand, we weren't particularly busy at the moment and I was sympathetic to Miss Spencer's loyalty to her uncle. "I'll compromise with you. I'll do a preliminary survey, talk to Mr. Carr, review the police reports, look around a little. That'll take a couple of days. I'll let you know what I've found out and what I recommend, and then we can discuss whether or not it's worth pursuing the matter further. Is that agreeable?"

"Perfectly." She reached for her bag, removed several folded sheets of typescript and placed them on my desk. "That's all the information I have on the four partners. I'll call Avery and tell him about our arrangement, and there's a letter of introduction there as well. I assume you'll want a retainer?"

I touched a button on the intercom, summoning Steve. "My secretary will take care of that on your way out. I have to caution you once more not to read too much into this. People sometimes act impulsively and irrationally, particularly when they're in pain or under stress. Your uncle probably did kill himself, Miss Spencer." I stood up.

Steve pushed the door open but she hesitated a moment longer. "There's one other thing I should tell you. About my uncle, I mean."

She fell silent and I finally prompted her. "Yes, Miss Spencer?"

"Uncle Walter used to be married to one of the other partners, Kristina Kwan. She was twenty and he was almost forty at the time. It didn't last long and the breakup was unusually civilized. They were still friends after a fashion. Neither of them ever re-married and about three years ago they started seeing each other again, romantically I mean. There was even talk about making it permanent, at least on his side. I don't know if she felt the same way at the time. But then something happened about six months ago. Uncle wouldn't tell me about it but they'd obviously had some kind of falling out. And as far as I know, they never spoke to each other again."

"Are you suggesting that Miss Kwan killed your uncle?"

She shook her head. "I'm not suggesting anything, Mr. Birch, but she was the only one of the partners who didn't go to his funeral. Even Earl Garner came, and he almost never leaves his place in the mountains."

"I'll speak to her, if I can. She's under no obligation to cooperate, you realize?"

"Oh, she'll talk to you. She won't want to be left out of the loop. Just be careful she doesn't get more information than she gives." And with that she turned and left.

It was pretty evident that Kari Spencer didn't much like her uncle's ex-wife. I wondered why.

CHAPTER TWO

Dusty shouted at me from the second floor the moment I opened the door. "If you go into the dining room, don't knock over the Eiffel Tower. I spent most of the afternoon getting everything set up right."

That may not be the kind of greeting most people hear when they get home from work, but I've adjusted to Dusty's idiosyncrasies rather quickly if I do say so myself, and I took this latest in stride. Of course, with a lead in like that, I had to go look into the dining room. The oversized redwood dining table I'd inherited from my mother had been stripped of its damask cloth and was now covered by an array of unidentifiable shapes most of them constructed from children's building blocks, Lincoln Logs, and Tinkertoys.

Darla appeared in the opposite doorway, gave a perfunctory sniff at the table, then wandered over to brush against my leg. Darla is a buff colored stray cat who moved in with me two years ago. She tolerates Dusty, barely, but is quite obviously my cat and not our cat. And no, she doesn't help me solve cases unless you count the fact that having her around helps me to relax.

Dusty hadn't made an appearance yet so I raised my voice so that she could hear me. "Let me guess. You're building a particle accelerator out of wood."

I jumped as she touched my shoulder from behind, having descended silently in her stocking feet. "Don't make fun. You have your ways of getting a job done and I have mine. This is a working model." She slipped past me and walked slowly along one side of the table, admiring her handiwork.

"Couldn't you have used the kitchen table? I like eating in here."

Ignoring me, she continued her slow circuit around the room. When she reached the end of the table across from me, she pointed at the tallest structure. "That's the Eiffel Tower there, and see, this is the Champs Elysees, and over there are the Tuileries and the Louvre."

A faint glimmer of light stained my mental horizon. "This is Paris? I never thought of it as quite so lumpy."

Dusty nodded vigorously. "Daniel Craig followed Beaulieu to Paris but he still doesn't know who has the jewels. And the Pirelli brothers are after them both, along with the rogue Interpol agent."

This is probably a good time to mention that Dusty makes a tolerably good income as a freelance writer. Her latest project is an international crime thriller, which she hopes will be the first in a series.

"And that explains all of this how?"

"It's a visual aid. Look this is Craig right here." She pointed to a toy soldier standing in front of the Louvre. "And these are the Pirelli brothers." Her hand moved to the far side of the Tuileries. "It helps me keep track of things if I can come down and see where everyone is in relation to everyone else."

"You couldn't just have written up a time line?"

She gave me a dirty look. "That wouldn't have been half as much fun. So how did your day go?'

Dusty had been living with me for only a few weeks now, but we'd adjusted to each other with surprisingly little trouble. My house was larger than it needed to be, but I've always liked having lots of space and we were far enough out of Providence that I'd been able to buy it at a reasonable price. Dusty had converted one of the guest rooms into an office, and it was now crowded with two desks, one for each of her computers, three filing cabinets, and an elaborate stereo system. She'd lined all the walls with shelves which were now filled to the bursting point with reference books, CDs, and occasional paperback novels, all arranged apparently haphazardly although she insisted they were grouped by mood, whatever that meant. Despite my occasional teasing about her informal lifestyle, Dusty works hard, a minimum of six hours a day and usually considerably more. I manage to pry her loose on weekends most of the time, but not always.

I left Paris for the kitchen with Dusty in my wake. "Closed out two cases and sent the bills. The first client is going to be unhappy; we didn't find any evidence of irregularities by his business manager. I think he wanted an excuse to fire the woman. Costs are up, business is slow, and profits drop. It's a simple formula but some people just don't get it. The second should be satisfied though. We figured out who was stealing finished items and how they were doing it. One of the stock clerks would drop it out a window into a dumpster in the alley and come back later to pick it up. Nelson Kidd got it all on video tape the second night he staked the place out."

"Sounds pretty dull." She stood watching as I opened the refrigerator and took out the salmon steaks I'd left to defrost.

"Dull but profitable." I poked around, looking for the leftover Hollandaise. "And in my business, dull is a good thing. Your man Craig has some government agency to pay all his bills, and he can risk his life because he's got the author on his side."

"So do you. Have the author on your side, I mean. This author, at least." She put her arm around my shoulders as I squatted, still unable to find the Hollandaise. "What are you looking for?"

I told her.

"Oops! Had it for lunch."

I straightened up. "You had Hollandaise sauce for lunch?"

Her eyebrows went up. "Not by itself. I melted it on some green beans."

"Those very same green beans I told you we were going to have with the salmon tonight?"

"Oops again. There's a package of lima beans in the freezer."

"It's not the same," I pouted.

"Don't be a grump, just because you have an unfulfilling job and get bored is no reason to let it affect your home life."

"It's not unfulfilling. It's very rewarding. Today wasn't boring at all in fact. I'll have you know that I was offered a murder case today. And by an attractive young woman."

I'm very discreet about my work, and I also dislike taking it home with me. Although I sometimes talked to Dusty about cases we were working on, I never mentioned names and sometimes fudged the facts so that she wouldn't be able to recognize who my clients were. To be honest, it wasn't all that difficult because she rarely showed any particular interest in fraud, embezzlement, or similar white collar crimes. When I had once suggested that I could provide her with a sophisticated plot for a murder mystery involving intricate manipulations of a corporation's accounting system, she had leaned over and patted me on the knee. "Paul dear, the idea is to make the stories interesting enough that people actually want to buy them."

"A murder? Really?" Her face lit up like a Christmas tree.

"You don't have to sound so happy about it." I carried the frozen lima beans and the salmon over to the stove. "Besides, it probably wasn't actually a murder and I'm not sure I'm going to take the case anyway."

"Why not and why not?"

"Because the police have already determined that it was a suicide and there's no real reason to believe otherwise. And I'm not taking it if I think it's a complete waste of the client's money."

"But you are considering it." Dusty had dropped the light tone and switched to inquisitorial.

"There are some aspects that might fit well with our expertise. The dead man was a partner in a profitable business and there's a possibility that something fishy was going on there. It's more likely that the suicide resulted from an unwillingness to face some kind of personal crisis. He was an older man, he had health issues, his only relative was a niece who had drifted away in recent years, and a winter romance had just gone awry. Odds are he did shoot himself despite what the niece thinks."

"The dead man wouldn't be Walter Spencer, would it?"

Dusty, whose real name was Emily Rhodes although she wrote under two or three different pseudonyms, had surprised me more than once during the few months that we'd known each other. But I think this was the first instance that left me momentarily speechless. "How in the world did you guess that?" I asked at last.

Her face twisted into an expression of exaggerated smugness. "I have clandestine sources. In this case, the *Providence Journal*, to say nothing of the evening news. If you bothered to read the papers yourself, you'd know that. Walter Spencer was a prominent sculptor and part owner of the Tontine Art Gallery over on the East Side. I've been to the gallery a couple of times, actually, but everything there is way out of my price range. Anyway, he was found dead in his office there a couple of months ago. The papers said he hadn't been able to work for the last few years because of a serious health problem and that he'd been depressed. It was on the front page when it first happened and there was a feature on him in the arts section a few days later. If you actually read the newspaper instead of skimming to the financials, you'd know about it."

"I read the newspapers," I said defensively.

"No, you read the business section, the editorials, and occasionally the front page. You skim through the rest just to make sure you get your money's worth."

"Point taken."

"I don't remember if they mentioned how he did it."

"Shot himself."

"Easy enough to fake."

"Don't start. I really don't want to talk about it right now. I'm hungry."

I whipped up an entirely unsatisfactory cream sauce and we opened a bottle of Zinfandel to drink with supper. Dusty knows when to give me space and we spoke only of inconsequential things until the food was gone. She split what was left of the wine between our glasses, then sat back in her chair, holding her glass with both hands, an amused expression on her face.

"You're going to take the case, aren't you?"

It was no use pretending that I didn't know what she was talking about. "I'm going to do a preliminary survey. That's all. If I don't do it, the client will just keep contacting agencies until she finds someone willing to take her money. At least I can try to minimize the damage."

"Who's your client, anyway? The niece, or another family member?"

"If you read the newspapers," I answered haughtily, "you'd have known that he died a bachelor. And childless. And don't bother asking again. You know I can't tell you the client's name."

"That's okay. I'll figure it out."

I had spent the balance of that day at the office clearing up loose ends and trying not to think about my new, provisional client. Steve ordered lunch for me and I ate a sandwich while reading quickly through the handful of typed pages Kari had left behind. It was all background information, except for the last page which was a photocopy of the disposition page of the police report, and the first, which was a letter to Avery Carr identifying me as Kari's agent and requesting that he provide any help within his power. The investigating officer, Detective Raymond Harris, had left himself some wiggle room but essentially had deferred to the medical examiner's judgment. The trajectory, powder burns, bruising, position of the body and the weapon, were all consistent with a self inflicted gunshot wound.

The brief history of the Tontine Art Gallery was only marginally more interesting. It had been founded in 1970 by seven independent artists, all of whom had until then enjoyed marginally successful careers. For the first decade they had shown only their own work, but beginning in the early 1980s they had acted as agents for other artists as well. The most famous of the seven was, or rather had been, Peter Trentano, whose canvases had commanded impressive prices during the 1980s and even greater ones following his death—lung cancer—in 1991. The oldest, Phyllis Reynolds, died in an automobile accident less than a year later. The four surviving partners were Avery Carr, who served as manager of the gallery, Kristina Kwan, Earl Garner, and Michelle Bernstein.

After we'd cleared away the dishes, Dusty and I adjourned to the screening room, my name for the home theater I'd had installed in what had formerly been the den. I suppose it was wasteful to use such a high end sound system when most of the movies I watched were produced before 1960, but even monaural sounded better when it was carried on first class equipment. Tonight we were watching George Sanders as Gay Lawrence in *A Date with the Falcon*, but it wasn't one of the better entries in the series and the Falcon's complicated troubles with his female companions didn't hold my interest. My thoughts kept returning to the morning's interview and the documents I'd read during the afternoon. This wasn't at all my kind of case and I had begun to feel guilty even agreeing to conduct a tentative investigation. I was aware enough of my own chauvinism to suspect that I'd allowed myself to be influenced by my reaction to the client and not to the facts.

The credits began to roll up the screen. Dusty leaned over and nudged my shoulder. "That last scene almost made up for the dull plot."

I perked up. "Yeah, I guess so. I liked Sanders better as the Saint."

"But he looked really impressive when he wrestled his girl away from the gorilla and carried her to safety by swinging on those vines. And the special effects when the flying saucer landed were surprisingly good for 1941."

I blinked. "Huh?"

"You stopped paying attention halfway through, Paul."

"I guess I'm just tired. I didn't sleep too well last night."

"That wasn't my fault."
I grinned at her. "Oh yes it was."

Dusty was up before me in the morning. I heard her pecking away at the keyboard when I passed her office and found a pot of coffee waiting for me in the kitchen. She had put food down for Darla, who was sitting to one side, waiting for me to certify that it was okay before she'd eat it. I nudged the bowl with my foot, which was our secret approval code, and she deigned to try a taste. Fortified with caffeine, I showered and dressed and then went to say good morning before leaving for work. There was no answer when I knocked on her door and called her name, but I found her downstairs, hunting through the closet for a jacket.

"Going out before you've typed your quota for the day?"
She gave me a quick smile. "Research. I won't be long."
"You will be if you're going to Paris."
"Not quite that far. I'll tell you about it later. You're going to be late for work."
I helped her slip into her jacket and the closeness was stimulating. "I'm the boss, remember? By definition, I'm never late. In fact, I don't think I need to leave for another hour."
She pushed me away. "Down boy. We both have work to do. But don't lose that thought."

I did check in at the office, but only long enough to be certain that there was nothing there requiring my immediate attention. I folded Kari Spencer's letter of introduction and put it in my jacket pocket, told Steve to keep the staff in line, and then went for a drive.

The East Side of Providence is a sometimes uneasy mix of cultures and lifestyles. Brown University and the Rhode Island School of Design attract a steady flow of foreign students as well as our native brand of domestic nonconformists, interspersed with frighteningly earnest would-be professionals. Student and faculty housing are intermixed and have spread down toward the river where much of the city's wealthy population lives in homes that go for half a million dollars or more, while on the city side Benefit Street is partly lined with well preserved colonial buildings, each identified by an historical society plaque. Both schools have been spreading into the downtown as elderly buildings abandoned by their original owners lose their viability as offices and shops and end up as dormitories, classrooms, and studios. Coffee shops, a variety of restaurants specializing in foreign cuisines, music stores, and antique dealers are all mixed together in a handful of commercial strips scattered through the area, which is often clogged by traffic, both vehicular and pedestrian.

It didn't take long to find the Tontine, although it was further away from the downtown than I remembered. It took almost as long again to find a parking space reasonably close. The fall term was about to start and students and their families were busily moving personal goods from cars and vans into apartments, condominiums, and dormitories. I ended up walking three blocks, which wasn't bad except that a pesky wind kept blowing grit into my face and I had to walk with my face half turned to avoid sand blasting.

The Tontine dominated its block, flanked by a bagel shop on one side and a small furniture store on the other. There were three paintings and an elaborate display of handmade jewelry visible through the front windows. The paintings included a landscape, a bizarre still life in which each object was almost but not quite recognizable, and an abstract piece that looked like a printed circuit with an overlay of spaghetti sauce. I tried the door, found it locked, and belatedly noticed that the gallery didn't open until ten. A quick glance at my watch told me I had almost half an hour to kill, so I had a bagel with cream cheese, plain and plain thank you, and a rather good cup of coffee.

I returned to the door still a few minutes early but it was unlocked this time and I stepped into a small carpeted lobby with subdued lighting. Directly facing me and mounted on a column well above my head was an elaborately framed painting whose significance struck me immediately. Seven people in medieval costume sat at an elaborate, circular table. Three of the figures were female and four were male, and one of each gender had slumped forward over their dinners. A brass placard beneath the painting identified it as The Tontine.

A very thin young woman with unflattering glasses and her hair tied back in a bun appeared from one of the two corridors which branched away from the column. "Oh, hello! Welcome to the

Tontine. We're not actually open for another few minutes yet but you're welcome to come in and enjoy the artwork." She shifted her weight back and forth from one foot to the other, her eyes downcast.

"Actually I was hoping to speak to the manager, Mr. Carr."

"Oh!" She looked briefly unsettled. "I'm sorry. Mr. Carr isn't in yet."

"But you expect him?" I prompted.

"Yes, certainly. He should be here very soon. Would you like to wait in our reception area?" She gestured in the direction from which she'd just come.

"I'll just look around a little if that's all right."

"Certainly. If you need anything, I'll be at my desk. My name is Wanda."

The gallery was larger than I expected, extending all the way through the block, although the rear was closed off. There were four separate display rooms on the right hand side of the central corridor, three more plus the office/reception area on the left, with two larger rooms at the rear, each marked "Studio: No Admittance". The main corridor was interrupted by three staircases, two leading to the second floor, the third to a basement. All three were roped off with "No Admittance" signs. The seven rooms were each named after one of the partners, but only Kwan, Bernstein, and Trentano contained material produced exclusively by their namesakes. Each of the others displayed work by a variety of other artists as well as by the relevant partner. Reynolds had been dead for years and was represented only by a dozen black and white photographs, copies of her two published books, and one small portrait of three fishermen standing on a dock, but Trentano's paintings filled his room, at least in part because the canvases were so large. There was only enough space to display five of them, one on each wall and two mounted back to back on a sturdy partition in the center of the room. All five were elaborate, landscapes whose trees and hills seemed to shift position when I moved. I vaguely recalled that Trentano was famous for his lighting effects but to my unpracticed eye they just seemed dark and muddled.

Of all the work displayed, it was Michelle Bernstein's slightly surreal paintings that appealed to me the most. Every object was recognizable and reproduced in sometimes astonishing detail, but their arrangement was frequently striking. A galleon sailed across a sea of cloud above a modern urban landscape in one, for example, and in another a flight of birds made unlikely patterns in a red sky above a landscape whose trees were arranged to suggest a congregation of humans.

I was examining Earl Garner's dark and indistinct studies of decaying farms and snow covered hills when the receptionist—who now wore a name tag that read "Wanda"—found me.

"Mr. Carr is in his office now, sir. May I ask your name?"

I took out one of my business cards and handed it to her. "Please tell him that I'm representing Miss Kari Spencer and that I won't take up much of his time."

Wanda went away and I had time to look at another couple of paintings before she returned. "Mr. Carr will see you, Mr. Birch."

She led me to the front stairway and unhooked the rope. "Turn left at the top of the stairs. His office is right there." Her smile was just the faintest bit uncertain.

The stairs were thickly carpeted and I couldn't help noticing that it would be very easy to climb them without making enough noise to alert anyone above that they were no longer alone. When I reached the landing I turned to my left. There were two doors visible, one open and one closed. I was halfway to the open one when Avery Carr stepped out.

"You must be Mr. Birch. Please come in."

Carr was a few inches shorter than me, and a few pounds heavier. Not fat, but definitely drifting toward the shores of obesity. He was wearing a three piece suit and had his hair expertly styled to disguise the fact that he was going bald. If he'd been an actor in one of the movies I watched, he'd have been the hero's valet, perhaps providing a bit of comic relief.

I followed him through the door. Carr's office was quietly luxurious and almost obsessively neat. A quartz and gold pen and pencil set with matching clock were the only items on his glass-topped, teakwood desk. The walls were covered with framed paintings, or perhaps prints, in a variety of styles. There was a computer at a workstation in one corner, but the monitor was covered and it was obviously powered down. The desk itself was old, ornately appointed, but in excellent condition.

"Please have a seat, Mr. Birch. I imagine I know why you're here."

"I have a letter of introduction from Miss Spencer." I started to fumble in my pocket as he took his own seat, but he waved me to the chair.

"I'll take your word for it. Kari told me she was going to hire an investigator to look into her uncle's death."

"She indicated that you supported her, or at least felt that there were unresolved issues."

He sighed and sat back in his chair, his weight making the springs complain audibly. "When someone takes his own life, there are always unresolved issues."

"Then you don't think he was murdered?"

"Walter had not been a happy man of late. I don't think it probable that someone killed him, but I can't rule out the possibility."

"Do you know of anyone who might have had a good reason to want him dead?"

"No, but what might seem an insufficient reason to you or I might be more than adequate for someone else. Walter was not always the easiest person to get along with but I'm not aware of any extraordinary animosities. He left behind a not inconsiderable estate, I believe, but Kari herself was the chief beneficiary."

"Other than his share of the gallery."

Carr acknowledged this with a nod. "And he did die here, of course. The police entertained the same suspicion. I'm not sure that Detective Harris was completely satisfied. He seemed to have an innately suspicious nature, but I suppose that's a prerequisite for his job. And for yours as well, I imagine."

"I'm not suspicious, Mr. Carr, at least not yet. I'm just trying to decide whether or not there is sufficient reason to justify a formal investigation. May I ask why you've taken Miss Spencer's part in this?"

"But I haven't. I simply want the young lady to have some peace of mind. I think Walter killed himself. He was in a great deal of pain and he wasn't able to work. Other than his niece he had no surviving family. I know for a fact that he was being treated for depression as well as arthritis. If I was surprised at all it was the way he chose to end it. I didn't even know that he owned a handgun."

"According to the police report, he bought it less than a month before he died."

"Which I presume implies that he may have been considering suicide for some time in advance."

I thought of the bottle of pills Kari Spencer had shown me. "Most people buy handguns for self defense, not self destruction. If Spencer was murdered, he might have had reason to believe that he was in danger."

Carr was obviously skeptical. "I imagine we could sit here and concoct any number of scenarios, but I'm not sure it would advance the issue. Would you like to see where he died?"

I was caught off guard by the sudden shift, tried not to show it. "Yes, if you don't mind."

"Of course not. We must be thorough, after all." He stood up and came around the desk. "If you'll come this way."

Spencer's office was on the opposite side of the landing, two doors down. It was a remarkable contrast to Carr's, cluttered to the point of chaos with pieces of art, not all of it mounted on the walls, sculpture, wood carvings, scrimshaw, pottery, and some objects I couldn't begin to identify.

"I'd like to say that the police made this mess during their investigation, but I'm afraid that's not the case. Walter was not the most orderly of people except in his workshop. I can show you that as well if you like, but I don't think he'd used it for at least a few months."

The floor was hardwood and completely exposed. "I thought there was a rug."

"Yes, a very fine Persian. As soon as the police released the scene, I had it sent out to be cleaned. I'm not sure the bloodstains will ever come out completely. It belongs to Kari, not the gallery, but I thought it was the least we could do for her, under the circumstances."

"He was sitting at the desk when he died?"

"That's right."

"Who found him?"

"It was one of the cleaning women, but I'm afraid I don't know her name. They have a very high rate of turnover. We had quite a time calming her down and she never did come back to work. I had just come in the door and was talking to Wanda about some changes I wanted to make when the woman screamed. She was sitting on the floor outside his office when I got there and I thought at first she'd had some kind of attack. Then I looked inside and saw the blood, then Walter, and it wasn't obvious at first that he was dead. His eyes were open and for a moment I thought he was looking at me. Then I saw that the side of his head was covered with blood and that his stare was fixed on the opposite wall. It was clear that he was beyond help so I sent the cleaning woman downstairs, closed the office door, and called the police."

"And you didn't notice anything out of the usual?" It sounded stupid as soon as I said it, but it was too late by then.

"A dead man sitting in a pool of dried blood is hardly usual, Mr. Birch, but no, nothing otherwise."

"Did you see the weapon?"

"Not at the time. One of the policemen asked me to come up again later to confirm Walter's identity and I noticed it then. It was on the floor beside his chair."

I made a show of looking around, but it was more to gather my thoughts than anything else.

"What was he doing here that night?"

"I have no idea. He had his own key and knew how to disarm the alarm system. He could come and go whenever he wanted. Back when he was working, he'd come in late at night occasionally. This was his primary studio. He had no formal duties with the gallery, of course, but he conducted a lot of his private business out of his office. It was more professional than doing it from his house."

"Did anyone see him come in that night?"

"No. He wasn't here when I locked up a few minutes after eight."

"Were the alarms on in the morning?"

'Yes, but he could easily have reset them himself once he was inside. That's what I do when I come in during the off hours. We don't have motion sensors. It's just the doors and windows."

"Miss Spencer seemed to think that the gallery was experiencing financial difficulties."

I was watching him closely and hopefully without revealing how interested I was, but he responded promptly and, as far as I could tell, candidly. "In that she is mistaken, but I don't imagine you'll take my word for it. We're making a reasonable profit. It's inconsequential to Kristina and Earl, of course; they're both doing quite well on their own. But we each receive a quarterly check dividing the profits evenly. I could live on my share of the proceeds quite comfortably even if I wasn't drawing a salary as director."

"Then there's no chance that the gallery will be shutting down."

He hesitated perceptibly. "That's not entirely certain, Mr. Birch."

CHAPTER THREE

When Carr seemed disinclined to explain, I decided to prompt him. "Would you care to expand on that point?"

Carr sighed. "I suppose I must. Let's go back to my office shall we? I'm sure it's just my imagination but I still smell the blood in here." It wasn't his imagination; I had picked up the faint coppery scent the moment we'd entered the room.

As we walked, I made a mental note. Why had Walter Spencer purchased a handgun? If he had owned one all along, I could understand that he might have used it to end his life rather than resort to the medication he had set aside for that purpose. But if he was already planning to kill himself a month beforehand, there was no reason not to use the more certain, less messy, and potentially less painful method. Which meant that regardless of whether or not he had taken his own life, he almost certainly had had a separate reason for arming himself. That suggested that he thought himself in danger and that in turn raised the possibility that his suicide had been orchestrated by someone else.

"How much do you know about Peter Trentano?"

We were back in Carr's office, where I would have expected him to feel more at ease, but his demeanor had taken a different turn. He was less certain of himself, obviously uncomfortable. I took my seat before answering. "I know his name and I've just looked at some of his work. It's a little too moody for my taste, but I can see why he's popular. His style is certainly distinctive and the attention to detail is impressive."

"Peter was a man of excesses, in his private life as well as his work. The official cause of his death was cancer, but he might have survived that if he hadn't treated his body so badly otherwise. He ate rich foods, drank incessantly, smoked constantly, and bedded beautiful women until the day of his final confinement. At times I envied him that last. He was a handsome man and he cultivated an air of mystery that was apparently irresistible for a certain type of woman. But for all his faults, he was a good friend. I still miss him."

Carr was quiet for so long that I was trying to decide how best to prompt him when he finally stirred again. "When Peter died, he left the Tontine several pieces of his work, five completed canvases—which I gather you've seen—and a collection of sketches, a few early and atypical pieces, and a variety of odds and ends. If they were placed for auction, they would probably net a total of something in the area of four million dollars, possibly more."

"I noticed the sign downstairs that said they weren't for sale."

Carr nodded. "We might be willing to sell one or two of them, but by the terms of Peter's will, we can't. Or at least we can't do it unless we're ready to close down the gallery." He moved restlessly. "Kristina has invested considerable time and money challenging the terms of the will, but Peter was quite explicit. If we close the Tontine, his work becomes just another disposable asset owned by the surviving partners. But as long as the gallery is open, we're enjoined from selling or even temporarily loaning the paintings to any other party. We can't even put another artist's work in his show room." He chuckled softly. "Not that there's much room left to do that in any case. So far the partners have voted to remain open, but it's been a majority of one for the past three years. Walter has always voted with Michelle and I against closing."

"If Spencer favored keeping the gallery open, that could be construed as a motive for wanting him dead." But it might mean that either Carr or Bernstein would have to die as well to actually change the outcome of a vote. "What happens now that you're divided evenly?"

"That's a source of no little concern, frankly. As I understand it, the status quo remains in effect until a majority votes to change things, although I don't doubt that Kristina will be on the phone with her lawyers soon if she hasn't already. But there's good reason to think that Walter was considering shifting his position anyway. I don't think he wanted us to continue once he was gone. And he didn't talk about it, but I gathered he'd had some financial reversals recently. "

Which gave the other two parties a motive to want him dead. I didn't say that, but I didn't have to be much of a detective to interpret the way Carr was looking at me. He knew what I was thinking.

"Michelle would be unhappy to see the doors close, but she wouldn't be materially affected. Her work has never commanded the high prices that Kristina and Paul enjoyed, but she's been working steadily, her work sells readily, and her husband has his own not inconsiderable income, I understand. They live quite well and I suspect she has enough salted away to support her nicely for the rest of her life even if she never sells another painting. I, on the other hand, would lose my comfortable salary and find myself unemployed, but I have a nest egg and my share of the proceeds of the liquidation would be considerable. It would be inconvenient rather than catastrophic."

"I didn't see much of your work on display downstairs." Some charcoal sketches that weren't bad at all and a pair of unmemorable paintings.

"I have no intention of being an artist who produces inferior work after the muse has deserted him to inspire another." He leaned forward with both forearms on the desk. "The only time I ever made good money was doing caricatures of celebrities and politicians back in the 1960s. There's not much market for that today even if I were in my prime, and even then I was more a craftsman than an artist. Technically I was as good as Paul, I think, but I lacked his eye for things. We both had a talent for reproducing what we saw, but Paul could perceive aspects of the world that were invisible to me. He could create where I could only imitate." He sighed theatrically. "I suppose that I have the most to lose if we close, but on the other hand, my share of the proceeds would be somewhere in the area of two million dollars, Mr. Birch. I could retire early and live happily ever after."

"I never suggested that you killed Walter Spencer."

"No, but the police did, and the thought was probably in your mind as well. I am a logical suspect."

Carr was enjoying this, I suspected. Becoming a murder suspect, however briefly, was probably the most exciting thing that had happened to him in years. "Was there any particular reason why the police pursued that line of inquiry?"

He shook his head. "Not that I know of. They questioned all of us, but I think it was a matter of procedure rather than definite suspicion. Detective Harris appeared to be bored half of the time, although I suspected all along that he cultivated that impression to make us overconfident. I think it actually pained him to conclude that Walter committed suicide."

I decided to shift gears. "The partners divide up the income from the gallery on an equal basis?"

He nodded. "That's correct. We do a quarterly accounting. I write the checks myself. We hold a certain amount for contingencies in an escrow account, and that fluctuates slightly depending on the value of the work we have on consignment. All of our financial matters are transparent and we use an outside auditor once a year to double check our regular accountant. I don't have any objection to your examining the records for yourself." He opened a desk drawer and took out a half inch thick bound document. "This is a copy of the last audit. You're welcome to take it with you." He slid it across the desk.

I opened the cover. The auditing firm was well known and dependable. "Thanks. I will borrow this, but I'm sure there's nothing wrong with your bookkeeping."

"Is there anything else I can do for you?" For the first time I heard a note of impatience in his voice.

"Would it be possible for me to talk to the other partners?"

"I'm sure Michelle would be willing to see you. I have her card here." He opened another drawer and drew out three business cards. "Here are all three of them. Michelle comes into the gallery about once a week, usually to work in the studio, but I never know when she's going to be here. Kristina drops by even less frequently, and Earl only shows up for board meetings. He's rather a recluse, frankly. Lives in a cabin up north."

I slipped the business cards into a pocket in the sleeve of the auditors' report. "I think that's it, at least for now. Thank you for your time and your frankness, Mr. Carr."

We both stood up and shook hands across the desk. I was just about to turn away when one more thought occurred to me. "Sorry, but I forgot to ask. Do all the partners have keys to the gallery?"

"Of course. We all had studios here originally, and sometimes one or another of us would work well into the night."

"Does anyone else have a key?"

He frowned thoughtfully. "Wanda does, of course. She opens up every morning, and I do the closing. No one else that I can think of.

The other help is all part time and we don't let them come in on their own."

"How about the cleaning people?"

Carr shook his head. "No. They're bonded, but I wouldn't take that kind of chance. As I said before, the faces change at least once a month. Wanda comes in early when they're scheduled to work and lets them in."

"So she was there the morning that Spencer's body was found?"

"Yes, of course. I was speaking to her when all hell broke loose."

"How about the keys that belonged to Reynolds and Trentano? Could they still be circulating somewhere?"

He shook his head. "We changed all the locks when we upgraded the alarm system two years ago."

"Thank you, Mr. Carr. You've been very helpful."

He walked me as far as the landing. "I hope you'll be able to put Miss Spencer's mind at ease."

I drove back to the office with a strong feeling that while Avery Carr may not have lied to me, he hadn't told me the complete truth. But then again, no one ever tells the complete truth.

"Take a look at this when you have a minute." I dropped the financial statements on Barry's desk.

"What's that?"

"Audit results. I don't think there's anything wrong with them, but it wouldn't hurt to take a look."

Barry picked up the folder, paged through it briefly. "Looks pretty straightforward. Is there anything in particular I'm looking for?"

"A motive for murder."

"Ahh!" He nodded knowingly. "The Spencer case."

"It's not a case yet, and how do you know about it anyway?" Steve was very discreet, which was one of the many reasons why I'd hired him. He wouldn't have told Tina and Barry anything unless I specifically authorized it.

"Dusty called and asked me how to get copies of corporate charters. She explained that she was working on a lead for you."

I tried to control my expression but almost certainly failed. "Dusty sometimes runs with the ball before it's handed off to her. What else did she say?"

Barry shrugged. "Just that you were looking into the possibility that Spencer was murdered and that it might have something to do with the finances at the gallery he co-owned."

"I very much doubt that Walter Spencer died by any hand other than his own. His niece just wants reassurance on that point."

I went to my office and buzzed for Steve, who appeared almost immediately. "Yes, boss?"

"I understand that Dusty called today."

"Yes she did. Just after you went out. She said she needed to ask Barry a financial question."

"Did she say anything else?"

"Not to me. Is anything wrong?"

Yes there was, but I wasn't about to discuss it with Steve. "No. I just thought she might have left a message for me. Did you open a folder on the server for Miss Spencer yet?"

He nodded. "It's under Preliminary. There's just an expense sheet and a blank log so far."

"I'm going to post some contact information for Spencer's business partners. Would you try to set up appointments with all of them except Avery Carr?"

"Will do."

I made more typos than usual entering the information. It was flattering that Dusty was so interested in my job, but I wanted our relationship to be separate and distinct from my work. Birch Investigations has an enviable reputation; we're good at what we do. Treasure hunts can be exciting, but when the treasure is no more than a clever accounting trick, it loses some of its luster. Hollywood detectives sit around waiting for beautiful women to walk into their offices, then dodge heavies and corrupt police to uncover the truth. Real detectives spend most of their time going through piles of documents, our clients are more likely to be middle aged business executives than distraught beauty queens, and if there is any possibility of violence we defer to the police rather than defy them.

Dusty's enthusiasm for everything around her was part of the reason I loved her. Her good judgment, alas, was not. She could quite easily get herself into trouble, or more likely tarnish the image of the agency if she represented herself as working for us in any capacity. I finished inputting the information Avery had provided and then punched up my private line and called home.

The answering machine picked up after the fourth ring. I left a message asking Dusty to call me at the office.

I had a late lunch, a personal gourmet pizza from across the street. Steve was waiting for me when I came back. "Miss Bernstein can see you this afternoon at 3:00 if that's convenient. Miss Kwan's assistant tells me that her schedule is very full and that she would need to know more precisely why you wanted to see her before she could even attempt to schedule an appointment."

"What about Garner?"

"I was unable to reach Mr. Garner, but I did speak to his brother, Mr. Carl Garner. The brother was quite annoyed at me; he was apparently taking a nap. He wishes it to be known that he is not his brother's goddamned secretary and that he has no idea when his goddamned brother will be home or whether or not he would be goddamned interested in meeting with you."

I sighed. "I don't suppose he suggested any goddamned time when it would be convenient for you to call back. Preferably some time God doesn't frown upon?"

"I think he made it quite clear that as far as he was concerned, any time at all would be inconvenient. I thought I might try again late in the afternoon or early evening."

Garner lived in a small town in New Hampshire. I checked my notes to get the name and went to see Tina who, as usual, had her face almost pressed against the screen of her computer. No wonder she wore contacts.

"Tina, you visit relatives in New Hampshire, don't you?"

She glanced up impatiently. "Henniker. That's my home town."

"Ever hear of a place called Jaffrey?"

"Sure. I go through it every trip. Pretty little place. Not much there except for the mountain though. Monadnock State Park."

"How long would it take to drive there?"

"Depends on when you go."

"Sunday night, after rush hour."

She pushed out one cheek with her tongue. "A couple of hours probably."

"Okay, thanks." Kwan and Bernstein were both local. Garner was within commuting distance. Any one of them could have driven to the Tontine for an unannounced visit.

I tried calling home again with no better luck than before, then used Google maps to print out directions to Michelle Bernstein's studio. It was in Lincoln, a mostly bedroom community north of Providence. Google estimated a twenty-minute drive but I decided to give it twice that, just in case, and ended up spending ten minutes circling the neighborhood, admiring the expensive homes sprinkled through a heavily wooded area.

Bernstein's house was set well back from the road, almost invisible thanks to a row of thick privet hedge that lined the semi-circular driveway. I parked behind a Lexus and watched two squirrels playing on a marble bird bath before ringing the doorbell.

I half expected a maid to answer, and the woman who opened the door certainly looked the part. She was about my height with handsome features that must once have been beautiful, wearing stained jeans and a torn sweatshirt, her long black hair tied back in a bun.

"Hi, my name is Paul Birch. I have an appointment with Miss Bernstein."

"That would be me." She opened the door wider and nodded me in. "You'll have to pardon my appearance, Mr. Birch, but these are my work clothes."

The house, what I could see of it, was tastefully and expensively furnished. "I appreciate that you're letting me intrude, Mrs. Bernstein."

"It's Ms. Bernstein actually, or preferably Michelle. Can I offer you something to drink?"

"No, I'm fine. This won't take very long. Would you mind answering a few questions about the Tontine for me?"

We sat down opposite one another in a spotlessly clean sitting room. No television, I noticed. "You're investigating Walter Spencer's death." I must have looked momentarily startled because she laughed at me. "Avery Carr called me this morning to let me know, Mr. Birch. It's not a conspiracy. He'd warned me that Walter's niece might stir things up."

"Why would he feel the need to warn you?"

"Oh, there's nothing sinister involved. Kari made quite a scene when the police closed their investigation. It's a pity she didn't take more interest in her uncle while he was still alive. Walter was a very lonely man."

"I thought they were close."

"Years ago maybe. Not since she went off to college. I don't think she was unkind or anything, but she had her own life with people her own age, and it was natural for the two of them to drift apart. Unfortunately, it happened just when Walter was feeling a bit adrift himself and needed her the most."

"I understand that Mr. Spencer was married to one of the other partners at one time."

"He and Kristina tried to make something permanent out of a brief fling. It didn't work. No one was surprised."

"And he never married again?"

She shook her head. "Never even came close. Lots of lovers but no one to love."

"Anyone in particular recently?"

There was an awkward silence as she decided how much to say. "I don't know how serious it was but he and Kristina were together again for a while and they talked about remarrying, but I don't think either of them really thought it would happen. I certainly didn't. Then they had some kind of fight and that was the end of that. By then I think Walter was in a lot more pain than he let on. He had periods of irritability and flashes of temper that were quite unlike him. It must have been obvious to Kristina that he wouldn't be able to sustain the relationship physically or emotionally for much longer, and I suspect she told him so. Kristina is painfully blunt at times. That must have been quite a blow to his ego. I wasn't surprised when I heard that he'd killed himself."

"Had he ever mentioned the possibility to you?"

"Not in so many words, but there were hints. I can't claim to have recognized them at the time, but in retrospect it was obvious that he was winding up his affairs. He gave away a few things to friends that he had always kept close, and he cancelled his annual vacation trip to Block Island this past year."

"Do you have any idea why he would have bought a gun just a few weeks before his death?"

"None at all." She sat back in her seat and crossed her arms. "That was the one jarring element, frankly. You'd never know it from his office, but Walter hated messes. He had the neatest studio I've ever seen, and I think he was sometimes physically ill when he visited mine." She laughed. "My mother tells me that I used to play with my own feces when I was an infant. A born painter, I guess."

"Mr. Carr told me that there'd been some tension at the gallery in recent months, some question about its future."

"More like the last two years. Avery and I want to keep the gallery open. It's particularly important to him because he hasn't worked, at his art I mean, for several years now. Without the gallery, he'd be lost."

"But he'd come out of it well off financially if you closed down."

"You don't need me to tell you that life is more than just physical comforts, Mr. Birch."

"And may I ask why you feel the same? You seem to have a full life."

"Part of it is because Avery and I have been friends for more than thirty years, but most of it is because of Peter Trentano. He was my mentor, Mr. Birch. Without his encouragement and guidance, my career would have ended during the 1970s. The others were all reasonably successful when we organized the Tontine. I was just a talented amateur with an inheritance. Phyllis and Earl objected to my being included but Peter talked them into accepting me. Paul wanted the Tontine to stay open and I feel constrained to honor his wishes."

"Earl Garner and Kristina Kwan both want to close the gallery, don't they?"

"That's right. Kristina's work is so popular that she has a waiting list for items she hasn't even designed yet. Financially, she's done better than the rest of us combined. Her income from the Tontine is inconsequential."

"She'd make more if it was closed and the assets sold."

"Yes, but I don't think that's her motivation. She doesn't lead a flamboyant lifestyle, and I think it's the public acclaim rather than the money that keeps her working."

"Then why does it matter to her?"

Bernstein hesitated and I wondered if she was going to tell me a lie. "Kristina was always a little bit spoiled. She had money, family money, right from the start. She's used to having her way and I think she's just pissed off that Avery and Walter and I thwarted her. I'm sorry, that probably sounds a bit catty. Kristina's not a bad person, actually, but she can be very stubborn sometimes. She also tends to be secretive, so I'm just guessing about her motivation. It could be something else entirely."

"What about Earl Garner?"

"Earl plays his cards very close to his chest. He has a decent income as I understand it, but he lives in a glorified log cabin up north. I've never known Earl to be extravagant, so he should have a nice nest egg somewhere, but it's possible that he's frittered his money away. I know that his recent work has not done well."

"Has Garner ever said why he wants to close the gallery?"

She shook her head. "Only by implication. He talks about times changing and the need to move on. He's not the most sociable member of our circle. He and Paul had some serious fights early on and the Tontine might have broken up very quickly if we hadn't made the charter so restrictive. Just about the only time I ever see Earl is at the annual Board meeting, and he doesn't say much even then."

"That leaves us with Walter Spencer himself. Avery Carr said that he was opposed to the sale as well, but that he might have changed his mind recently."

An elaborate wall clock began to chime the hour. Bernstein waited for it to end, apparently using the diversion to decide what she wanted to say. "Yes, that's probably true. Walter was an odd character. Financial rewards were of less interest to him than to any of the rest of us, although he didn't do at all badly during his good years. But even before the arthritis made it difficult for him to work, he'd suffered from...let's say a loss of inspiration. Many of his last sculptures were variations of work he'd completed years before. They were technically brilliant but they didn't have anything new to say. I think that Walter felt increasingly divorced from his art, and that staying involved with the gallery was his way of compensating. And he was a good speaker and in considerable demand, right up until the end. An attentive audience was more important to him than a sale. He was the unofficial spokesperson for the Tontine."

"He took an active part then?"

"Oh yes. Walter attended almost every opening. He was very good with customers, even lectured a few times, and most of the local reporters knew him well enough to be on a first name basis. Up until three years ago, he ran a small summer workshop in conjunction with the School of Design. The students loved him and the college was very unhappy when he told them he didn't want to continue. He was still physically up to it, but his enthusiasm was gone."

"So what changed?"

"Walter became aware of his own mortality and frailty. It was bad enough to lose his art. Losing his craft as well left him with nothing. His sister died years ago and while he and his niece got along while she lived with him, their lives and interests were so different that they had little to offer one another after she left for college."

"How would closing the Tontine help any of that?"

"Walter wanted to set up a scholarship fund in his name at the School of Design. I think he intended to contribute his share of the proceeds for that purpose."

"I see. Was his intention generally known?"

"I have no idea. He told Avery and I that he was seriously considering reversing his position, but we argued with him until he seemed to have taken our part again. You'd have to ask Kristina and Earl if he spoke to them about it." She smiled. "I suppose that gives me a motive for murdering him." She was the second person I'd talked to who seemed perversely pleased at the idea.

I considered my reply very carefully. "The police have ruled his death a suicide."

"The police closed the case in just over a week, Mr. Birch. I believe they spoke to me for a total of ten minutes."

"Did you tell them about Spencer's recent change of heart?"

"They didn't ask."

"Well, thank you very much, Mrs. Bernstein." I rose slowly to my feet and she followed suit. "I appreciate your frankness."

"So what's next, Mr. Birch?"

"I beg your pardon?"

"You're being paid to prove that Walter Spencer was murdered, aren't you? You can't have his body exhumed because he was cremated, so how will you proceed?"

"I've been asked to examine the circumstances of his death and that's all. I haven't seen or heard anything which causes me to believe the police were mistaken. My objective is to set his niece's mind at rest, not to cause trouble for anyone."

"Of course. But have you considered the most obvious suspect?"

There was a teasing tone in her voice now that hadn't been there before. "And who would that be?"

"Who had the most to gain from Walter Spencer's death, Mr. Birch? Who inherited the bulk of his estate?"

"You're talking about his niece. If she was involved in his death, why in the world would she hire someone to stir things up again? The police are satisfied and no one is contesting the will." That I knew of, anyway.

We were walking toward the door. "Oh, I can think of a couple of reasons why she might do such a thing. If you uncovered any flaws in her plan, she would be forewarned and have time to smooth them over. Or perhaps she intended to implicate someone else and the police were too unimaginative to find the clues she left, and she's hoping you're smart enough to tumble to them, but not smart enough to recognize them for what they are."

There was obviously no love lost between Kari Spencer and Michelle Bernstein. "You should meet my friend Dusty," I said lightly. "She writes murder mysteries. The two of you might have a lot in common." A thought occurred to me. "If you have a studio here, why keep a second one at the Tontine?"

"I don't like conducting business out of my home. If I'm meeting with a client about a project, I almost always do it there. We all had studios together back when we started the gallery, but Earl rents a barn up in New Hampshire, Kristina has her own elaborate showroom and studio, and Avery has pretty much abandoned his artistic career. Walter's space will probably be converted into another gallery if we stay open."

"What happens now that you're evenly split on the issue?"

"I have no idea." We had reached the door, where I thanked her again for taking the time to see me. I was on my way back to the car when she called after me. "Can you keep a secret, Mr. Birch?"

I hesitated. "I'm obligated to report my findings to my client, Mrs. Bernstein."

She considered that. "It's only my opinion, but I don't think Walter killed himself either."

"May I ask why not?"

"Because he left too many loose ends. Most artists have unfinished projects laying around, either because we've lost interest, or encountered technical problems we haven't solved yet. But not Walter. He couldn't even start a new piece until he'd finished the last one."

"Sometimes desperate people act out of character."

"Walter was discouraged and depressed at times, but he was never desperate. That's probably why he was never a great success as an artist. And another thing. I don't think Walter would have left a mystery behind. He would have provided a suicide note, probably a very lengthy one." She half turned away. "Have a nice day, Mr. Birch."

And the door closed firmly between us.

CHAPTER FOUR

I took my time driving back to the office. Between Carr and Bernstein, I'd gotten a pretty consistent and plausible description of the internal politics at the Tontine. But so far I'd heard nothing from the opposing group, Kwan and Garner. It was entirely possible that they saw things differently and that I lacked relevant information. But I couldn't remedy that unless one or both of them agreed to speak to me, and so far they hadn't seemed to be so inclined.

I stopped for gas and used my cell phone to call home. Still no answer. I told myself not to get angry until I knew that I was justified, but it didn't work. I was quietly fuming.

Steve was on the phone when I arrived so I waved at him and went into my office. Half a dozen invoices sat on my desk, awaiting my approval before they were paid. I started to go through them but found it difficult to concentrate and finally set them aside. I reached toward the intercom, then stood up and walked out into the reception area. Steve was still on the phone, looking uncharacteristically dour, and I decided to see if Barry had had a chance to go over the Tontine financials.

He had. "Pretty clear cut, actually. Almost all of the expenses are periodic and consistent. The income varies dramatically from month to month, as you might expect given the nature of their business. The profit to asset ratio is off, but only because of the high value assigned to the Trentano materials. The appraisals are from a reputable firm and show a modest appreciation from year to year. Nothing to get excited about but the bottom line is black."

"How about disbursements?"

"Nothing out of the ordinary there either. The five partners—four now I guess—split the profits evenly at the end of every fiscal quarter, less a modest reserve held for contingencies like extraordinary maintenance or insurance expenses. They take a standard commission on everything sold, including work by the partners, and that's the biggest part of their income. There's a bit more from lectures, classes, and things like that, but it's not significant. Avery Carr also receives a handsome stipend as gallery manager, but it's not grossly inflated and he hasn't had an increase in six years."

"The gallery is a viable entity then?"

"Over the course of a year, yes. Individual quarters vary considerably. The partners each received almost two hundred thousand dollars last year, not counting Carr's salary or their take from the sale of their own work."

"And there's nothing odd or unusual?"

Barry shook his head vigorously. "Not in these numbers. It's possible that they're understating their sales figures, I suppose, but they'd have to be very clever about it. The auditors sent statements to randomly selected clients and no discrepancies turned up. If there's something funny going on, I'd need access to a lot more than this in order to find it."

"Okay, thanks Barry."

Steve had called Kristina Kwan's assistant again. "I hinted that there might be legal problems that would require even more of her time if she couldn't clarify a few points quickly. She didn't like it, but she put me on hold and talked to her boss and you have half an hour tomorrow afternoon at two o'clock."

"Great! Anything from Garner?"

His expression turned sour. "No, I got the answering machine when I tried to call back." I wasn't relishing the prospect for a four or five hour round trip even if it was going on the expense account, so I wasn't tremendously disappointed. I considered the fact that Michelle Bernstein shared Kari Spencer's doubts about her uncle's alleged suicide, but I had yet to hear anything that made me want to seriously challenge the medical examiner's verdict.

The balance of the afternoon passed relatively uneventfully. I had a late meeting with one of our subcontractors on the Sheffield case. The estate in Managansett had been in limbo for several years and we'd been hired to track down a rumored distant relative who turned out to be not only unrelated but also quite dead. Then Barry came by to tell me that there were indeed some irregularities in the Merrivale Rental Service's accounting, but they were probably the result of incompetence rather than fraud and the amounts were too small to be suspicious. I told him to write up a summary of his findings and forward it to me.

I left the office on time for a change, made a stop to pick up my dry cleaning on the way home, deliberately taking my time in an effort to cool off before confronting Dusty. Her Volkswagen was in the driveway, which meant she was finally back, and I began rehearsing what I was going to say to her as I carried my briefcase and my shirts to the door. All of the scenarios I'd rehearsed became irrelevant the moment I stepped inside the house.

I should explain that Dusty insists on doing her share of our normal household chores, but that I do almost all the cooking. She can charbroil a hamburger or microwave a heat and serve meal, but anything that requires reading detailed instructions or taking incremental steps between the time the stove is turned on and the time the food is served strikes her as unnecessarily complicated. Not that I'm an expert chef myself, mind you, but I know my way around a food processor. On the rare occasion when she feels compelled to have supper waiting for me, it's usually a fancy salad, pasta and out-of-the-jar tomato sauce, or burgers and baked potatoes.

It took only a couple of sniffs to tell me the delightful aroma pervading the house wasn't her handiwork. It was takeout. Darla was curled up on the couch. She raised her head, waited until she knew I was looking, then sniffed disapprovingly and went back to sleep.

I followed my nose into the kitchen—the dining room was still mimicking Paris. The table was set for two, my best set of china incongruously intermingled with cardboard cartons.

"Hi! You're late." Dusty was measuring grounds into the coffee maker.

"Actually, I'm earlier than usual."

"But you left the office almost an hour ago. I know because I called and Greta told me you were just driving out of the lot." Greta vacuumed the offices and emptied the wastebaskets every evening.

I held up my shirts. "Had to run an errand."

"Well, let's eat before it gets cold. I have spring rolls and shrimp Szechwan and Moo goo gai pan and beef with orange sauce. Oh, and hot and sour soup, or at least lukewarm and sour soup."

"I'll be right back." I carried my shirts up to the bedroom, taking my time in order to factor these new circumstances into my strategic plan, but when I got back, Dusty handed me a glass of white wine and diverted me again.

"This is all from that new place that opened on Broad Street. We keep saying we're going to try them but we never seem to find the time, so since I was driving by on my way home tonight, I just stopped on impulse."

"I tried calling a couple of times," I said carefully. "But you weren't here. I thought the new book was going well and you were planning a marathon session."

"It is, actually, but I felt like I needed a break. You'll never guess what I did today."

"Let me try. How about you spent several hours prying into the corporate structure of the Tontine Art Gallery?"

That stopped her, even made her pout, but only for a few seconds. "Oh, Barry must have blabbed."

"Barry works for me. He's paid to tell me what's going on."

"Well I didn't do anything wrong and I was just trying to help. It's all a matter of public record anyway, and the nice people at the state office building were very helpful. There's a copy of the corporate charter on the coffee table in the living room. You owe me six bucks for copying. I left the receipt with it."

"Barry had a copy faxed to our office this afternoon. My people do know how to do their jobs, Dusty."

She ignored me completely. "Sit. Eat before it gets cold. I tried the soup and it's just so-so, but the spring rolls are quite nice."

I was hungry as a matter of fact, so I let her talk me into it. The white rice was done properly, firm and not all stuck together. I sampled all three main courses; Dusty has an aversion to shrimp so she only had two. We ate silently for a minute or two. The food wasn't bad, although the orange beef was just a trifle too sweet for my palate.

"So what did you find out at the gallery?"

"You know I can't talk about the case, Dusty."

"I thought you hadn't really taken the case. If you're just thinking about it, it doesn't fall under the confidentiality restriction, does it?"

"I'm taking the client's money. She's entitled to discretion."

"But I'm discreet!" She pointed her chopsticks at me. "So did Walter Spencer kill himself or not?"

"One or the other. I didn't hear anything today that makes me think the police got it wrong. There are a few loose ends, but there always are when there's an unexpected death."

"What did you think of Avery Carr?"

I wasn't going to be allowed to eat in peace until I conceded something to her and, to be completely honest, I hadn't really learned anything that could be construed as confidential or even controversial. "He seems to be competent and above board. If he was broken up by the death of his partner, there was no evidence of it, but I gather they'd ceased being close friends years ago. He answered all my questions honestly, as far as I could tell. I'm sure there's more to the story, but I don't know that any of it is relevant."

"But he stands to gain quite a bit from Spencer's death. His share of the gallery goes from twenty percent to twenty-five."

"Which won't amount to a great deal unless the gallery closes and sells off its assets, and in that case he loses his high paying job, which would offset at least a part of what he stands to gain. And that's all I'm going to tell you about our conversation."

Dusty tried to tease more information but I stuffed my mouth and refused to answer. She followed suit and we put a significant dent in all three cartons before she changed tactics.

"So what did you think of Wanda?"

I almost choked on a shrimp and had to drink some wine before I could answer. "What do you know about Wanda? And how do you know it?"

It was her turn to be unresponsive. I glared across the table while she refilled her plate, taking her time, before answering. "Wanda and I had a long talk when I went to the gallery today."

"You went to the Tontine?" I wasn't sure if I was more angry than surprised or vice versa.

"I certainly did. It's a public place, Mr. Birch. I have just as much right to go there as anyone else."

"And what did you do while you were there?" I tried to eat through gritted teeth. It doesn't work very well.

"I admired the artwork, most of it anyway. The Kwan display was way below her usual standards, I thought."

"And you talked to Wanda. What about?"

Dusty apparently decided that she was full because she pushed her plate away and poured herself another glass of wine, deliberately taking the time to sip at it before answering. "Wanda Fredericks, age twenty-five, single, high school graduate. Grew up in Braintree. She has worked at the Tontine for just under two years, has been studying nights to get a degree in art history from Providence College. She's single, divorced after a very brief and unhappy marriage, has no steady boyfriend, and lives in Warwick. Wanda always liked Walter Spencer and is greatly saddened by his death. There were tears, quite genuine I'm sure. She seems to be less fond of her boss, Avery Carr, although she has no specific complaints, or none that she would mention to a casual acquaintance no matter how sympathetic. Doesn't know the other partners well enough to have an opinion of any of them except Kristina Kwan, whom she described as a very nice lady. At the moment, she's a bit concerned about her job because she's not sure if the gallery is going to stay open now that Spencer is gone, but she's also not sure she wants to stay even if it does."

"What did you do? Lure her into a back room and grill her under hot lights?"

"Not at all. I took her to lunch. Told her I didn't know a thing about art and wondered if she'd be willing to get me started in the right direction. Turns out she doesn't know much more than I do, so the subject changed a few times. Once she got started, it was hard to turn her off."

I knew that I should be annoyed by her interference, but I was too curious to indulge myself just now. "Did she say anything about the day that Spencer died?"

She shook her head. "Nothing useful. The cleaning lady found the body and started screaming, Carr told her to stay at the front door while he investigated, then had her call the police a few minutes later. She didn't even know who had died until the police told her."

"So she didn't see anything suspicious?"

"No, and she was quite upset by the way the police treated her. They only spoke to her for about five minutes, apparently. They asked if Spencer made a habit of coming in at unexpected hours, and she told them she didn't know, since she was never at the gallery except when she was scheduled to work."

"Does she believe that he killed himself?"

"As far as I can tell. I sort of hinted that it sounded mysterious to me but she didn't take the bait."

"Anything else?"

"Not that I can think of. Wanda is smarter than she lets on, but I don't think she lied to me. Now it's your turn. Tell me all about Avery Carr."

I sighed. "You know I can't do that."

"You trust Tina and Barry. Don't you trust me?"

"It isn't a matter of trust, Dusty. It's professional ethics. You're not an employee and you're not assigned to the case."

She gave me a dirty look which I pretended to ignore while I served myself the last of the very good shrimp dish, carefully saving one for Darla. She wasn't partial to table scraps but she made an exception for shrimp. I had just set the carton aside when Dusty abruptly stood up and walked around behind me. I felt her arms around my shoulders and figured she'd decided to drop the subject in favor of a more physical pleasure when her hand slipped inside my jacket and deftly removed my wallet from the inside pocket.

"And just what are you doing, young lady?"

Ignoring me, she opened the wallet, riffled through the paper money, and extracted a five.

"Is that for my share of supper?"

"No, supper is on me. This is my retainer."

"Now wait a minute." I'm pretty fast on my feet and I knew where she was headed.

But she dropped my wallet on the table and skipped back out of reach, folding the bill and slipping it into her own pocket. "You hire subcontractors all the time, Paul, and I work cheap. Since you've now retained my services, there's no reason why you can't provide me with the background I need to continue my investigations."

"I don't want you to do any investigating, particularly not without clearing it with me first. Among other things, you don't have a license. You can get into considerable trouble representing yourself as something you aren't."

"That's all right. I work best undercover anyway."

I shook my head with exasperation. "You're not going to work undercover either. If this was just a suicide, you could stir up a lot of unnecessary trouble. And if by some chance it really is a murder case, the consequences could be a lot worse."

She went back to her chair and picked up her wine glass. "I'm not a child, Paul. I've done things like this before."

"Oh? Like what exactly?"

"I pretended to be a college student when I wanted background for my first murder mystery. And there was that strip club I went to just before we met, the one I used for the crime scene in *Bare Essentials*."

"Wasn't that the time you sprained your ankle running away from the two guys who thought you were a prostitute?"

She parried my thrust easily. "But I did get away. I sprained my ankle later because I cut across an empty lot on the way back to pick up my car." Her voice changed, softening. "Don't worry, lover, I won't be taking any chances. I'll just talk to people and listen to what they have to say."

I wasn't satisfied. "What people?"

"Why, whoever it seems might be able to help us with our case."

It was "our" case now, apparently, and I could tell by her tone that nothing I could say would change her mind. My only hope was that she'd lose interest quickly and devote her time to getting Craig into more trouble in Paris.

The phone rang at a very inconvenient time about two hours later. I was slow getting up because Darla was sleeping on my right hip and grumbled as I eased her off, then answered it dressed only in a bathrobe, ready to jump down the throat of any salesperson who dared to ignore the do-not-call list. But it was Steve, calling from home.

"Sorry to disturb you so late, Mr. Birch, but I finally got through to Earl Garner. He wasn't inclined to be helpful, I'm afraid, but he finally said that if it was really necessary for you to speak to him, he could arrange to be at his cabin all day on Friday. I told him I'd call right back once I'd checked with you."

Friday? I wasn't about to retrieve my day planner and check, but I was almost certain I had kept it free. Dusty and I had been promising ourselves a three day weekend for over a month now and I had set the day aside a month ago, but hadn't gotten around to making any actual plans. I was still sufficiently mad at her to derive a small amount of pleasure from scheduling work that day. "That should work for me. Tell him that I'll be there sometime before noon. Ask him for directions."

"Will do. Good night, Mr. Birch."

So it looked like I would get to meet all four partners after all.

Most of the following day, Thursday, I spent in the office. We worked up the final report for the Merrivale stockholders and sketched out our preliminary plan of attack for a review of the inventory shrinkage at Eblis Manufacturing. Barry thought that it might just be a fault in their stock keeping programming, but Tina's initial review had turned up no significant flaws in its logic. So either we had clever thieves stealing finished goods out of their warehouse, incompetents who were entering transactions inaccurately, or a subtle computer glitch that overstated production or understated shipments.

Merrilee had sent a request to add two people on a temporary basis and I okayed it immediately; she had an uncanny knack for anticipating our workload. I had asked her about it once and she'd just smiled mysteriously and tapped the side of her head with one finger.

Our meeting ran longer than expected so I had a late and rather abbreviated lunch before driving across the city to keep my appointment with Kristina Kwan. Her showroom was set well back from the main road and there was only enough space for a half dozen vehicles in the parking lot, but I suspected that most of her sales were mail order or through wholesalers. The sign identifying her business was small and subdued and not visible until you were already on the property.

The receptionist wasn't much of an advertisement for her employer's work. She wore no jewelry except a pair of very plain earrings and a practical, inexpensive wristwatch. After granting me just the faintest sketch of a smile, she took my name and asked me to take a seat in the waiting room. This wouldn't have been the first time I'd wasted an hour so that the person I was interviewing could feel that I'd been put in my proper place, but in fact a tall, thin woman with her hair cut surprisingly short came out within a minute or two.

"Mr. Birch, I'm Kristina Kwan. My office is this way." Based on her name, I'd been expecting an Asian American, but other than a faint hint about the eyes, that part of her heritage was very thoroughly diluted.

She led me down a narrow corridor whose walls were decorated with printed posters advertising one or another of her product lines. I noticed the usual, ear rings, necklaces, pendants, and pins meant to be worn in a woman's hair, most of them quite gaudy if I was a fair judge, which I probably wasn't. We passed three doors, all closed and unlabeled, before the corridor turned to the right and opened into an oversized office.

"Please make yourself comfortable."

It wouldn't be accurate to describe her very large desk as being glass topped because it was in fact glass from top to bottom. It was more properly a table than a desk, since it had no drawers, but she sat behind it, steepled her fingers, and waited until I had settled into a very fragile looking and quite uncomfortable chair facing her. The décor was relentlessly modern, straight lines and subdued colors, and felt almost antiseptic, as though I'd stepped into a futuristic medical clinic.

"Would you like some coffee or tea?"

"No, thank you. I just had lunch. I appreciate your taking the time to see me."

"Your secretary was apparently quite persistent. Faith, my assistant, is very careful about wasting my time."

"Then I'll try to be as brief as possible. I believe you know the matter that brings me here."

"I assume it's Walter Spencer's suicide."

She was so obviously sure of herself that I found myself bristling. "Walter Spencer's alleged suicide, yes."

"Do you have reason to believe it anything else?"

"There are a number of open issues that I'm hoping to resolve."

"Which issues? My understanding is that the police were completely satisfied."

"The police are not the only parties concerned." She wanted to know who had hired me. There was no reason why I shouldn't tell her, since at least two of her partners knew, but I had a feeling that the only way I would learn anything from Kristina Kwan was if I traded for the information. "Since you are among those who benefited from his death, I thought I should offer you the opportunity to help clear the air."

The corners of her mouth twitched in what might have been an amused smile. "You are referring to the Tontine, I assume?"

I nodded.

"If you've come from Avery Carr or Michelle Bernstein, I can save us both considerable time. I have made my position clear in the past and see no reason to change it now. The gallery is of no interest to me and as an investment, it is under producing. The proceeds of a liquidation could be put to much better use, for all of us, as a matter of fact. But while I can't say that the money would be unwelcome, they would not significantly alter my personal circumstances, Mr. Birch. Walter was an old friend and I valued him much higher than I do my share of the gallery."

"I'm sure his loss was a blow to all his friends."

"He was a child in an adult's body, wondering at the world. It was always a pleasure to look at things vicariously through his eyes."

"It's my understanding that two of the partners, and Walter Spencer as well, disagreed with you about the benefits of closing the gallery."

She shook her head impatiently. "Then you're misinformed. There's never been any question that we would all benefit from closing the Tontine."

"Then why has a majority opposed it?"

"Sentiment." Kwan said it as though it was a dirty word. "Michelle idolized Peter Trentano and tries to honor his wishes even when it no longer matters to anyone but herself. Avery simply doesn't like changes in his life and he's happy in the niche he's fallen into. Walter," she hesitated, "Walter was a bit of a mystery. I'm not sure he understood his own motives. Sometimes I thought he took the position he did simply because he knew it would annoy me."

"There was friction between the two of you then?"

Kwan regarded me coolly. "Our relationship was much more complex than that. We were married once and lovers since, Mr. Birch. And friends always. It may be hard for you to accept this, but even though we saw each other no more than a few times each year, we still felt affection for one another. We fought constantly and sometimes quite viciously, but our feelings remained constant. I don't expect you to understand that."

"Do you know of anyone who might have wished him harm?"

"He could be quite short with people, and sometimes was unintentionally cruel, but no, I can't think of anyone who actively hated him."

"Did he seem to you like the kind of man who would kill himself?"

Kwan took her time answering, seemed to be considering the possibility for the first time. "I am inclined to say that he was not, but I confess that when I think back over the past several months, I can recall more than one occasion where he said or did something that struck me as odd at the time, and more so in retrospect."

"Could you be more specific?"

She hesitated again and I thought she might balk, but then she visibly relaxed and settled back into her seat. "Walter was always skeptical about academic art. He used to say that schools can teach the craft of painting or sculpting or design, but they can't instill a talent or a vision that doesn't already exist. But about a year ago he started talking about establishing a scholarship in his name and a few months later he began negotiating with someone about an endowment. It was so completely unlike him that I asked about it, and he told me that he'd decided that second rate immortality was better than no immortality at all."

"Do you think Walter Spencer killed himself, Miss Kwan?"

She was silent for so long that I wondered if she was going to answer. When she did, her words were slow, deliberate, and without emotion. "He certainly had sufficient cause and I wouldn't have blamed him. I suppose I believe it, intellectually, but there's another part that says he wouldn't have done it, or at least not the way he did. Walter would have set up his scholarship, paid a last visit to each of his old friends, and then found a quiet, efficient way to end his life. I can't imagine what could have driven him to such an ugly death, and I find it hard to accept that he would leave us with no explanation. If you find out why, I would very much like to know."

We talked for a few minutes longer, but were twice interrupted by the buzzing of her desk phone and by then I'd run out of questions to ask.

CHAPTER FIVE

Dusty was typing away in her office when I got home that evening, and I almost had to physically drag her away from the computer when I had supper ready. For the most part, she's a methodical person who approaches her writing as a job, keeps regular hours, and writes even when she's not in the mood. I've only known her to have writer's block once and it lasted just over a day. Once in a while she gets on a roll though and sits hunched over the keyboard for ten, twelve, or even fourteen hours at a stretch.

She doesn't like being interrupted when that happens and she sulked at the table for several minutes before admitting the beef Stroganoff was quite good. By the time she'd finished a glass of wine and half her plate, the mood had lightened and she asked if I'd found out anything new related to the Spencer case. I winced, because I'd hoped that she'd forgotten about it overnight, but I should have known better. She's like a terrier when she gets hold of something that interests her.

"Nothing of consequence." I pitched my voice to seem casual, but decided to throw her a bone. "Did you know he used to be married to Kristina Kwan?"

"They seem like an odd couple."

"How would you know? You've never met either of them."

She tossed her head indignantly. "Maybe not, but I watched when Kwan was interviewed on A&E and she seems entirely businesslike and practical. I can't imagine her having much in common with an ivory tower artist type like Spencer."

"And how do you know what Spencer was like?"

"Well, I have that at second hand." Dusty glanced down at her plate and speared a piece of beef. "Wanda really admired him and he seemed to welcome the attention. He was the main reason she stayed at the Tontine, apparently. I think she had a crush on him, but she said he was a perfect gentleman and even got a little cranky when I suggested that he might have been flattered by the attention of a young woman. He used to tell her long stories about the early days, when they were pretending to be struggling artists even though they were all pretty well heeled."

"You and Wanda must have really hit it off."

"I think she just wanted someone to talk to. Apparently Avery Carr treats her like a piece of furniture. He's not nasty to her or anything, but if she quit one day and another woman showed up in her place, he probably wouldn't even notice the change."

"So she doesn't like her boss."

A shrug. "I don't think she dislikes him, but there's certainly no office camaraderie there."

"What did she say about Kwan?"

"Her name didn't come up. I'll ask her on Saturday."

I froze with a bite half way to my mouth. "You'll do what?"

She tossed her head. "Oh, didn't I tell you? We're getting together again. I offered to buy her a nice lunch if she took me around to some of the other galleries and educated me about art."

I put my fork down without relieving it of its burden. "What do you think you're doing, Dusty?"

I was using my stern voice and my serious face, but she ignored both. "Just trying to educate myself."

"Since when have you had more than a casual interest in art?"

"You never know when an odd piece of knowledge might come in useful. Maybe I'll write a murder mystery set in an art gallery. Besides, it'll be fun and the poor girl needs to be cheered up. Don't worry. I won't spill the beans. Do we even have any beans to spill?"

Choosing my words very carefully, I tried to explain why I thought this was a bad idea. "I know you mean well and that you're the soul of discretion, but if Wanda or anyone else ever found out that you were involved in this investigation, formally or otherwise, it could be very awkward. You might let slip something that she shouldn't know..."

Dusty interrupted me, shaking her head. "Not possible. You haven't told me anything that isn't part of the public record, remember?"

"That's beside the point."

"Besides, you don't really think Wanda might be involved, do you?"

I hadn't, but now that she mentioned it, the thought wouldn't go away. If Spencer had in fact been murdered, she would certainly need to be included among the suspects. She had known him, quite well in fact, and she had a key to the Tontine, was familiar with the routine there. It was entirely possible that she could have returned during the night, murdered him, locked up and gone home. She hadn't been the one to find the body, but she was on the scene and could have been watching for anything she might have overlooked. Her fondness for Spencer could be pretense, or she might have been infatuated with him and killed him impulsively when he refused to reciprocate.

"I don't know who's involved," I said slowly. "But if a crime has been committed, she'd certainly be someone I'd be interested in."

Dusty made an exasperated sound. "But she didn't have a motive and she has an alibi."

"Oh?"

"She went to a concert the night Spencer was murdered, at the Performing Arts Center."

"Who did she go with?"

Her eyes drifted away from me. "I think she said she went alone. But there'd be a seat number and we could check with the people who had the adjoining seats."

"Slow down, Dusty. First of all, unless she kept the ticket stub, there's probably no way of finding out her seat number. And even if it all checked out, Spencer might have died as late as 1:00 in the morning. She could have stopped back at the studio after the concert. Hell, she could have stopped for pie and coffee and still have had time to kill him."

"All right," she admitted sullenly. "I'll be careful. She'll do most of the talking anyway. I think she's very lonely and I'm the first person in a long time who's been willing to listen to what she has to say."

I still wasn't happy about it, but I knew from experience that Dusty would only be more determined to meet with Wanda if I tried to forbid it. And I was still leaning toward suicide, despite the skepticism of Kari Spencer, Kristina Kwan, and everyone else concerned including my own nagging subconscious. We're all surprised when someone we know takes their own life. If we had known, we would have done something about it, so we can't admit even to ourselves that we might have had any real suspicion of their state of mind.

"I might be late getting home tomorrow. You may have to shift for yourself for supper."

"I can probably manage a single meal on my own." Dusty helped herself to another dish of noodles and drowned them in the cream sauce. "What's up?"

"I'm going to visit the last of the partners, Earl Garner, and he lives up in New Hampshire."

"Whereabouts in New Hampshire?"

"Jaffrey, just a little way across the border from Massachusetts."

"Oh, I know Jaffrey. We used to climb Mount Monadnock every summer when I was a kid. Our church youth group would rent a bus and we'd all spend the day hiking and, when we could slip away from the chaperones, making out."

"Do you remember much about the town itself?"

"Sure. Pretty little place. Real small. Great scenery. There was this neat little ice cream shop on the way to the town beach. Hey, why don't I go along with you?" My face must have telegraphed my reservations because she hurried on before I could refuse. "Just for the ride, okay? You can drop me off in town and pick me up afterward. I won't mess up your interview, honest."

Truthfully, I wasn't looking forward to the long ride alone. I didn't even have an audio book worth listening to and it would be at least four hours round trip. Still, this was supposed to be business.

Dusty pressed her momentary advantage. "I can ask around about bed and breakfasts. We keep saying we need to get out of the city for a weekend."

I felt a twinge of guilt, quickly suppressed. "All right. If you really want to go, you can. But it might take me a while. Garner's not the easiest person to pin down and he might not be sitting there waiting for me to show up."

"I'll bring a book. Two books."

Bereft of my last argument, I capitulated.

It was actually a rather pleasant morning. I was up first and took a casual walk around the yard with Darla sitting in my arms so that she wouldn't get her feet wet with dew. Dusty is often a bit grumpy when she gets up before mid-morning and for the first twenty minutes of the ride she said very little, but then the coffee kicked in and by the time we stopped for breakfast in Fitchburg, she was her usual cheery self. Through some unique magic of her own, she managed to discover the names and ages of our waitress' three children, the fact that her husband disliked his boss at the garage across the street, and that she herself was considering applying to one of the chain restaurants that was opening near the new strip mall. She managed all this while devouring a lumberjack's plate, the largest breakfast on the menu, while I struggled to finish my omelet.

We reached Jaffrey late in the morning, too early for lunch and an awkward time to drop in on Garner, so I let Dusty act as tour guide for awhile, although her memory wasn't always as accurate as she expected. Either she'd forgotten where things were or, more likely, they'd disappeared during the previous decade, replaced by newer names. After a light lunch at a low profile but surprisingly good sandwich shop, formerly a used book store according to Dusty, we drove back into the town proper and I let her out in front of an antique shop.

"Got your cell?"

"In my bag."

"I'll call you as soon as I'm done, or sooner if something goes wrong."

"Don't worry. I have a P.D. James novel with me if I get bored." She tapped the side of her oversized bag.

Steve had typed up the directions Garner provided and I had no doubt that he had done so accurately, but there was something wrong with them. The first few landmarks were right, but then things turned hairy. Garner lived on an unnamed dirt road on the north side of town, but when I made what should have been the final turn, keeping a close eye on the odometer, there was no side road to the left. I went on for almost another mile, explored one dirt road that ended at a boat slip, then slowly made my way back, searching for another. Nothing, and nobody around to ask. I tried calling Garner's number on my cell phone but there was no answer.

I retraced my route until I reached the town proper, then tried again, with the exact same results. This time I returned only as far as a rather rundown gas station and convenience store, with an unbranded gasoline and old fashioned pumps that wouldn't accept credit cards. There was a dingy looking bar and grill next door with a shared parking lot.

I sat at the pumps for at least two full minutes before a young woman came out of the store and walked around to my side of the car. "Fill her up?"

"Yes, please." I waited until I heard the dinging of the pump, then stepped out of the car. "Excuse me; I wonder if you might be able to help me."

She appeared disinterested but not hostile.

"I'm looking for someone named Earl Garner. He's supposed to live in a log cabin somewhere around here. I have directions, but they're wrong."

The woman shook her head very slowly. "Never heard of him. Sorry. Has he lived here long?"

I tried to remember what the file had said. "A few years, at least."

"What's the name again?"

"Garner. Earl Garner."

She seemed to be making an honest effort to remember, but failed. "Can't help you. You might try Zach. He knows just about everyone in town."

"Zach?"

She raised her hand and pointed past me. I turned, following her finger, and saw the sign. Zach's Bar and Grill.

"Thanks. I'll do that."

I paid her and moved the car to one of the parking spaces. Zach's was open, apparently. There were three cars and two motorcycles out front, and a pickup truck with exposed undercoating at the rear. A thin line of smoke curled up from behind the building, and a mangy looking dog was prowling around the trashcans. It didn't look promising, but I couldn't think of anything better to try.

I was expecting the blare of country and western, but when I stepped inside, I was greeted by almost subliminal Irish folk music. That wasn't my only surprise. The exterior was weather worn and disreputable; the interior was clean, attractive, and well lit. The decor was unremarkable, with a vaguely Irish tone. Lots of green, a shamrock pattern in the curtains. There were two rows of booths, a handful of tables, and a good sized bar. An elderly couple sat in one of the booths, and three men, all close to retirement age if not past it, were grouped together at the bar. I wondered which two of them belonged to the motorcycles.

The bartender clearly was not Zach. She was fortyish, had a pleasant face, and one of the largest bosoms I've ever seen, with shoulders to match. Her arms were thick and muscular. She glanced up when I came in and watched as I crossed the room, her expression neutral but watchful.

"What can I get for you?"

I wasn't particularly thirsty, but I decided to invest in some good will. "Sam Adams? On tap if you've got it."

She served it in a mug so quickly that it looked like Irish magic. I put some money on the bar. "I wonder if you could help me. I'm supposed to be meeting someone near here but I think there's something wrong with my directions. His name's Earl Garner and he has a cabin not far from here."

The threesome to my left had stopped talking when I ordered the beer, and now I was aware that they had turned to stare at me. "Don't know anyone named Earl Garner." My hopes sank. "But everyone here knows Carl Garner, don't we?"

They responded with nods and some low laughter.

"That's his brother," volunteered the closest of the three. "Carl says his brother doesn't take to alcohol, so he has to drink for the both of them." That brought louder laughter.

The bartender smirked. "Carl's in here every few days. Drinks a couple by himself, then buys for the house until I throw him out. He has a nasty temper and a foul mouth and I wouldn't let him in at all if he wasn't one of my best customers."

"Can you tell me where he lives?"

"He told me once that he's staying at his brother's place, but never said where it was. Hiram, didn't you take him home one night last year?"

The middle member of the threesome nodded. "Coupla times. If he'd killed himself driving home, I'd have missed a lot of free drinks."

"Can you help this gentleman then?"

"I have directions." I took the slip of paper out of my pocket and handed it to Hiram, who scrutinized it as though it was a legal document governing the distribution of a fortune.

"You'll never find him this way."

I was relieved to know that it wasn't my interpretation that was at fault.

"See here, where it says take the first left and then the second right? That's ass backwards. You take the first right and then the second left. That's Prescott Road, but there's no sign to tell you that. Snow plow knocked it down last winter. About half a mile up you turn off to the left. It goes way back so don't get discouraged. Road gets real narrow, too narrow for the plows. When it snows, those two aren't going anywhere except on skis."

He handed the directions back and I thanked him, then glanced down at the money I'd left on the bar. "Will that pay for a round for the house?"

The woman nodded. "More than."

"Keep the change."

I followed the elderly couple back out to the parking lot, and had to hide my amused smile when they climbed onto the motorcycles.

Hiram's directions worked just fine. I found the turnoff with no difficulty this time and followed it around a winding, slightly uphill course until it passed through a stand of thick pine trees. Just beyond was a cleared patch in the center of which stood what technically, I suppose, was a log cabin. It was two stories tall and probably had as much floor space as my house in the city. Maybe more. There was a jeep parked out front. To the left was a detached, prefabricated garage that looked completely out of place. The garage door was up, and I could see skis mounted on the wall, at least three pair, a snowmobile, and a set of shelves filled with camping equipment.

I parked beside the jeep and got out, glancing around. There was a series of steps, outlined with half buried logs, that led me to an open porch, although once I was on it I could see the fittings where screens or even storm windows could be installed to enclose it completely. There was no doorbell, so I knocked as hard as I could. Nobody answered and I hadn't heard the sound of movement from inside.

I waited a minute or so, then repeated the process, with no better luck. Irritated, I took out my cell phone and tried calling again, but the tinny buzz threatened to go on forever. With no clear idea of what to do next, I retreated down the steps and started around the left side of the house. It was then that I heard the first thud and, a moment later another. Several more seconds passed before I realized that what I was hearing was the sound of someone chopping wood.

I circled around the cabin and found the source. There was an enormous pile of firewood stretching along the back wall of the cabin, and just to one side a man wearing a flannel shirt stood with his back to me, carefully setting another piece onto a chopping block.

"Hi there!" I called out, not wanting to get too close to a man carrying an axe without letting him know that I was coming. "Are you Earl Garner?"

He turned around calmly and stared at me for a second or two before responding. "Yes, I'm Earl Garner. Who are you?"

"Paul Birch. We had an appointment today."

Garner was still holding the axe so I decided not to get any closer just yet. He wasn't a young man, but he looked fit and alert. "I'm not aware of any such thing, Mr. Birch. What makes you think that might be the case?"

"My office called two days ago and set it up. I'm representing Miss Kari Spencer."

He turned and buried the axe in the chopping block, then crossed his arms and started toward me. "I've been out of town for the past week, Mr. Birch. I haven't spoken to anyone in your office."

I was suddenly at a loss for words and stammered something barely intelligible, but Garner smiled and waved it off. "Don't fret yourself. I know what happened. My brother lives with me and he has a rather twisted sense of humor sometimes. We're identical twins, you see, and ever since we were kids he's enjoyed pissing me off by pretending he was me and getting me into trouble. I have no doubt that he's the one your people talked to, but I assure you he never passed the word along to me."

"I see. I apologize for intruding then, but I wonder if you might have time to talk to me for a few minutes about Walter Spencer?"

"You said Kari Spencer hired you?"

I nodded. "She has some doubts about the manner of his death."

Garner grunted. "What? Let me guess, she thinks someone killed him and made it look like suicide."

"She would like some reassurance that the police came to the right conclusion."

"She'd probably also like the proceeds of his insurance policy, which is void if he took his own life, Mr. Birch. Let's go inside. I have a pot of coffee brewing or there are soft drinks if you prefer. Nothing alcoholic, I'm afraid. I leave that to my brother."

The inside of the "cabin" reflected either Garner's excellent taste or the efforts of a professional interior designer. We settled in a small den where I admired the paintings, including an original Trentano, a small one, while Garner fetched coffee and the fixings.

"Now what exactly can I do for you, Mr. Birch?"

I ran through the usual questions. No, he had no reason to believe that there was any hanky panky going on with the Tontine's finances but yes, he favored shutting it down. "If it was in New York City, it might be worth keeping open, but frankly there just isn't enough of a market in the Providence area anymore."   He couldn't suggest anyone who might have hated Spencer enough to have murdered him, but he had known that he had purchased a handgun. "He called me to ask my advice when he first when shopping for one. I told him he was a damned fool more likely to shoot himself than someone else, but I steered him toward the safest weapon I could think of. He wouldn't tell me why he wanted it and I couldn't venture a guess. Walter and I spoke once or twice a year, at board meetings, and that was about it. There was no hostility between us, but we've moved in such different directions, both artistically and personally, that there's little left for us to talk about."

"But you were close friends at one time, weren't you?"

"Very close. Walter helped me when we were young, introduced me to the right people, PeterTrentano and Phyllis Reynolds, both gone now. The four of us came up with the idea for the Tontine, you know, but we couldn't quite swing the finances. I brought in Avery Carr, Paul recruited Michelle Bernstein, who'd just come into a nice little inheritance. I'm not sure exactly how Kristina Kwan joined the group."

"Wasn't she married to Spencer for a while?"

"That's right. I suppose he must have brought her into it. I never cared for Kristina, frankly. She was something of a cold fish and she always had secrets she wouldn't share with the rest of us. Walter and I drifted apart when they got married, and even though it didn't last very long, we never managed the old warmth after they divorced. I think he was embarrassed because I'd told him not to marry her and didn't want to admit that I'd been right."

I was beginning to think this trip had been a complete waste of time when Garner hesitated a second, then apparently made a decision to be more forthcoming. "You know why they divorced, don't you?"

"The subject hasn't come up actually."

"I've been remembering the old times more and more lately. I guess that's a sign of advancing age. We were a pretty wild bunch back then, at least by the standards of the time. We were artists, you see, so we had to live up to some vague code of nonconformity. We dressed oddly, said outrageous things in public, and drank a lot. I did a lifetime's drinking in just a few years, which is why I stay away from the stuff now. And we ingested a few substances which the government believes are bad for us. Avery even got busted once. He didn't smoke any more than the rest of us but we were careful. Most of the time he was careful too, but he mouthed off to a police detective and two days later they planted a few joints in his apartment and arrested him. After that he never trusted the police, even though he got off with a suspended sentence and probation."

He was drifting so I nudged him back toward the subject at hand. "Was this before or after he married Kwan?"

"A little before. Walter always said society's mores were artificial and didn't apply, particularly in sexual matters. He and Kristina had separate apartments, but he slept at her place most of the time. Michelle was obsessed with Peter and spent most of her nights in his bed. When she wasn't there she was with Avery Carr. This was all before she married Benjamin, of course. She'd settled down by then."

I remembered the name Benjamin Fogle from Bernstein's file. They'd been married for more than twenty years.

"Kristina played the untouchable back in the early days. You know, the virgin muse who was supposed to inspire the rest of us. She got very annoyed when we wouldn't play along. But somehow she and Walter got very tight after awhile. Walter was a real hellion. I'm sure he had more sexual partners than the rest of us put together. But he and Kristina started getting exclusive during the late 1970s and the next thing we knew they were announcing their engagement. We all found it perfectly shocking."

"Their marriage didn't last long."

"No, and I have to admit that it was pretty much Walter's fault. How much do you know about Phyllis Reynolds?"

There was a paragraph about her in the files. "Not much. It doesn't seem likely that she's connected with Spencer's death."

"You might be surprised. Her spirit lingers even now that she's gone. Phyllis was a lovely woman, and sexually insatiable. Walter always claimed that she led him astray, but the rest of us never believed it. He just wasn't the type to tie himself down to a single woman. He and Phyllis had an affair; Kristina found out about it and filed for divorce. Walter couldn't contest the issue because there was some rather damning evidence in the matter. Phyllis was pregnant."

"Spencer had a child?" There was no hint of this in anything I'd seen to date. "Do the others know about this?"

"Of course. It was no secret at the time. The baby was put up for adoption and we never spoke of her again. Walter never mentioned the child in my presence until about ten years ago when we went out for a few drinks and he told me that he'd been keeping an eye on her but that she didn't know that he was her father."

"I don't suppose you know her name?"

"Not a clue. She'd be somewhere in her twenties now, probably married and raising a brood of her own. Kristina kept her distance from the rest of us from that point on, as though we all shared in Walter's guilt. Walter must have felt some degree or remorse because he immediately broke things off with Phyllis, who became very bitter because she thought the rest of us blamed her for wrecking a happy marriage. It wasn't true, of course. If we blamed anyone, it was Walter, and really we'd never expected it to last long anyway. And about a year after that, Peterl and Phyllis were both dead and the rest of us had begun to drift apart."

I had a question, but I wasn't sure I should ask it. It proved unnecessary, because Garner read my mind.

"You're wondering where I fit into all this, aren't you? I've just revealed the sexual misadventures of all my partners with no mention of my own indiscretions."

"The thought had occurred to me."

"Well, let me put your mind at rest. I was just as much a libertine as the rest of them, but I always chose my partners from outside our little circle. I had no choice in the matter, actually. The only one who appealed to me at all was Avery, and my one attempt to feel him out on the subject, no pun intended, ended disastrously."

Garner fell silent, perhaps lost in memories, and I fumbled around for something to say. "Do you agree with the others that Walter was not likely to have killed himself?"

For a moment I thought he might not answer, but he turned to look at me directly. "Not at all. I'm surprised he didn't do it weeks earlier."

"When he first bought the handgun, you mean?"

"Well, shortly after that. He'd been receiving mysterious, unsigned letters, you see, which he thought were threats directed at his daughter. That's why he bought a weapon. He was determined to protect her."

I tried not to react. "Then why would he kill himself?"

"Because he had just found out that he'd been looking out for the wrong person. His daughter had already died."

CHAPTER SIX

For a few seconds, my head spun as I tried to digest this new information. "How do you know all this? I thought you only spoke to him at board meetings."

Garner nodded, not bothering to disguise a smirk. He might be reclusive but he still delighted in gossip. "Ordinarily, that was the case. But during the last few weeks before he died, Walter called me several times. The first call was to ask my advice about handguns, like I said before. He didn't know the first thing about the subject but he remembered that I do some hunting. Even over the phone it was obvious to me that Walter was under a lot of stress. My first thought, of course, was that he was going to kill himself, so I tried to draw him out. He wouldn't be too specific but he insisted it was for self defense or, as he put it, to defend his family. I had misgivings even then, but he made it sound plausible enough. And besides, he was going to go out and buy himself a weapon anyway. The least I could do was suggest a comparatively safe handgun."

"He might have meant that his niece was in danger."

"No, he specifically mentioned his daughter, but he wouldn't tell me who she was, only that he'd been aware of her identity for some time but hadn't revealed himself. He didn't think it would be appropriate after so long, or at least that's what he said. It was more likely that he was afraid of what the reaction might be. Walter was never at ease when emotions were running high. I pressed the issue and he said that he'd received some abusive letters regarding the girl, but he wouldn't be more specific than that."

"Had he gone to the police?"

"I have no idea. Walter didn't mix well with authority. I may have suggested something along those lines when we spoke, but I honestly don't recall. If Walter didn't want his daughter to know of their relationship then I suspect he decided to deal with the situation himself."

"Did he say anything else about these letters? When or how he received them, anything like that?"

Garner shook his head. "I don't think so. He was pretty close mouthed about details and we really weren't as close as we used to be. I eventually steered him to a relatively safe weapon, but any handgun is potentially deadly, as Walter subsequently demonstrated. And no, I don't feel any sense of responsibility. If Walter was determined to take his own life, he'd have found another way to do it. In fact, I'm surprised that he chose the method he did. He always hated making a mess."

"You said he called more than once?"

"Twice more, the last time just the day before he died. That's when he told me that he believed the letters had been a cruel hoax, that he'd found out his daughter had died as a child. He rambled a bit and I thought he might have been drunk, although with Walter it was sometimes hard to tell because he was taking a lot of pain killers and sometimes his voice was slurred. I made the usual sympathetic sounds but I don't think he heard me. He was so distraught that I actually thought about driving into the city to see him the following week but by then it was too late."

"And you think this revelation drove him to suicide?"

"Walter Spencer was a strong man, Mr. Birch, but he had been hammered in recent years by a series of setbacks. He could no longer work, he was in constant physical pain, his attempt to renew his relationship with Kristina had failed miserably, his scholarship project had fallen through, and now the young woman he believed to be his daughter turned out to be a stranger and his real daughter, his only child, was dead. Yes, I think Walter shot himself. I might have done the same in his position."

I sorted through my thoughts. "What happened with the scholarship?"

He shrugged. "I don't know the details, but either the School of Design was unwilling to accept some of the terms Walter had specified or he had second thoughts of his own. You could ask them, or Avery might know. I believe he helped write up the proposal."

"Assuming for the sake of argument that Spencer didn't commit suicide, can you think of anyone who might hate him enough to kill him?"

"Well, whoever sent those mysterious letters about his daughter certainly seems vindictive enough."

"What about Kristina Kwan? They'd broken off their relationship recently."

"You don't really expect me to point fingers at my partners, do you?" He laughed. "Kristina may have a violent temper hidden behind her ice queen image, but I've never seen any sign of it and in her own way she has always loved Walter Spencer. I don't know why they broke it off this latest time, but I'd expect her to be saddened rather than angry. As far as I know, he was the only man she ever allowed into her life."

"I understand that you're in favor of shutting down the Tontine."

"That's true. I was the first to suggest it after Paul died, but no one would hear of it then. Kristina joined me a few years later, but we were still a minority."

"I've been told that Spencer was about to come over to your side. That would have given you a majority."

Garner laughed. "Walter played that card every few years. He'd pretend to be wavering so that he'd be in Kristina's good graces for a while, but he always backed away when it came to a vote. I think the Tontine had some vague mystical importance for Walter. He was there almost as much as Avery. No, that's unfair. Avery works very hard and does an excellent job under the circumstances. But Walter maintained an office there and he'd stroll through the galleries, talk to customers, things like that. He was our spokesperson back when we were a more cohesive group. Audiences liked him and he enjoyed being the center of attention."

"So you don't think the Tontine would have closed if he hadn't died?"

"No."

"How about now? What happens in the event of a tie?"

"I haven't the faintest idea. Avery is Chairman of the Board. I imagine it's up to him to cast the tie breaker, which means the status quo continues."

"Until another one of you dies."

Garner gave me a long, appraising look. "You think Walter was murdered, don't you?"

And much to my surprise, I realized I was leaning in that direction. "I haven't ruled it out. Just out of curiosity, where were you on the night in question?"

He laughed, genuinely I thought. "I have an alibi. I was right here."

"And presumably your brother will confirm that?"

"Carl? No, I'm afraid not. He was out that night and didn't get back until well after midnight. I was in bed by then."

"Well then, theoretically, you could have driven down to Providence, shot Walter Spencer, and then driven back."

"Except that I can prove I was here from eleven until almost midnight. I was in a teleconference with my agent, who was at the time in Sydney, Australia, arranging an exhibition. I assure you, Mr. Birch, that I didn't kill Walter Spencer. Leaving aside the fact that he was one of my few friends, however infrequently we were together, I simply had no motive to do so."

I started to leave a few minutes later, but Garner insisted on giving me a tour of his cabin. All of the rooms were spacious, well lit, and expensively furnished. "I close off some of the rooms during the heating season. You'd be amazed how much wood I burn annually. I've cleared a couple of acres since I've been here, and I buy more cordage than I cut for myself."

The second floor consisted of a small studio plus three bedrooms, one of which I was not allowed to see. "That's Carl's room. I try to respect his privacy."

"Is he in?"

"No, he spends a lot of his time off by himself. He's a fair hunter although I don't think he takes any pleasure in it."

"You'll have to thank him for me. I got to see a lot of extra scenery thanks to his misdirection."

"I am sorry about that. Carl tends to be impulsive and antisocial. He's never been able to hold a job and I've supported him for the last several years. Most of the time he behaves himself but he's even more of a hermit than I am."

I glanced around the open space. "Is this where you work?" There was an easel in one corner of the room and an oversized worktable, but no work in progress and none of the disorder I expected.

"Not really. I do some sketching here from time to time, but I rent a converted barn. I find that I'm more inclined to actually work if I'm not in my own home. The distractions here, even when Carl isn't around, would inhibit me." It sounded plausible, but Garner had turned away from me as he spoke, and I sensed that he wasn't being completely truthful.

He walked me back to my car and I hesitated with the door open. "Will you be coming in to Providence any time soon?"

"Not before the board meeting next month. I drove down when Walter was buried, of course, but I don't get into the city very often anymore."

"I understand that Kwan didn't attend the funeral."

"That's right. She didn't." I waited for him to say more, but he didn't, so I shook his hand and left.

Dusty answered on the third ring. "I'm here."

"Where's here?" I asked. I was at the end of Garner's dirt road, waiting to finish the call before going further.

"Ummm, across the street from Jolene's Flower and Gift Shop."

I sighed. "Across what street?"

"I don't know. I can't see any signs from here. Just come back into town. It's the last left before Route 12. I'm about a block down."

"All right. Give me ten minutes."

It didn't take that long. Dusty was sitting on a bench in a tiny park, a book open in her lap. There were two bright yellow plastic bags on the seat beside her. Apparently she'd managed to get some shopping done.

"So how'd it go?" she asked as soon as her baggage was stowed in the back seat.

I hadn't intended to tell her much but my thoughts were so jumbled that it all spilled out, including my growing feeling that Walter Spencer had been murdered, despite all the evidence to the contrary.

"You should go with your instincts," she told me.

"It would be easier if my instincts pointed in a specific direction. I can't come up with a plausible motive for any of the partners to have killed Spencer. If he really had planned to change his vote, Carr and Bernstein might have been objected strongly enough to take direct action, but Garner insists that it was just a tactic to get some sympathy from Kwan and that he'd raised similar false alarms in the past."

"That doesn't mean they didn't believe him this time. Or that he wasn't serious."

"No, but I'm not sure the motive is really strong enough. Both Carr and Bernstein are well-heeled, or would be if the gallery closed and its assets were sold off. I'm having trouble casting either of them as a killer."

"What about Garner?"

"Spencer's death probably doesn't change the status quo. He gets a larger percentage of the profits from the Tontine, but that's all. He also has a very good alibi if it checks out, and I'm sure the police checked it out." But I wasn't, actually. There was no mention of it in the summary portion of the police report which I'd read.

"He'd be even better off if someone else died."

"Another violent death would probably make the police very suspicious."

"That might be a risk he's willing to take."

I shook my head. "I'm not seeing him in the part. You should see where he lives, Dusty. Even way out here it must have cost him better than a half million dollars. And he rents a separate studio. I'm not saying he wouldn't welcome the proceeds if the gallery closes, but it doesn't look like his lifestyle is going to be affected appreciably."

"Appearances can be deceiving."

There was a tone in her voice that told me she was holding something back. "All right, out with it. You obviously know something that I don't."

"What? Are we finally going to admit that this amateur over here might have something to contribute after all?"

"I never said you had nothing to contribute and I'm not going to be trapped into another round of twisted reasoning on the subject. Do you know something or don't you?"

"Well, I did talk to a couple of people. I stopped at the real estate office right where you dropped me off and asked about log cabins for sale or rent. Miss Fairfax was very sorry but the only ones she had listed were pretty run down. I mentioned that I had heard that the artist, Earl Garner, lived in a cabin somewhere in the area and she told me that he had a very nice place but that it was really too grand for its location and that she'd already told Mr. Garner that he would be lucky to get his investment back if he sold it.

"So his place is on the market?"

"Not yet, apparently. But he's been making inquiries. And he declined to renew his lease on the barn studio three months ago. It runs out a few weeks from now."

"Which could mean that he's gotten tired of the frigid winters up here, or just wants a change of scenery."

"That doesn't explain why he sold his Porsche."

"Does the real estate agent handle auto sales in her spare time?"

"No, I heard that from Ed at Logan's Garage. He's the only mechanic Garner ever let touch his car. He sold it over in Keene six months ago and now he drives around in a three year old jeep."

"A jeep is more practical for this area."

Dusty's snort dismissed my comment. "I bet if you asked Barry to do some checking, you'd find out that Mr. Garner's income has dropped below his expenses. It looks to me like he's cutting corners and hoarding cash."

"Your evidence is pretty slim."

"Then we need to widen it. Did you meet the brother?"

"Carl? No, he wasn't there." I recounted my misadventure with the set of bad directions and my visit to Zach's. "Garner seemed embarrassed about him."

"Do you think he might have killed Spencer?"

I had to mull that one over for a minute or two before admitting that yes, there was a certain plausibility to that. "If he thought Spencer's death might materially help his brother, he might have taken a hand either through self interest or misguided loyalty. Earl did say that Carl wasn't home that night."

"Did he take the jeep?"

I shook my head. "I don't know. It's possible, I suppose."

"I have another scenario for you. What if Earl did commit the murder after all?"

"I told you he has an alibi. A conference call during the critical period. I haven't checked it yet, but I don't think he'd have volunteered the information if it wasn't true."

"That doesn't mean Carl couldn't have done the murder for him." She gasped suddenly. "Wait! It could still be Earl for that matter. Maybe Carl was the one on the conference call, covering for his brother who drove down to Providence to kill his partner."

"I'd be more willing to accept that possibility if we had a more concrete motive. Even if Garner is having financial difficulties, Spencer's death isn't going to make a substantial difference."

We would have been back in Providence in time for supper if Dusty hadn't insisted on stopping at four yard sales and a flea market on the way back, adding a handful of purchases to what she had already accumulated in the back seat. It was getting dark by the time we reached Leominster and I remembered a nice seafood place in Sterling from several years back, although the reality didn't live up to the memory. The fish was obviously frozen rather than fresh and the vegetables were so overcooked that they lacked both taste and texture.

During one of the stops I called the office. Steve gave me a brief summary of what had obviously been a very quiet day. I talked to Barry and asked him to see what he could find out about Earl Garner's financial situation. "Don't leave any footprints, Barry. Garner seems to be cooperative and I don't want him getting mad at us."

I tried calling Kari Spencer twice, got her answering machine both times. I left a message indicating that I'd completed my preliminary survey and would like to meet with her to decide whether or not she wanted to proceed. "Please call my office and set up an appointment at your convenience."

I wasn't sure whether or not I wanted her to go forward. My instincts told me that there was something strange about Walter Spencer's death but logic led to a different conclusion, and even if my instincts were right—and they aren't always—I wasn't sure that I could pick out a path that would lead to the truth. Like I said, I leave murder investigations to the police.

It was Friday, and there was no reason why I should have to think about business over the weekend. I decided to push the Spencer case to the back of my mind and let it sit there until Monday morning.

Unfortunately, the rest of the world often declines to play by my rules.

We got back to the house just before nine. Dusty had been napping the last half hour and she went upstairs to get out of her clothes and into a nightgown. I finished unloading the car; Dusty had added to her stores of children's building blocks and I had visions of London appearing in the living room, or Tokyo in the bedroom. Her James Bondish protagonist had followed the villains to both locations during the course of the as yet uncompleted novel, but Paris remained undemolished in the dining room because "the climax is going to be on the Eiffel Tower". I mixed myself a weak drink and took a couple of aspirin; prolonged driving occasionally gives me a blinding headache. I almost went upstairs without checking the answering machine.

Almost.

It was blinking. Two messages. The first was a reminder for Dusty that she had a doctor's appointment. The second was for me and it was Kari Spencer, her voice thick with tension.

"Mr. Birch? I'm sorry to disturb you at home but I just found something in my uncle's papers that might be relevant. It's rather disturbing, in fact. I wonder if you could call me as soon as possible. I'd really appreciate it." She gave the number but I was too befuddled to memorize it and I had to play the message back in order to write it down.

I glanced at my watch. It was late. But not too late. Sighing, I dialed the number. She answered on the second ring and I identified myself.

"Thank you so much for calling, Mr. Birch. I suppose I should have waited until Monday but I just had to tell someone about this right away."

She was talking very quickly and I could almost feel the tension in her voice. "What can I do for you, Miss Spencer?"

"I've been sorting through my uncle's papers, sending unpaid bills to the lawyers, answering some correspondence, things like that. Uncle Walter was a bit of a packrat, you understand. He has receipts going back to the 1950s and what looks like every personal letter he ever received. Anyway, I found a folder with some legal papers and some letters and a lot of handwritten notes he must have added."

I immediately thought of the threatening letters Spencer had supposedly received in the weeks leading up to his death and assumed that Kari had stumbled upon them but I was wrong.

"They're not really specific, but when I read through them I realized what they meant." She paused, either for effect or to gather

her own thoughts. "Mr. Birch, I think I might have been Uncle Walter's illegitimate daughter!"

Rarely have I been in a more awkward position. It seemed unlikely that Walter Spencer had believed Kari to be his daughter, but if I could trust Earl Garner's version of things, Spencer had recently discovered that he'd been mistaken about her identity. Assuming, of course, that Spencer's mistake hadn't been in doubting his original theory. My head started to spin. And some people think spreadsheets are bewildering. Now I was in the position of probably knowing more than my client, but not knowing if what I knew was accurate, or if she would best be served by my silence or by hearing what I'd learned. I certainly was in no position to comment usefully.

"I thought your mother was married to Walter's brother," I said carefully.

"Yes, at least she raised me. Her husband, the man I originally thought was my father, died when I was two. When I turned fourteen, she told me that I'd been adopted and that she didn't know who my real parents were."

"These papers you found. Were they from the adoption agency?"

"No, but they refer to it."

"Is there any mention of your mother? Your birth mother, I mean."

"Only indirectly. Not by name. If you could come over, I can show them to you."

"It's rather late, Miss Spencer."

"Oh, yes. Of course. I'm sorry. I just sort of lost track of time."

I suppressed the urge to sigh. "Why don't we get together tomorrow morning? Can you bring the papers in question to my office?" I'd have to open up. The others didn't come in on Saturday, except sometimes Tina when she was working on something that intrigued her.

"Yes, certainly. But it would be easier if you came here."

"All right. I assume here is your uncle's house?" That was the address she had provided to Steve.

"Yes, I'm staying here temporarily. Do you know where it is?"

"I do. I'll see you in the morning, Miss Spencer. About 9:30."

We both hung up and I went upstairs. Dusty was already asleep and I eased into bed beside her carefully so that I wouldn't wake her. Darla jumped up onto the bed and insisted on having her ears scratched, as well as the hard to get at areas inside her collar, and I obliged absentmindedly. I was exhausted but it took quite a while before I finally closed my eyes.

Much to my surprise, Dusty was up and about before I left the house. "Meeting Wanda at 10:00," she explained. I still had misgivings about that, but decided to keep my mouth shut. I was sure Dusty wouldn't violate any confidences and it could be worse. She could be stalking Avery Carr or applying for a job at Kwan and Company.

I had no trouble finding the late Walter Spencer's house. It was on the East Side of Providence, but north of Swan Point Cemetery where the real estate prices weren't quite as outrageous. It was an older place, brick fronted, two stories, crowded with shrubs, evergreens, and a prolific climbing ivy. There was a Volkswagen Golf parked in the driveway, but the garage door was down. I pulled in beside it.

Kari Spencer answered my ring promptly. She looked considerably different from the last time we'd met, wearing a plaid men's shirt and mildly disreputable jeans, her hair tied back into a pony tail. I knew that she was at least twenty-five years old but she looked like a high school student.

"Please come in, Mr. Birch. You'll have to pardon the mess. I've been trying to sort things out."

Her industriousness was self evident. The living room was barely visible under stacks of paper, some gathered in cardboard boxes, some arranged on the couch and chairs, others on the floor. There was one trash bag tied off and another in progress. An empty pizza box sat on a card table in front of the fireplace along with two empty bottles of Sam Adams.

"You've been busy."

She gave an exaggerated sigh. "I always knew Uncle Walter saved everything, but I didn't realize the scale of things until I started going through them. These are all from his home office, and I'm only half way. And there are more files at the gallery and in his bedroom and the den, six file cabinets in the basement and at least a dozen boxes in the attic."

"Who's the administrator of the estate?"

"I'm co-executor with his lawyer, a Mr. Judson. I've been separating out anything I think he should look at."

"I hope you've consulted someone about his correspondence. It might have some value."

She nodded vigorously. "Quite a bit, actually. There's a whole folder of letters from Peter Trentano, and he used to doodle in the margins. And I found a bunch of photographs of them all together, the partners I mean. It all has to be appraised before we can settle the estate."

"You said you found some documents you wanted me to look at."

"Yes, this way." She led me through a rather cluttered but reasonably orderly house to what was obviously meant to be an office. There were more piles of paper here, mostly on the floor and on top of a row of three filing cabinets, but the ornate mahogany desk was bare except for three folders.

"The top folder is mostly correspondence between Uncle Walter and a detective agency he hired during the 1980s. It's not complete apparently. I'm sure he must have known the name of the mother—my mother—but it's not mentioned anywhere. They weren't much help. The records were sealed and they say that without some overriding necessity like an hereditary disease, there's no likelihood that he could get them released. They were able to provide at least a partial list of placements during the period in question, and one of them is me."

"That doesn't necessarily mean anything." I picked up the folder in question and thumbed through it. The list of placements was three pages long. "If your uncle had wanted his daughter to be raised by his sister, why not do so openly?"

"I don't know, but that second folder is all about me. Uncle Walter secretly paid for my college tuition and my first car and took care of a lot of other things I didn't know about or assumed my mother had handled."

"Were your parents, your adopted parents I mean, well off?"

"No, not at all. Mom supervised an office but she didn't make a lot of money. I guess I should have figured she couldn't have saved as much as she said she did, but she always told me that her husband had been heavily insured when he died."

"It's possible that your uncle was frustrated by his inability to find his own daughter and took a strong interest in you as compensation. He could afford to indulge himself that way."

"I suppose." She didn't sound convinced. "Anyway, there's also some correspondence between Uncle Walter and the Lincoln Child Services, which is the agency that handled my adoption. They very politely refused to identify my birth mother—but he would already have known that - or any of the details of the adoption except to say that the arrangements had been unusually secretive and that I'd only been in their care for a few days. And there's a page from another investigator's report with some passages underlined. My birth mother and my adopted mother contacted the agency together even before I was born and asked them to handle the adoption. They must have known one another."

"What's in the third folder?"

"I think you should look for yourself."

CHAPTER SEVEN

"I hadn't found these yet when I called you." Her voice trembled.

There were three sheets of white bond paper, each folded multiple times. They hadn't been signed and they'd been printed from a computer in what looked like 24 point or larger. None of them were dated but it wasn't hard to figure out their order of precedence..

The first said simply: "KARI SPENCER IS NOT THE PERSON YOU THINK SHE IS."

The second read: "KARI IS NOT YOUR DAUGHTER. OPEN YOUR EYES AND SEE THE TRUTH."

The third was the most ominous. "YOU ARE WASTING YOUR AFFECTION ON THAT BITCH. I COULD KILL HER FOR THE WAY SHE TREATS YOU!" None of the notes bore a signature or any other distinguishing marks.

I read through them three times before I said anything. "Did your uncle ever mention anything to you about these? Even a hint that he'd heard something disturbing or that he thought you might be in danger?"

She shook her head. "But we hadn't talked a lot those last few months. I've been busy at work and you know how time slips away." There was a hint of guilt in her voice but I pretended not to notice.

"He might have gone to the police." I knew that was impossible as soon as I made the suggestion. If Spencer had shown these to the authorities, they would have insisted on interviewing Kari and probably her friends and co-workers, even if they didn't take the implied threat seriously.

"No, I'm sure he didn't. Uncle Walter didn't think much of the police. He would have to be pretty desperate to talk to them voluntarily. He always called them the 'arms of oppression' or worse."

I waved the notes gently. "These might explain why he bought a handgun. He may have become convinced that you were in danger."

She bit her lip. "I suppose so. But I can't imagine how he thought he was going to protect me; I'm not even sure he knows where my office is. And frankly I can't imagine him hiding in the bushes outside my apartment building waiting to ambush a prowler. But then again, he never was a very practical man and he might not have thought things through. He used to say that you could have a creative imagination or a thorough grounding in reality but not both." A more troubling thought rippled across her face. "Do you think I'm in any real danger, Mr. Birch?"

I shrugged. "I couldn't answer that intelligently based on these." I waved the notes at her again. "It's obvious that someone doesn't like you very much, but that doesn't mean they would do you any harm. And with your uncle dead, whether by his own hand or another, this might all be irrelevant now. And these are vague enough that I doubt the police would do anything more proactive than sending extra patrols through your neighborhood." I hesitated. "But it wouldn't hurt to be cautious. Keep the doors locked when you're alone, be careful when you go out, particularly at night. At least for the time being."

My cautions were alarming rather than reassuring her so I turned back to the notes, reading them once more. "May I borrow these for awhile?"

"Sure. If it'll help. Does that mean you've decided to continue with your investigation?"

"I've uncovered nothing which contradicts the conclusions in the police report, Miss Spencer. There's no evidence that your uncle had any serious enemies and while there are always people who profit by a death, particularly of someone so prominent, none of them had particularly strong motives for murder."

Her face fell. "Then you think he killed himself."

"I think it probable that he did just that, but I might be wrong. There are a few questions that I could pursue further but before I ask you to commit any more of your money I have to say first, that they may be no more than ordinary loose ends leading nowhere, and second, that even if your uncle was murdered, we might never be able to prove it or identify the party responsible."

"But you think there's justification for going on with this?"

I chose my words carefully. "I think another couple of days work might prove enlightening but I can't promise significant results."

"Then go ahead, Mr. Birch. I've already told you that I want to know the truth, regardless of the cost."

Dusty was gone when I got home. I'd forgotten to open a can of food and Darla made sure I knew how outrageously I'd abused her. Once that crisis was remedied, I took the three folders up to my office and read through them all in detail. The agency Spencer had hired was defunct now, but I'd heard good things about them. They appeared to have done as thorough a job as possible under the circumstances. Adoption records are almost as hard to access as the Vice President's working notes. They'd tracked down a few of the women who'd given their children up for adoption through Lincoln Child Services, an upscale adoption agency and foster home center north of Providence. Phyllis Reynolds was not on the list, but a false name wasn't out of the question. They'd also identified a number of adopting parents for the year in question, including Arthur Rayburn and Heather Spencer. Kari's mother had kept her maiden name when she married and had passed it on to the baby. I wondered if that had been her idea or if Walter had influenced her. It was obvious that he had been troubled by his abandonment of his daughter as a child and it wouldn't surprise me if he had been trying to replace her. If he was predisposed to cast Kari as his quasi-daughter, it wouldn't have been that big a leap to deciding that she really was his flesh and blood.

The notes offered no solid evidence that Kari was or was not in fact Spencer's daughter, nor was there anything remotely suggesting that the child had died in infancy. Something must have convinced him not only that she was unrelated, but that his real daughter had been dead for years. Was there another note? More than one?

Impulsively I reached out and dialed. Kari answered almost immediately this time. "Miss Spencer, have you gone through the papers at your uncle's office at the Tontine yet?"

"No, I haven't even been there since...since he died. The police told me that I couldn't remove anything until their investigation was done and there was enough here to keep me busy anyway."

"Would you mind if I took a look through them?"

"Of course not. Do you need me to call Mr. Carr?"

"No, I don't think so. You wouldn't happen to know if the gallery is open today."

"Of course. Saturday is their busiest day."

"Thank you. I'll be in touch."

It was much harder to find a parking space this time and I had to walk eight blocks to the gallery after squeezing into a barely adequate gap on a side street near the Brown University athletic field. There was a light drizzle just to add to my discomfort and I had to fish around in my overcrowded trunk for a couple of minutes before I found the umbrella I'd stowed there.

The Tontine wasn't exactly mobbed, but there were several people browsing when I arrived. Wanda had been replaced by an earnest looking young man whose name tag read "Eric" and who was busy with a young couple when I came in. Avery Carr was not visible and the upstairs was cordoned off. I was considering stepping over the rope anyway when the door opened again and Carr bustled in, collapsing his umbrella in the process.

I waited until he had shaken it relatively dry before approaching.

"Oh, Mr. Birch. I didn't know you were coming by. I hope you haven't been waiting long. I had an errand to run."

"I just got here actually. Miss Spencer gave me permission to look through her uncle's papers."

"That's no problem at all, but I can't promise that they're in the same state as they were when Walter left us. The police, you know. They went through all the files."

That came as no surprise, but if they'd discovered any kind of death threat, there would at least have been a mention of it in the case file, which there wasn't. On the other hand, they hadn't been looking for anything specifically involving Spencer's niece, or daughter.

"Is his office locked?"

"No, not now. I've left it open since the police released it. To air it out, you see. You know the way?"

It took almost an hour to go through the desk. Most of the paperwork was related to Spencer's lecture appearances including an impressive collection of flyers and printed programs. There were also some recent financial reports from the Tontine, which looked routine, some correspondence from the School of Design discussing the proposed Walter Spencer Scholarship, and a few random letters from fans and friends. I read the material from the college thoroughly but found nothing indicating that the project had run into any difficulties, and the most recent letter was dated only a few days before Spencer's death. I made a mental note to find out if Garner's account was accurate.

The filing cabinet was better organized but I spent another hour there. Some folders were easily dismissed, like the one that held menus from East Side restaurants, plus a street map of Providence. Others took longer. There were some photographs of Spencer with one or more of his partners, including several with Kristina Kwan, but in none of these did they look like a couple. A tall, ascetic looking woman appeared in some of the older ones and I surmised this must be Phyllis Reynolds. She was not the femme fatale I'd expected, her features rather sharp, her expression not exactly unfriendly but certainly stern. She looked like a stereotypical old fashioned schoolteacher. There were quite a few letters sent care of the gallery, some expressing admiration for his work, some soliciting donations, plus invitations to speak or conduct workshops. I went through these very carefully, but there was nothing menacing or angry in any of them, and the most recent was in any case almost two years old.

I closed the last drawer on the file cabinet and looked around wearily. There was a full sized print of one of Peter Trentano's paintings, rolled up and sitting in one corner, and I recognized it as one of those displayed downstairs. The lower right hand corner had been neatly cut off, about four inches square. A three part picture frame stood on the desk, with three photographs of Kari Spencer, as a child, as a gangly teenager, and the last fairly recent.

There was an appointment book on his desk, but it held very few entries for the month preceding Spencer's death and none at all on the critical weekend. I went back through the entire year anyway, but nothing stood out except one: "Call Carl about gun". The rest of that particular page was blank.

Carr stuck his head in the door as I was nearing the end of my search. "Find anything?"

"Nothing worth mentioning. Did Spencer ever throw out a piece of paper?"

That earned me a chuckle. "Walter wouldn't even throw out junk mail until he'd conducted an extensive internal debate. He was a bit of a nut about keeping records, reducing everything to paper. He'd write down notes for Wanda and I and leave them in our offices when it was just as easy simply to tell us verbally. He insisted that he was a visual rather than auditory person. I sometimes teased him that he'd missed his calling, that he should have been an accountant."

I glanced down at the desk. "There's not much in his appointment book."

"No, there wouldn't be. Walter began disengaging himself from the world about a year ago. He shocked us all by turning down several speaking engagements early in the year and word got around so the invitations dried up. It was very much unlike him. Walter did love to talk. But he said he was getting tired of hearing his own voice and that he'd said everything that he intended to say and was just repeating himself. I think the pain was wearing him down."

"You knew he and Reynolds had a daughter together, didn't you?"

His face sobered. "I wondered if you'd find that out. It didn't seem right for me to just come out and tell you and in any case that was a long time ago. They put her up for adoption, or Phyllis did, actually. Walter never wanted to talk about it. I think it was one of the few things in his life that he regretted."

"He never tried to find her?"

"Not that I know of, but he may have. We were friends, but neither of us felt comfortable talking about personal matters."

"How about Kwan? She obviously knew Spencer had a daughter and they were intimate recently. Did she ever mention the girl?"

Carr looked as though I'd asked how often it rained frogs. "I doubt that Kristina spoke of personal matters even when she was married to Walter, let alone just his lover. We used to call her the Ice Princess, you know."

"They sound like an unlikely couple."

"Well, they lasted less than a year, after all. The breakup was the only time I've ever seen Kristina visibly shaken. She went off to Europe somewhere and we didn't see her for more than a year. When she came back, the mantle of ice was firmly back in place and there hasn't been even the hint of a thaw since. Their recent reconciliation was more intellectual than emotional, and the closeness didn't last more than a few months, although that was mostly Walter's fault, I fear. He was never happy committing himself to a long term relationship, even though he desperately wanted to."

I opened one of the desk drawers as Carr wandered off. I'd looked into it before; it was full almost to overflowing with business cards, thrown in randomly, apparently an exception to Spencer's mania for orderliness. I almost closed the drawer but some impulse made me stop and began to sift through them. When a person does something this far out of character, it suggests significance. A few seconds later I found a file folder at the bottom of the drawer. Inside were three envelopes, each addressed to Walter Spencer, the last postmarked three days before he had died. The return address in each case was Furtado Investigations, a detective agency based in Taunton, Massachusetts. The first envelope was a terse letter of acknowledgment indicating that Furtado Investigations welcomed Walter Spencer as a client and informing him that a detailed contract would be available for his signature shortly. The letter had been written in January. The second envelope contained an interim invoice for work performed, referencing a contract number, but the detail page or pages were missing. The third envelope was empty, but the postmark was less than two months old.

I poked around in the drawer, but nothing else of interest showed up. I folded the three envelopes and put them in my jacket pocket, then got up and checked to see if Avery Carr was in his office. He was. He was sitting in his chair, staring at a blank spot on the wall so intently that he didn't even notice that I was standing there until I cleared my throat.

"Oh, my apologies Mr. Birch. I was daydreaming. Can I help you with anything?"

"No, I just wanted to let you know that I was leaving."

"Find anything to justify your effort?"

"Not really. I'm afraid Miss Spencer is wasting her money, but she is determined to have her way."

"If that's the greatest mistake she makes in her life, she'll be a very lucky woman." He sighed as though he was remembering the great mistakes of his own life, as perhaps he was. I thanked him for his cooperation and left him there to stare at the wall in peace.

I didn't know anyone at the Furtado Agency, though I'd heard the name before, and when I looked up their number and called, there was no answer. Probably all at home or out enjoying the weekend, which is what I should have been doing myself. I called the house on the chance that Dusty had returned early, but there was no answer there either. She'd told me not to expect her before late afternoon. I stopped at my own office which was similarly deserted, and spent an hour sifting through paper without accomplishing anything. The cases we handle mostly involve abstracts like financial transactions or bureaucratic artifacts—public records, statistics, old police reports, newspaper morgues—and a slow, rigorous, methodical approach is the best strategy. The Spencer matter was personal, wrapped up in human emotions, and I felt an uncharacteristic impatience to get to the heart of the matter, and frustration because I couldn't immediately resolve the situation. I wished that Kari Spencer had never walked into my office, or that I'd had the sense to send her on her way.

When it became obvious that I wasn't accomplishing anything, I drove home and tried, with reasonable success, to lose myself in a book, a new thriller that had attracted my attention, and eventually I got caught up in the story, handling the thick hardcover carefully so that I wouldn't disturb the cat sleeping in my lap. When Dusty finally came home, I was surprised to see how early she was, until I glanced out the window and saw the long shadows creeping across the lawn. It was almost five o'clock.

I displaced Darla, used a business card to mark my place in the book, and went downstairs in my stocking feet. Dusty was in the kitchen, making a pot of coffee.

"So how'd it go?"

Her voice sounded tired. "Well, we looked at a lot of bad art. Wanda doesn't have any formal training but I suspect she has a good eye for what will sell and what won't. She also has a good business sense. After each stop, she gave me a detailed evaluation of the physical layout and presentation, and critiqued the staff's method of greeting and follow up with potential customers."

"Is she a frustrated artist herself?"

"No, not at all, but she's very bright. She has a good sense of the business of art rather than the creative side. This is the first job she's ever had that actually interests her."

"How'd she end up at the Tontine?" I opened a cabinet and found a package of shortbread cookies, put several of them on a plate.

"They were originally looking for part time help on weekends clearing up paperwork. Wanda was unemployed at the time and someone recommended her for the job. She got asked to watch the desk a couple of times and she was so good with the customers that Avery Carr offered her a full time position. He's apparently very short with her and she believes that Spencer talked him into keeping her on while she was still new and making mistakes. And she's been there ever since."

The coffee was ready. Dusty got the mugs while I went after milk and sugar. We sat at the table and sipped hot liquid. "Did she have any great insights into Walter Spencer's death?"

"Not really. She liked him a lot, thought he was the best artist of the lot of them. I think he may have flirted with her a little, and even if he was old enough to be her grandfather, it still must have been flattering. I don't think she's ever had a boyfriend, maybe not even a date. I asked if she had any idea why he might have killed himself and she got very upset and said she couldn't understand it. She knew he'd had bad news recently but he hadn't seemed that upset and she was convinced that his spirits would have picked up soon."

"Why would she say that? His physical condition was deteriorating and incurable."

"I asked her something along those lines, as a matter of fact, but she just gave me a blank look and said that things always look brighter if you're patient enough."

"Did she say anything else about Avery Carr?" I took one of the cookies. "I know she didn't like him particularly, but I don't know if there was anything beyond the usual boss vs. subordinate adversarial relationship."

"That's most of it, I think. She doesn't like the way he checks up on her all the time. He praises her infrequently and never misses a chance to find fault with something she's done, and he has to be kept informed of every little detail. Wanda's not allowed to make even minor decisions. She says he treats her like an old piece of equipment that he's thinking about replacing."

"Carr has managed the Tontine for a lot of years. It's probably hard for him to relinquish control, even in little things. Wanda could stay there ten years and she'd probably have no more authority than she does now."

"If she makes it to three years, she'll have set a personal record. She got her first job at eighteen, and this is her seventh, not counting the time she spent temping." Dusty ate a cookie and washed it down with coffee. "Laid off or fired three times, quit the rest. Mostly clerical. One of them might interest you. She worked for an adoption agency for a year."

That did get my attention. "Lincoln?"

She shook her head. "Nope. That would have been neat though, wouldn't it? She was with Little Darlings in Woonsocket. Worked as a file clerk and did some typing, until she got fired for falling asleep on the night shift. She was moonlighting a second job, waiting tables, and it caught up to her one slow night. At least that's her version."

Dusty appeared to have nothing further to say. We finished our coffee, and she poured herself a refill but I declined. "Is that all you found out?"

"Pretty much. Unless you count a lot of good background material I picked up about the art scene. I think Craig is going to battle art thieves in his next adventure."

"You haven't sold the first one yet," I pointed out.

"Simply a technicality. So where does this all fit on your spreadsheet?"

This was a standing joke between us. Dusty insisted that I leeched all the romance out of my cases, reducing them to spreadsheets that I could analyze on my laptop. I usually responded that there was precious little romance to be found in double entry bookkeeping, even when there were two sets of books, or in boxes full of shipping manifests, invoices, bills of lading, and appraisals or even worse, official government documents.

"Not yet. Want to help me create one?"

She wrinkled her nose at me and finished her coffee, but her implied suggestion wasn't entirely without merit. I always felt better when I had reduced a problem to something organized and visual.

We adjourned to the den where I kept a box of columnar pads. "Ready to be helpful?"

I was sitting at the writing table and Dusty had flopped down on the couch, kicked off her shoes, and put her feet up. "Sure, as long as I don't have to move from this spot. My feet hurt." Darla poked her head around the corner of the door, then trotted off disdainfully.

"Okay. We have two possibilities to start with. Either Walter Spencer killed himself for reasons known or unknown or he was murdered. I think we can rule out an accident while cleaning his handgun."

"How about someone else causing the accident?"

I gave her a skeptical look. "Someone didn't realize the gun was loaded and fired it at Spencer's head from close range? I think we can safely discard that scenario."

"Yes, of course, Holmes."

"If it was suicide, then that's the end of it. Tragic, out of character, but leading us nowhere. But if he was murdered, we have a wealth of suspects." I labeled three columns, one for name, one for motive, and one for opportunity. "As far as we know, only five people stood to benefit financially from Spencer's death—the four surviving partners and his niece." I wrote down each of the five names, leaving ample space between them for the other entries. "I'm lumping the Garner brothers together because it seems likely that their motives are identical and for all practical purposes they're interchangeable."

"You're forgetting someone."

I looked up at Dusty. She was wearing her serious face. "Who might that be?"

"Michelle Bernstein's husband. I don't remember his name."

"Fogle. Benjamin Fogle." I had forgotten him. "All right, I'm adding him at the end, although the two of them are in pretty much the same situation as the Garner brothers. Anyone else with an obvious motive, non-financial?"

"Well, someone was sending him anonymous notes."

"They weren't hostile to Spencer, only his niece. But that does bring us to the second category—people with no obvious motives but a clear connection. Let's call Spencer's mystery correspondent "Mr. X". I added the entry to my list. "Who else?"

"Well, Wanda Fredericks, of course. We only have her word for how she felt about Spencer, and even if she's telling the truth, something might have happened to change her attitude. Maybe they had a fight."

"Okay, she's on the list." I made it so. "Who else?"

"Kari Spencer?" Dusty sounded uncertain.

I thought about it. "Let's include her for the time being. I can jury rig a case that she wrote the threatening notes herself and hired me as part of an elaborate cover, but given that the official investigation is already closed and that no one else seems inclined to ask questions, I just can't believe it."

"There could be someone we haven't even heard of yet."

She was right, but I didn't like dealing with complete unknowns. For the sake of thoroughness, I wrote "Stranger" at the bottom of the list. "All right, now we need to consider motives. All four partners gained through their share of the Tontine and Kari inherited the bulk of his remaining estate, which is considerable."

"Were there any other beneficiaries?"

The folder Kari had provided had included a copy of the will. "No one of any significance. A few gifts to charities, a few personal items to friends. Certainly nothing that seems likely to have led to murder."

"Who benefits the most if the Tontine is closed?"

"Garner and Kwan have advocated that all along so they're obviously expecting to benefit from it. If Spencer really was going to change his vote, then they had the least to gain from his death, and conversely Carr and Bernstein had the most to gain. But it's not clear that Spencer really had decided to switch. If that is the case, then Garner and Kwan gain from his death, and the other two have the most to lose. Unfortunately, there is no clear proof in either direction."

"Which means that any of the four could have killed him over the issue."

"Theoretically. And Fogle and Carl Garner fall into the same ambivalent limbo."

"But Fogle's motives could be more confused." Dusty sat up, swinging her legs down onto the floor and leaning forward. "He might have supported his wife's desire to keep the studio open, but it's also possible that he hoped to gain from the sale of the gallery, but didn't want his wife to know how he really felt."

My head was spinning but Dusty was right. I wondered if I could contrive a way to meet Bernstein's husband. "Kari's motive is obvious, but like I said I can't quite see her then hiring a detective to investigate after the police were satisfied." I had already dismissed the suggestion that she had done so in order to implicate someone else. There are degrees of complication that transcend common sense.

"Could she have been concerned about being disinherited? I mean, if her uncle discovered, or at least believed, that she was not his daughter after all, would he still have left her the bulk of the estate?"

"That thought had occurred to me, but again, why would she stir things up when they'd already been settled in her favor? And if I'm any judge of character, she was genuinely surprised and shocked when those notes showed up. How would she have found out that he no longer believed it when she apparently never knew previously that he did think she was his daughter?" The effort to wrap my brain around the possibilities made my head hurt.

"Still, it's a possibility," she insisted. "She might have guessed somehow."

"Both times?" I gave her a skeptical look but made an appropriate note. "Now what about Wanda, since you nominated her? Could she have killed him on some passing impulse, or might she be lying about their relationship?"

"Wanda as the spurned lover of an elderly man with arthritis? I don't think so. She might have killed him for some reason, but it wouldn't have been on the spur of the moment. Wanda is meticulously organized. She would have planned it in advance and carried it out coolly and efficiently."

"That would fit with the way it was done. Again, assuming it wasn't suicide."

"I don't think she was faking her admiration for him, but they might have had a falling out. Maybe he was going to ask Carr to fire her, or maybe she made a pass at him and he laughed at her."

"He was twice her age. Almost triple."

Dusty's eyes twinkled. "But he was a handsome man. I wouldn't rule it out. And I don't think Wanda has had much experience with the opposite sex."

"Okay, we'll leave her on the list, but I'm not satisfied she had sufficient motive. How about Mr. or Ms. X?"

"There's obviously considerable hostility there. It was directed toward Kari Spencer initially, but maybe it changed. Maybe when he didn't immediately renounce his niece, the anger turned toward him for being so gullible."

"If he was threatened directly, that would be a more plausible reason for his purchasing a firearm, but Spencer held onto everything and no other notes have shown up."

"That doesn't mean they didn't exist."

We were both quiet for a moment or two. I got up and walked to the bar, poured myself a brandy. "Want something?"

"An amaretto, a small one. What's next? Alibis?"

"Not quite." I delivered the drink and went back to my seat. "We've listed all the financial motives for the partners, but what if this was more personal?"

"Well, he and Kwan had just broken off their relationship again."

I made a note. "Spencer and Carr were supposedly close friends, but I thought Carr was a little too aggressive when he mentioned their friendship, as though he was trying to ensure that I made note of it. It's possible there was some tension there. Carr was the gallery manager but I understand Spencer spent a lot of time on the premises and he may have interfered from time to time. Wanda's strong feelings toward him may have some connection to behind the scenes political maneuvering."

"Spencer went to Garner for help when he wanted a weapon, so they were presumably on friendly terms. What about Bernstein?"

I shook my head. "Unknown. They don't appear to have been as close as they once were, but I don't know of any antagonism between them. Ditto for the husband. He's not an artist. It's possible that he knew Spencer only casually."

"Paul, these are all wealthy people, except for Wanda. Unless something turns up suggesting that one of them was overextended, I don't think money was the motive. Maybe Walter Spencer really did kill himself."

CHAPTER EIGHT

I'd been intellectually convinced all along that Walter Spencer probably committed suicide, but a little voice in the back of my mind was whispering otherwise. Dusty had lusted after a juicy murder case from the outset, which was probably why she'd involved herself in the first place. When she admitted the possibility that we were on a wild goose chase, my little voice took a serious body blow and, oddly, I felt a twinge of disappointment. On some atavistic level, I had cast myself as Philip Marlowe or Sam Spade, despite my protestations to the contrary. I finished my drink to cover my momentary uncertainty, considered another brandy but decided against it. Whatever kind of detective I was, I was not a hard drinking private eye like Robert Parker's Spenser.

"If we can prove that to the client, I'm sure she'll be satisfied with the results. Not necessarily happy, but satisfied."

"But you don't think that's what happened, not any more. Am I right?"

"I still haven't decided," I hedged. "Spencer might have been capable of killing himself, but I'm not sure he would have taken this particular route. Splattering his brains on one of his most prized possessions doesn't fit the profile. Even more significantly, I can't see him ending it all without leaving a suicide note, or perhaps a suicide manuscript. He was apparently long winded."

"So we still have doubts. What's next on the list?"

I glanced down at my pad. "Opportunity. If we can provisionally eliminate some of our suspects, that might point us in a new direction. Or at least reduce the number of directions to choose among."

"And can we eliminate anyone?"

"Let's look at the police files again." But they were less than useful. Bernstein and her husband had been home, asleep. The same was true of Kari Spencer and Avery Carr, both of whom lived alone. The first two had provided each other with alibis, such as they were. The second pair had no independent corroboration, but that was hardly suspicious. Kristina Kwan had been attending a conference in Boston, but it was not impossible for her to have driven back to

Providence to commit the murder, leaving ample time to return to her hotel before her absence was noted. Pretty much everyone could have managed the murder although in Bernstein's case, she and her husband might not have been able to pull it off without the other knowing, or at least suspecting, the truth.

Earl Garner's teleconference story satisfied the police, but only because they hadn't been skeptical enough to pursue things further. "If I had to choose between the brothers, I'd guess that Carl Garner is more likely the killer. Earl would certainly have been more convincing on the phone and I gather Carl's the more aggressive of the pair."

"But his brother controls the money."

"Yeah, they obviously have a complicated relationship. Other than our unknowns, the only other name on our list is Wanda, and we already knew that her alibi was shaky."

"Maybe not," objected Dusty. "That's one thing I did find out today. Her car broke down that night. She called AAA and they couldn't get it started so they towed it to a garage. She eventually got a cab and arrived home around two in the morning."

"We only have her word for that."

"But it could all be checked, couldn't it? I even know the name of the cab company because she said the driver was very helpful and she was recommending them whenever she had a chance. And a state trooper stopped by to find out what was going on and stayed until the tow truck arrived."

I wrote down the information on a blank page and tore it out. "I'll call Tony Wilson Monday morning. He'll find out if she's telling the truth."

"It wasn't Wanda," said Dusty firmly. "She really admired Spencer. I could hear it in her voice when we were talking about him."

"Maybe she's adding actress to her resume. Or maybe she killed him because she couldn't stand to see him in pain and unable to work."

"Cynic." She yawned. "Are we about done?" She stretched out on the couch again, very slowly this time.

I closed the notebook. "No, we're just about to begin."

I spent most of Sunday mowing the lawn, cleaning out the garage, washing down the driveway, and trimming the privet hedge. Dusty worked in her office all morning and most of the afternoon, came out to join me when I started the charcoal in the back yard. "How's it going?" I nodded in the general direction of her office to indicate I meant the current novel.

"Oh, Craig just spent a lovely night with Tatyana."

"Last night was research then?"

She reached over and slapped my leg. "If I included anything like last night, I'd have my editor blushing."

We ate grilled sausages and vegetables and sat outside listening to the mosquitoes toasting themselves on the bug zapper. The distant sounds of a ball game at the nearby playground were not loud enough to disturb us and we both dozed off once or twice, not necessarily at the same time. It was quite dark when I finally roused myself and turned on the floodlights so that I could clean up. Dusty carried dirty dishes inside and loaded the dishwasher while I made certain the coals were out and that we hadn't left anything behind.

There had been some vandalism and petty thefts in the neighborhood a couple of years ago, almost certainly kids, so I routinely locked up anything portable in the gazebo that stood in one corner of the yard. It was too small to hold even a small table and chairs so I used it as a tool shed. There were rakes and shovels, a can of paint, drop cloths and brushes, a few tools that duplicated what I had in the garage, a box of nails, and the usual odds and ends that get tucked into out of the way corners rather than discarded. There were two windows, between which I'd hung a calendar that was now four years out of date and which had become effectively invisible to me, but this time I noticed it and stopped in my tracks.

The lower right hand corner had been badly torn when I'd accidentally hooked it with a rake some time ago. It reminded me of the Trentano print in Walter Spencer's office, a fairly expensive print in all likelihood. Why would Spencer have cut off one corner?

Monday morning was a disaster. I'd forgotten that it was Steve's physical therapy day and the temp sitting behind his desk was new and didn't recognize me. Tina had apparently oriented her, which meant that she didn't know where anything was, what to do with incoming calls, or how to make a proper pot of coffee. Barry had left a message saying he'd be in by late morning. The lawyer for the Dalglieshes called the moment I finally reached my office and wanted to meet right away. She was very indignant when I told her that the report wasn't due until Wednesday and wouldn't be ready until then. We went round and round on that one for awhile, with her insisting that our mutual client expected better service and with me explaining that the timeline had been agreed to by all parties beforehand.

It was lunch time before I had a moment's peace. I'd brought leftovers from home so I ate at my desk while making a few calls. The first was to a friend who was on the School of Design faculty. She wasn't in but I left a message asking if she knew anything about the proposed Spencer scholarship and if not, who could I talk to about it. Then I dialed the Furtado Agency and spoke to a strongly accented receptionist who kept trying to talk me into making a formal appointment.

"I'm with Birch Investigations in Providence," I explained calmly. "This is a professional call. I'd like to speak to someone who can tell me about the work you did for a Mr. Walter Spencer a few months back. Can you take down my number?"

She remained dubious, but agreed to take a message.

Tony Wilson answered his own phone and it sounded as though he had his mouth full, which was probably the case. Tony enjoyed eating, and not just at mealtimes. I told him I had a small job for him and read him the notes I'd made the day before. "Just do a quick pass on this, Tony. I'm tying up a loose end."

Someone knocked on my door almost the moment I put down the phone, then came in without waiting for an answer. It was Barry, with a fresh tomato sauce stain on his tie. Barry likes to have spaghetti for breakfast. There's probably a story there somewhere, but I don't ask. "I have something for you," he announced without preamble. "I dropped a few discreet questions and got some surprising answers. The Tontine appears to be exactly as represented; not a gold mine but a steady source of income for the partners. No suspicion of hanky panky there. But two of the surviving partners are in serious financial trouble."

I immediately thought of Avery Carr, but Barry surprised me. "Michelle Bernstein has been selling off several of the paintings she had previously declared as not for sale. Apparently her husband made some unwise, risky investments and has become seriously over extended. They had to come up with a lot of cash very quickly, and they're in debt up to their eyelids."

She couldn't have been completely desperate or she would have changed her position about keeping the Tontine open, but it was still an interesting point. Barry waited until I had absorbed that before revealing his more significant discovery. "Another partner is in even worse shape. Heavily in debt and with limited prospects. He hasn't had a major sale in four years."

"Avery Carr," I said quietly.

"No, he's actually surprisingly solvent. Must have made some good investments along the way because he's not bringing in that kind of income now. It's Earl Garner who's on the skids. He's very close to bankruptcy."

Now that was interesting. It gave Earl, not to mention Carl, an even stronger motive. "His place up north looked to be pretty valuable."

"Two mortgages, and the property isn't likely to attract hordes of potential buyers. He's been quietly trying to sell it for more than a year now. And he's liquidated most of his other investments, sometimes taking a stiff penalty in the process. It looks as though he's been bleeding money for at least the past three years, and it's progressed to a hemorrhage during the last six months."

The Garner brothers rose slightly on my list of suspects. "Thanks, Barry. That's good work. I appreciate it."

"No problem. I might have a little more for you later. Fogle used a couple of blind companies to conceal his involvement and it's going to take some time to peel off all the layers."

The morning was filled with similar tidbits of information, more than I had any right to expect. First Tony Miller called to tell me that Wanda Fredericks' alibi checked out. "The trooper noted her license plate and logged the time. He was apparently concerned because the young lady was very close to hysterics when he found her, stranded on a dark road with only her cell phone for company. Triple A also confirms her story. I have the name of the guy who serviced her— her car I mean." Tony had a weakness for coarse jokes which only he could find funny. "I haven't talked to him yet, but the dispatcher was very helpful."

"Don't bother, at least not yet. You've confirmed enough to satisfy me that she was where she said she was when she said she was." I asked about his daughter, who'd been going through chemotherapy for several weeks, and he was cautiously optimistic. She was a nice kid, and I wished her the best.

Ten minutes later, the temp told me that someone named Danny Silva was on the line. "Who is he and what does he want?" I asked. Even detective agencies are tormented by salespeople who use a variety of ploys to penetrate the defenses of receptionists and secretaries.

"He didn't tell me. Says he's with the Furtado Detective Agency. It doesn't sound like he's selling anything or asking for donations."

"I know what it's about. Put him through."

Danny Silva sounded young, with a hint of bluster and a slightly raspy voice that immediately got on my nerves. "This is a courtesy call, Mr. Birch. I was the one who handled the Spencer case. I got a message saying you wanted to talk to me."

"Yes I did. I'm working for Spencer's niece. I realize that you can't divulge the details of your investigation, but I wondered if you could describe its general nature. We're conducting another inquiry here and I want to eliminate that possibility if I can."

"I'm sorry but I can't help you, Mr. Birch." He didn't sound sorry at all. "It would be unethical to release any information without the permission of our client."

I kept my voice level. "Are you aware that Walter Spencer is dead, Mr. Silva?"

There was a short silence. "No, I was not aware of that fact. Can I ask how he died?"

"The police have tentatively ruled it a suicide," I hedged. "But the investigation is ongoing." Mine, not theirs. "I've been employed by his niece and primary heir, who believes it may have been a homicide."

Silva sounded relieved, and slightly defensive. "There was nothing in the work we did for Mr. Spencer that suggested he might be in danger."

"He'd been receiving anonymous letters just prior to his death." I decided that Silva might be more forthcoming if he thought I already knew at least part of what I wanted him to say. "They included threats against his daughter."

There was another, longer silence. "That's not consistent with our findings."

"Which were?"

I heard the sigh, probably was meant to. "I'd like to help you, Mr. Birch." That was also probably a lie. "I can talk to my boss and see how much he's willing to release. But he's on vacation this week so I won't be able to reach him before Monday."

"How long have you had your license, Mr. Silva?"

"What's that got to do with anything?"

"Are you aware that concealing information relating to a felony could result in suspension or loss of your license, to say nothing of civil penalties?"

"There's no reason to…"

"Particularly in a case where they may be an ongoing physical threat to another individual, specifically your client's niece."

"We can't be responsible…"

I didn't let him finish. I switched tactics quickly to keep him off balance. "Look, Mr. Silva, I don't want to make a federal case out of this. I just want a quick summary of what he hired you to do. Consider it a professional courtesy. I'll owe you one."

I let him think about it for a minute, and he took almost that long to decide. "All right, Mr. Birch. Since our client is dead, I suppose the usual rules don't apply. But I'd still appreciate it if you'd keep this conversation to yourself."

"Will do." Unless it was necessary to prove that Walter Spencer had been murdered, of course.

"Spencer wanted to track down a daughter he had out of wedlock when he was a young man. He knew that she'd been put up for adoption at a specific agency, but that was the extent of his knowledge. For reasons which he never explained to us, he had believed for some time that his sister's adopted daughter was the girl, but something had happened recently to change his mind. He didn't explain that to me either. We took the case with considerable reservations. As I'm sure you know, adoption records are very difficult to obtain, but we were fortunate in that there was an unusually small number of female children handled by the agency in question during the crucial period. That advantage was offset in part by a fire at the agency during the period of interest. Some of their adoptions were actually handled at other facilities and they told us off the record that even if we had a court order releasing the information, there might well be considerable difficulty in tracking down the paperwork. We caught a break because we were able to eliminate most of the candidates very quickly because we knew both parents were Caucasian or by other obvious physical characteristics. There were only three potentials left after we eliminated the obvious ones."

"Including the niece?"

"Yes, but we were able to rule her out very quickly. She was the wrong blood type. Mr. Spencer could have determined that himself if he'd checked it earlier."

So Kari Spencer was not Walter's daughter. His anonymous correspondent had been right about that. "What about the other two?"

"Both were matches bloodwise but we couldn't figure out how to get DNA samples from either of the remaining potentials without contacting them directly, which Spencer did not want us to do. One of them was in contact with her natural mother."

"So that left you with one candidate."

"That's right. But it didn't help. The last was a baby who died only a few weeks after she was placed. We assume that she was Spencer's daughter, but we can't actually prove the case."

"Did you convey this information to your client?"

"Yes, a couple of months ago. He sent the final payment and we haven't heard from him since."

"Thank you, Mr. Silva. You've been very helpful."

The morning had already been very interesting and there was still an hour to go before lunch. I figured I had time to take care of a few other items, particularly the invoices that were still waiting for my approval, but I had barely started when Tina buzzed me.

"There's someone here to see you, Mr. Birch."

"Where's the temp?" I had already forgotten her name.

"Powdering her nose. I told her I'd cover for her."

"I thought my calendar was open today."

"It is, but she's very insistent, and I think you might want to see her." Her voice dropped slightly. "It's Kristina Kwan."

"All right. Send her in."

I wasn't sure what to expect and there was no hint of her purpose in her demeanor. Kwan met my eyes levelly and seated herself so quickly that I never had a chance to offer. She was wearing an obviously tailored business suit and her hair was tied back in a tight bun, emphasizing her slimness and the flat panes of her cheeks and forehead.

"Thank you for seeing me without notice, Mr. Birch. I actually hadn't planned to come by, but I was called into the city on business, which took less time than I had anticipated, and I happened to have your card with me and hoped I might find you in. I've been thinking about our conversation the other day and I believe there is something that you should know."

I didn't believe for a moment that this visit had been made on impulse, but I nodded as though I did. "I appreciate your taking the time to stop by then."

"Yes, well, I don't know if you're aware of the fact that Walter fathered a child when he was much younger. It was unplanned and the girl was put up for adoption."

"As a matter of fact, I did know a little about it, but none of the details," I lied.

"The past really doesn't matter. It was a casual affair that Walter regretted later. For a long time he never spoke of it, but a few years back he told me that he was trying to track her down, the daughter I mean. I wondered if he had ever found her."

"I was hired to look into the circumstances of Walter Spencer's death, Miss Kwan. Unless there's some relevance, I try to avoid intruding into private issues."

"Of course." She sounded disappointed and she dropped her eyes. Was she trying to find out something about the daughter, or was she trying to find out how much I knew about the daughter?

"Unless you think that there might be some connection?" I prompted.

Her head came up and I could tell that she was evaluating me. I kept a poker face. If she was going to say something, I didn't want to reveal any foreknowledge. Poking and prodding wouldn't help and might make her defensive.

"I think he might have had a very great disappointment recently and that might explain why he chose to…do what he did."

I wanted to make it easier for her to say whatever it was that had brought her here, but I didn't know how and I was afraid that any tactic I might employ to encourage her would have exactly the opposite effect, so I said nothing and tried to look sympathetic. Either it worked, or she was so determined to talk that she wasn't bothered by my clumsiness.

"Walter thought that he had identified his daughter and it soothed his conscience considerably to watch over her and provide certain clandestine benefits. Financial mostly, although he also used his influence a bit when she went off to college."

"You're talking about his niece, Kari."

She was clearly surprised that I knew but she recovered quickly. "Yes I am. You know more than I expected, Mr. Birch."

"And you don't think she really is his missing daughter I take it?"

"I know that she isn't the person Walter believed her to be, but she appears to have turned into a reasonably competent adult. He could have found a worse object to squander his affections on." There was a hint of bitterness, quickly gone. "The point is that he had recently been disabused of his misconception and he was deeply affected. We only spoke of it once and I tried to convince him that his relationship with his niece was no less valuable simply because he'd been wrong about her origins, but Walter had become increasingly sentimental in his old age, and less amenable to reason."

I had coughed to cover my surprise when she used a phrase almost identical to one of the anonymous notes. Could she have been the author? It didn't seem likely. "Do you know how Walter discovered the truth?"

She shook her head. "He wouldn't tell me."

"And how is it that you knew before he did?"

I didn't think she was going to answer me. Her face was calm and emotionless and I could feel her weighing the issue before she spoke. "I knew the woman involved, the child's mother and I am aware of some of the circumstances surrounding her adoption."

"And you never told Spencer?"

"No. I'd given my word, and there were other considerations."

"Are you in contact with his natural daughter?"

"I heard that she'd been placed with a family, but her mother wanted to sever all the ties between her daughter and our circle."

She glanced away and I knew there was more there but I had no opening. So I switched tracks.

"Did you know that Spencer had bought a handgun?"

Kwan shook her head but didn't say anything, and her eyes still pointed in the general direction of a poster for Farewell, My Lovely.

"Did he tell you about the anonymous letters he'd been receiving? The ones threatening Kari?" That got her attention. "What are you talking about? What letters?"

I summarized the situation without being too specific. "The threats are implied rather than overt, but it was enough to alarm Spencer. There's reason to believe that it was receiving the letters that prompted him to buy the weapon he eventually used on himself." If he had in fact done so.

"Why weren't the police notified?" She shook her head, immediately answering her own question. "No, he wouldn't have gone to them. Walter never dealt well with authority. But surely someone has done so now."

"I've advised Miss Spencer to take steps to protect herself, but only as a precaution. There was no real evidence that violence was intended, and with Spencer's death, the basis for the animosity appears to have gone away."

"But you have no idea who the source was?"

"None whatsoever." But that wasn't true. I hadn't realized it until that very moment, but I was pretty sure that I knew who had written those anonymous notes. And I had an even wilder idea that might explain why.

"Were you and this other woman, the girl's mother, close friends?"

"Not really." She was lying now, and not very well. The mother had been Phyllis Reynolds, of course, the woman whose affair with Spencer had broken up her marriage. But if she did know what had actually happened to the child, why would Reynolds have told her the truth and then have lied to Spencer?"

I didn't want to let the point go, but I knew she'd bolt if I pursued things directly. "I went to visit Earl Garner the other day."

Kwan had half risen and she hesitated. "How is Earl? I haven't spoken to him in months. I had expected to see him at Walter's funeral, but I missed the opportunity." She essayed a smile but it didn't work. "I didn't want to admit that he was gone, I suppose, so I found an excuse to be elsewhere."

"Garner seems well. That's quite a place he has up there in the mountains. It's a shame he has to sell it."

She frowned and settled back in her seat. "I didn't know he'd put it up for sale. I know he's been short of cash lately, so I guess I shouldn't be surprised. I told Earl years ago that he needed to change with the times, but he was always stubborn."

"I had the impression his brother had something to do with it."

"Did you meet Carl?" There was something in her voice. Stress? Amusement?

"No, just talked to him on the phone. He gave me screwed up directions and never told his brother I was coming."

"That's Carl all right." She laughed. It was brittle but sounded authentic. "They're quite the character, those two." Without warning, she stood up, and I followed suit.

"I hope I haven't scared you off."

A sly smile implied that it would take something more frightening than Paul Birch to accomplish that, but she reached across the desk and shook my hand. "Not at all. I just don't want to waste any more of your time. I've gone back and forth on this, Mr. Birch, but I think now that it all just got to be too much for Walter. Too much pain, too much failure, too much loneliness. He was very difficult to get close to, even when we were married. I knew that beforehand and should have been prepared, but I wasn't."

"You might be right, Miss Kwan. Thank you for taking the time to stop and see me."

She started toward the door, then hesitated. "Someone is looking into this threat to Walter's niece, I assume."

"Miss Spencer is my client and I've expressed an opinion on the subject. But she's an adult. In my opinion, it's unlikely that she's actively in danger, but the degree of precaution she takes is up to her."

"Yes, of course." And she turned and left without another word.

CHAPTER NINE

As soon as Kristina Kwan was out of my office, I called Tony Wilson and asked him to check on a couple of things for me. If he was surprised by any of my requests, there was no hint of it in his voice.

"Might have something for you tomorrow, maybe not till the day after."

"That'll do just fine."

I actually managed to spend half an hour on paperwork before the next call came in, this one from my friend at the School of Design. We exchanged social pleasantries for a few seconds and promised each other, with some insincerity, that we needed to get together for lunch soon. We'd been a couple once, for about ten minutes. It had not been a success.

"What do you have for me, Claudia?"

"I don't know if this is going to be any help. There were indeed some sticking points between the school and Walter Spencer, but they were mostly ideological and would have been worked out one way or another. The actual reason that the scholarship fell through was that Spencer called a few days before his death and withdrew his offer."

"Withdrew it?" That wasn't at all the answer I'd been expecting.

"That's right. He was very apologetic about it but not particularly forthcoming. Asked that the project be shelved indefinitely."

"Thanks, Claudia."

"Hope that helps. We were all taken by surprise here." She was obviously curious about why I had asked.

"I'm not sure if it does or not. I'll tell you about it sometime. When we get together for lunch."

"Yeah, right." She didn't sound as though she thought that would be any time soon. She was probably right.

By the end of the day, I was feeling unusually tired, and more than slightly on edge. The feeling that I was missing something had been growing steadily stronger. I left early, shocking Tina and surprising Dusty, who acknowledged my return somewhat grumpily and immediately returned to her office. I figured she'd written her hero into some corner and had yet to find a way for him to escape. I felt the same way.

I decided to make a more than usually elaborate supper, but halfway through discovered that my heart really wasn't in it. The die was cast, however, and I had no choice but to continue, and for a change I actually resented the time and effort that went into preparing a really good meal. The delicious aromas lured Dusty downstairs and she kibitzed for a while, her sour mood muted and eventually fading as the chicken marsala approached completion.

"Anything new on the case?"

I knew which case she had in mind and I didn't want to talk about it. "Wanda's alibi checked out. She's in the clear."

"I told you she hadn't done it. She's the last person who would have wished Spencer harm."

"You've read enough mysteries to know that the person you least suspect is almost always the killer."

"Death is an intellectual puzzle in a murder mystery. In real life it's ugly, hurtful, and generally predictable."

"So who's the most likely person, regardless of the evidence?"

She pondered that for a while. "Earl Garner, I suppose. He had the most to gain and the greatest need."

"That's not entirely clear." I repeated what Barry had told me about the Fogel-Bernstein financial problems.

"But she was still going to vote to keep the gallery open," Dusty protested.

"So she says," I admitted. "But who knows what she'll really do the next time the board meets?"

"Okay, so who do you think is most likely the person who shot him?"

I thought about it. "Walter Spencer," I said at last, as I was fluffing the rice pilaf. "The police could have been more thorough, but that doesn't mean their conclusion wasn't the right one."

"Did you see the story about the Tontine in the paper this morning?"

I had glanced through the Journal before going to work, but I hadn't even opened the Arts section.

"No. What now?"

"They're having a reception Wednesday evening. Invitation only." She reached into her pocket and pulled out an envelope.

"Two invitations came in today's mail, compliments of Avery Carr. Paul Birch and guest."

"Trying to get back to business as usual, no doubt."

"Why don't we go? It might be interesting to see who shows up."

"I might just do that, but I can't take you with me."

She pouted. "Why not? Have I been helping you or haven't I?"

"Yes, you have," I said calmly. "But have you forgotten Wanda? She's not supposed to know that we're acquainted."

Crestfallen, she dropped her eyes. "Yeah, right. I forgot all about that." Her head came up suddenly, eyes flashing. "Maybe I can come separately. We just have to pretend we don't know each other."

She was right, and it might be useful to see how people reacted to my presence when my back was turned. "Let's see the invitations."

Unfortunately, one had my name on it and the other read "Guest of Paul Birch". I showed it to Dusty who looked even more unhappy than before.

Further conversation was delayed as I brought the food to the table. Dusty mumbled occasional superlatives around mouthsful of rice and chicken, but it seemed relatively bland to me and there was more left over than I expected, requiring me to reach up to the very top shelves for one of the larger plastic containers we stored there. Dusty watched as I carefully packed the remains.

"If you're going to go all moody on me, I'm going to wish I'd never talked you into taking this case."

I smiled at her. "That's not exactly how it happened and I'm not moody, I'm thoughtful."

She reached into her pocket, pulled out some loose change, and held out a penny.

"You wouldn't get your money's worth," I said, laughing slightly. "My mind is one big aching void right now." I scratched my head by way of illustration.

Dusty gave me an arch look. "I've got one of those myself."

"An empty head?" I said quizzically.

"No. An aching void."

So we went upstairs to fill at least one of them.

Steve was back the next morning and that lifted my spirits a bit. "Steve, I have a job for you. I need to know more about Peter Trentano. A biography. And something about his artwork." I dug through my memories. "Specifically anything about a painting called Lumber Mill at Dusk." That was the title of the painting a mutilated print of which sat in Walter Spencer's office.

"How fast do you want it?"

"Today if possible."

"I'll see what I can do."

Next was a call to Tony Wilson, following a totally illogical hunch. "Remember when I told you not to spend any more time on Wanda Fredericks?"

"The lady with the flat tire?"

"That's the one. I'm interested in her again, but a complete profile this time. All the way back to her childhood."

"Is this a rush job?"

I thought about it. "No, but don't put it on the back burner either. And I'll take interim reports as soon as you have them."

"I'll be in touch."

The rest of the morning was consumed by preparation of the Dalgliesh report. I'd jobbed out most of the field work and a courier had dropped off the raw information early in the morning. Steve had done a first pass at organizing it and I made only a few changes before sending it back to him for final preparation. We'd have a nifty little package to present at Wednesday's meeting. Barry stopped me as I was about to go out for lunch, obviously looking for an invitation so I obliged him.

"I have a little more on Benjamin Fogel. He started out as an investment counselor and had a pretty good reputation. Made a lot of money for a lot of people, including himself. Started dropping clients about ten years ago to devote himself to his own portfolio, but it looks like he lost the touch somewhere along the line, or had a string of bad luck and took some risks to try to recoup things. It turns out he's not quite as bad off as I originally thought, but without the income from his wife's work, he'd be in serious trouble."

"Not desperate enough to kill someone then?"

Barry shrugged his shoulders, but waited until we were seated in my car before answering. "I wouldn't think so, but he is still facing a considerable alteration in his lifestyle if things don't turn around. He has expensive hobbies. But that's not the most interesting thing I found out."

I started the engine. "And that would be?"

"Fogel eased himself back into his old line of work, quietly and unofficially. He lined up a few business partners, and used mostly their capital and mostly his judgment to make investments. One of those partners was Walter Spencer."

We were moving now, blending into traffic. There was a little sidewalk café that had just opened on the fringes of the Providence College campus that I wanted to try. "Let me guess. The money is all gone."

"Not quite. But Spencer lost a bundle."

"How big a bundle?"

"A couple million. About half his net worth."

I whistled, and made a mental note to ask Kari about it when we next met. And then another thought occurred to me. "When did this happen?"

"The bulk of the loss was experienced over a fourteen month period, but it probably wasn't obvious to the investors until the auditors blew the whistle."

"And when was that?" Barry mentioned a date and I whistled. Four days later, Walter Spencer had cancelled his plans to endow a scholarship. And a few days after that, he was dead.

The café's menu was too ambitious, three pages of offerings despite a kitchen not much bigger than my own. Our lunch took too long to arrive and was undercooked. Scratch another off the list. There are too many good restaurants in the Providence area to waste time on the marginal ones.

When we got back to the office, there was a courier in the reception area and Steve was signing his clipboard. I waved to say I was back and headed for my office, and a minute or two later Steve's voice came through the intercom. "I have the material on Trentano, Mr. Birch. Should I bring it in?"

"No, I'll come get it." Steve was perfectly mobile in his wheelchair, seemed more capable of moving gracefully and expeditiously around the office than I was, but I occasionally felt moments of quite irrational guilt about using him as a glorified clerk, even though that's in fact what he was. But I was also restless and wasn't looking forward to another session at my desk, so I went to his. He was thumbing through a coffee-table-sized hardcover titled *Through Different Eyes: The Art of Peter Trentano*. To one side sat a thick trade paperback from a university press: *Peter Trentano: A Life*. A very large cylindrical package balanced precariously on the floor to one side.

He closed the book and pushed it toward me. "Not the most cheerful art I've ever seen."

Steve was right. I'd been slightly put off by Trentano's paintings at the Tontine but I hadn't really understood why. They were dark, gloomy, emphasizing shadows and obscurity, and there was a suggestion of impurity, dirtiness. The artist had not been enjoying a rosy outlook on life when he'd painted them. I gathered up the two books and Steve leaned back and picked up the package. "I thought you might want this as well."

He was looking a bit smug as he crossed his arms expectantly, watching me. Sometimes Steve likes to suggest that he is a step ahead of me and there was a twinkle in his eyes that told me this was one of those times. I took the scissors from their resting place on his desk set and cut the strings. Plain brown paper uncurled revealing an oversized, full color print, neatly rolled inside. It was Lumber Mill at Dusk.

I unrolled one end just far enough to positively identify it. This wasn't the same print as the one I'd seen in Walter Spencer's office. That one had been bordered by a plain white band. This one had an ornate, probably digitally fabricated picture frame around it. I was quite sure it was nothing like the actual one holding the original painting at the Tontine. "Excellent work, Steve. Thanks a lot."

I carried all three objects into my office and unrolled the print fully across my desk. It wasn't quite as large a reproduction as Spencer's, but it still more than covered my desk on all four sides. I paid particular attention to the lower right hand corner, the portion which had been removed from Spencer's, which predictably included the artist's signature, or rather his initials. But there was nothing otherwise significant. The script lay over a patch of dark, spear shaped grass. After staring at it fruitlessly for a few minutes, I rolled it back up and turned to the larger of the two books.

It was a heavy volume. Trentano's career might have been truncated, but he'd produced a lot of work. There were more than two hundred full color plates plus scores of sketches and studies and even a series of cartoons he'd drawn for a newspaper early in his career. None of them seemed particularly funny and visually they were crowded and sometimes hard to resolve into individual images. I found the plate for *Lumber Mill at Dusk* and squinted at the lower right hand corner for a while, but without discovering anything of interest.

I picked up the phone and dialed Tina's extension.

"Yeah, what is it?" Her tone was terse. Obviously I was tearing her away from a particularly fascinating computer problem.

"Can you come to my office? I need your help with a problem."

"On my way."

She arrived promptly, looking harried. But then again, she almost always looked harried. I suspected that she looked very much the same even when she was asleep; it had become the indigenous expression on her face.

I pushed the open book across the desk toward her. "Can you scan the lower right hand corner of that painting?" I tapped the rolled print. "And the same area from this copy?"

"How much of it?"

"Six inches square on the print should be enough, and the same section from the book. And make the two scans the same size so I can compare them side by side."

She peered down to look at the corner of the print, glanced back and forth between it and the book. "The print's brighter. Should I adjust the hue and saturation levels?"

"Whatever you think would help."

"Give me half an hour."

It was almost exactly thirty minutes later when she came back, setting the book on my desk and propping the now rolled print against the wall. "Can I drive your computer for a minute?"

I stood up and stepped away. She pressed a few keys and an installation program opened on my screen. "Should I have Steve bring us coffee?"

Tina shook her head. "This won't take five minutes." Even as she spoke, the installation finished and she closed the window. Her fingers flew over the keyboard too fast for me to follow, but I could tell she was accessing the network. The screen flashed and some program I'd never seen before loaded, a large blank field rimmed with tool bars and bizarre icons. Another couple of keystrokes and the screen split into two identical but smaller versions. And then the lower right hand corner of *Lumber Mill at Dusk* appeared in each.

"The one on the left is from the print. The one on the right is from the book." She stood up and stepped back, inviting me to examine them. I sat down and leaned forward, peering back and forth. "There's some degradation, and the print is not as high quality as the plate in the book, so the first one seems fuzzier."

I could barely detect the difference. "They look exactly the same." But the question in my mind was whether the painting in the gallery at the Tontine would also be a match. If Walter Spencer had suspected that a substitution had been made, might he have taken a sample of his print down to check at first hand?

"Can I get a photo quality printout of these? Or just the better of the two, since they're the same."

Tina doesn't gloat. She works harder than anyone I know and achieves more than any two people I could have put in her place, but she always feels as though her work is barely adequate. But today she gloated.

"But they're not the same."

I looked again, but if there was any difference other than the mild loss of focus in the first, it was well hidden. "I don't see it."

"I didn't either," she confessed with a nervous laugh. "Human eyes see what we expect to see. But once it's been digitized, it's just data and two sets of data can be compared. That's what I did. Once you strip away the noise—the fuzziness—you get two very close parallels. Some of the fuzz was anomalous, which might just have been dust on the lens of the camera or the printing plate or even on the painting itself. The big discrepancy is in the grass."

I looked again. Trentano's initials floated on a bed of dark grass. "I don't see it."

"Count the blades between the top of the letter 'T' and the shadow of the tree stump."

I did. "Twenty-six."

Tina shook her head. "Try again. This time on the other one."

I counted, finished, then counted again. "Twenty-five."

"Bingo."

I picked up the book and opened to the copyright page. It was a brand new edition but its first publication had been in 1981. I had to unroll the print again to find the date printed on the back. 2004.

Sometime between those two dates, presumably, an extra blade of grass had grown near the Lumber Mill.

"Thanks, Tina."

"My pleasure."

ⵐ

I called Kari Spencer and told her that, subject to her approval, I wanted to continue the investigation. "I don't want to mislead you. We don't have a hot lead and I still think it probable that your uncle took his own life. But we have uncovered some interesting questions that bear looking into." I wasn't ready to tell anyone about the discrepancy until I understood more about it myself. And I hadn't been hired to look into art forgery in any case.

"Do whatever you think is appropriate, Mr. Birch. I trust you."

Her faith in me wasn't as welcome as you might think. I would feel exceptionally guilty if this all turned out to be a wild goose chase, or even if my suspicions were more or less true but had nothing to do with Walter Spencer's death. I reminded her to be careful even though I didn't believe she was in any danger from her uncle's anonymous correspondent and she assured me that she was being circumspect.

"It's unsettling having someone—possibly even a complete stranger—so hostile toward you. I can't imagine what I could have done."

"I don't believe it's what you've done so much as who you are, or maybe who you aren't." I gave her a brief, clinical summary of what I'd learned about Spencer's investigations. There was a short silence.

"That explains a few things. I always thought Uncle Walter's interest in me was because he'd never had children of his own. I suppose that in one sense at least that's true."

"There's nothing to suggest his affection for you was altered in any way by his discovery that he'd been deluding himself about your origins. It seems likely that the person who wrote the notes knew that you weren't his daughter, through some means we have yet to discover, although it's possible that there's another explanation that hasn't yet occurred to us."

"But who would have known the truth? My real mother? Could she still be alive?"

Not if she was the woman believed to have given birth to Spencer's child, which I was no longer sure I believed to be true. "It's possible. The investigators never considered you a suspect, so they never looked into your past. Even in their case, they would have needed probable cause to unseal the adoption agency's records." If Kari's mother had discovered her daughter's identity, it seemed to me she would be more likely to encourage Spencer's illusions than challenge them. If Phyllis Reynolds hadn't died, I might have been willing to accept the possibility that she was behind the letters, jealous of Spencer's affections for a child other than his own, but that too was out of the question.

We talked a few minutes longer and I realized that Kari Spencer was a very lonely young woman. She kept coming back to the possibility that her real mother might still be alive and I cut things short as gracefully as possible, before she could ask me to investigate that as well. There are few things more frustrating than dealing with adoption agencies.

I now had two potentially promising lines of inquiry. The disparity between the two reproductions of Trentano's painting suggested that one was a forgery, presumably the one currently on display at the Tontine. I suppose that it was possible for anyone with access to the gallery—which included all of the surviving partners—to have arranged for the substitution. The fraud wouldn't necessarily have been recent either. The authentic painting might have vanished as early as the 1980s or any time since, and there were sure to have been several employees with the required access during that period. I had to put Avery Carr at the top of the list of suspects simply because he was in the best position to have arranged the theft, but given the span of time which had passed, there were almost certainty multiple opportunities for connivance. Barry had mentioned that Carr was much better off financially than expected, which was another mark against him, but still not enough to merit a direct accusation. Regardless of the identity of the criminal, the theft of such valuable artwork provided more than ample motive for murder, and the torn print in Spencer's office suggested that he had discovered the truth. Had he confronted the culprit in his office that night, perhaps displaying his revolver in an effort to ensure his safety? Had his own weapon been turned against him to guarantee his silence?

My second lead was more tenuous and required knowledge of the circumstances surrounding Walter Spencer's real daughter, who reportedly had died at birth. Kari Spencer did look a great deal like her uncle, but that was apparently coincidental. Wanda Fredericks didn't resemble him at all, but I suspected that either Furtado's people had been wrong and that the child had survived, or at least that Wanda believed herself to be Spencer's illegitimate daughter. She was the right age, after all. If she was in fact his natural daughter, how did the records get so muddled and, given that fact, how had she eventually learned the truth? More likely, if I was right, she had drawn on the coincidences of age and the fact that she was also adopted to construct an elaborate fantasy linking herself to the older man. It was theoretically possible that she had claimed to be Spencer's child, that he had rebuffed her, and that she had known of his handgun and used it in a fit of rage. But her alibi had checked out. I hoped Tony Wilson would be able to throw some light on these particular shadows.

I skimmed through the biography of Peter Trentano, which was clearly written by an ardent fan of his work. Despite the bias, the picture that emerged was of a self-centered egotist who liked having his own way and was not above the occasional petty cruelty when he was crossed. Several angry outbursts and outrageous comments were dismissed as the result of a rarified artistic temperament rather than the tantrums of a spoiled dilettante. Familiar names impinged on Trentano's life but were minimized by the author. Reading between the lines, one could extrapolate Trentano's libertinage, and there were more references to Michelle Bernstein as his companion than as his business partner or fellow artist. They were apparently an item for about two years, which was something of a record in his case. Bernstein herself was presented as a prop, with no effort to bring life to her as a person.

Phyllis Reynolds was mentioned more frequently, and usually in unflattering terms. She was at various times vindictive, petty, and argumentative, caused a number of public scenes, and at one point— so the author contended—there was a serious effort by the other partners to buy her share of the Tontine. Kwan was barely mentioned; there was an allusion to her lack of commitment to the artistic ideal and her penchant for commercialization. Presumably she was suspect because she wanted to sell her work in mass produced quantities and at a profit. Carr and Garner were little more than footnotes. Walter Spencer wandered in and out periodically, and came across as a dyed in the wool radical but perhaps not as bright as he might have been.

I didn't find anything actively useful, but I would read the book more carefully when I had time. I tossed it into my briefcase to take home and spent the balance of the afternoon worrying about other matters. We had three big cases winding up and nothing to replace them with. In a business whose most effective form of advertising is word of mouth, it's not easy to solicit new clientele on short notice.

Dusty was in high spirits when I got home. Apparently she'd escaped the literary corner of the previous evening. I inquired as to the status of her dashing protagonist and she told me that he was on his way back to Paris. "I have the climax all planned out in my head. Now it's just a matter of writing it down."

"I imagine it'll be quite a relief to have it over with."

She considered the question with more seriousness than I had intended. "Not entirely. Once I get comfortable with my characters, it's hard to let them go. That's why I like the idea of an extended series. I know that they'll be back in my life as soon as I get an idea for the next book. I imagine you must miss your clients sometimes."

I laughed. "I miss their checks but not my clients. Most of them are lawyers, accountants, or company executives. They all like being catered to and I oblige within reason. But if I could conduct all our business by mail, I'd be perfectly happy."

"Kari Spencer isn't a stuffed shirt."

"No, she isn't." I didn't elaborate. "Let's see what we can do about dinner."

Dusty waited until after we'd eaten to ask the question I was sure had been on her mind ever since I'd gotten home. I decided to keep my discovery about the forged painting to myself for the moment, but I summarized my suspicions about Wanda.

"But we know she didn't kill Spencer!" she objected. "And if he was her father, or if she thought that he was, that's the last thing she would have done."

"I never said she killed him. But I do think she wrote those anonymous letters."

She started to digest that, along with the good sized portion of beef tips she'd just eaten. "She was kind of obsessed with Spencer. She cried when she talked about him. If you're right that Wanda was behind the letters, she might think that she was at least partly responsible for his death. I figured out how we could both be there, incidentally."

Dusty's ability to switch subjects with no obvious cue never ceased to amaze me and I hastily tried to catch up. "Are we talking about the reception at the Tontine now?"

She nodded. "I called Wanda and asked her if she'd like to go out to dinner tomorrow night. She told me she couldn't make it because she had to work, and then mentioned the reception, and I told her how interesting it sounded. So I'm invited."

I didn't like it, but I couldn't think of a valid objection. "But remember, we don't know each other. And you need to be careful around her for your own sake. Wanda might not have murdered Walter Spencer, but I'm not sure how balanced she is. She might be dangerous."

"I can be pretty dangerous myself if I need to."

CHAPTER TEN

Most of Wednesday was spent on the Dalgliesh case, the final preparations for the conference and the meeting itself. Barry and Tina came along because they spoke the two most important languages—accounting and computers—like native speakers where I would clearly have been at a disadvantage translating each sentence to or from English. The company lawyer—the same one who had harassed me on the telephone - might have been attractive if she hadn't expended quite so much effort to look like Professional

Barbie and if she had learned to smile once in a while. She tried to insinuate that we'd been taking our time in the investigation and I rebuffed her politely but firmly, pointing out that we'd come in at the short end of our projections and the low side of our cost estimate.

Barry and Tina took turns explaining what they'd found. The Dalgliesh Company was a kind of parasite company that acted as intermediaries between people who wanted things done and other people who could do those things. Their company charter said that they provided energy efficient solutions for businesses, but in fact they did no actual physical work. Everything was subcontracted to specialty companies, electricians, insulators, installers, and such. Most of their income came in the usual form of direct payments, but they had also been heavily involved in a rebate program offered by one of the major electrical companies in the area. Customers would sign over their rebates as payment for the installation of energy efficient lighting and other equipment.

Although the Dalgliesh brothers themselves appeared to be reasonably reputable, some of their subcontractors were not. Savings estimates were exaggerated and in some cases the new fixtures had not been any more efficient than the ones replaced. The power company refused to pay any further rebates until the entire program was audited, and they had also hinted that they suspected deliberate fraud. The fact that one of their own executives had been paid as a consultant by three of the subcontractors had muddied the waters even further.

"The bottom line," I said when Tina and Barry finished their presentation, "is that you're only entitled to slightly more than half of the total of the outstanding invoices, and some of that is offset by earlier overpayments. We've documented all of that, and we've identified six subcontractors who are guilty of fraud. There are two others whose figures are suspect, but we were unable to prove any deliberate falsifications there. You may be able to recoup some of your losses from them." I turned deliberately toward their lawyer. "I'm sure your legal counsel is ready to explore that possibility with you. Our recommendation is that you negotiate partial payments with your clients based on our calculations."

Neither of the brothers was happy with our findings, but once we'd shown them the evidence and the initial shock wore off, they declared themselves satisfied and promised to remit the agreed upon fee. One of them even thanked me with some warmth and made comments to the effect that he was unhappy with the results but pleased at the thoroughness of our investigation. I hoped he'd repeat that to all of his acquaintances. Good recommendations are almost as welcome as prompt checks.

The three of us stopped for a celebratory drink on the way back to the office—my treat—and Tina did her usual magic act of making a very large brandy and soda disappear in a very short period of time. She tended to do everything in a hurry. I had once speculated about her sex life, and retreated hastily from the images that rushed into my mind's eye. Barry was a sipper, and I swear half the alcohol evaporated before it reached his lips.

He was in the middle of a particularly languorous sip when his eyes widened and he put it down. "Damn! I forgot to tell you. I found out some more about our friend Benjamin Fogle. Got a call last night at home from a guy I know. Turns out Spencer isn't the only artist who unwisely chose to rely on the man's investment acumen."

I realized who it must be before Barry told me, but I didn't say anything.

"Turns out Earl Garner made the same mistake. It's not the only reason he's in deep trouble, but it certainly didn't help any. Lost a cool million, and even worse, what's left is tied up in a legal battle that isn't likely to be resolved until next year at the earliest. Hefty legal fees will eat into some of that before he sees a dime."

"So maybe Spencer talked him into investing and Garner figured he had had a right to be pissed."

Barry shook his head. "Based on the dates of the investments, it's more likely the other way around. Or maybe there's a third party who enlisted them both." He didn't need to tell me who the third party might be. Michelle Bernstein would have been in an ideal position to put her husband in touch with two aging and not particularly fiscally alert artist friends. She might even have thought she was doing them a favor. Fogle had, after all, been very successful earlier in his career.

I took out my tuxedo when I got home and brushed it off. I didn't wear it often, but in my line of business you never know where you're going to go or who you'll have to deal with, so I try to be flexible and prepared for any situation. I hated the thing, frankly, and barely tolerated the neckties that I wore to the office. I've always had an aversion to uniforms. It kept me out of the Boy Scouts and the military and my kids, if I ever have any, will never be sent to a school that requires uniformity in dress. I know it's supposed to make children who can't afford trendy clothing feel better about themselves, but the world is full of inequalities and it seems to me counterproductive to pretend that things are different. Not everything we learn in school comes out of books or the teachers' lips.

Anyway, a jacket and tie is just another kind of uniform, but I'm pragmatic about my quirks. If you want to deal with the shirts, you have to dress like one.

Dusty had bought herself a new dress for the occasion, which she paraded in front of me. It was low cut, like most of her formal wear, particularly in the back, although it didn't quite reveal a second cleavage. It was red, so dark that it looked almost black when she was standing in shadow, with the hint of a pattern and strategic swatches of delicate lace trim. "No one's going to be paying any attention to the art," I told her. "They'll all be looking at you."

"Thanks, but I doubt it. This class of people is too uptight to give in to animal impulses. Or at least in public."

Dusty wanted to show up as soon as things got underway but I talked her out of it. "Let me look things over first. I'll call your cell once I've got the lay of the land. Besides, you want to be stylishly late, looking like that. And remember, people are less likely to confide in you if you seem too interested. Be attentive but not eager."

"You're the boss. For the evening anyway. Anything in particular you want me to listen for?"

"Background mostly, and any gossip that might come your way. I'm curious about how people react to learning that a private investigator is looking into Spencer's death. They might hint at something they wouldn't tell me if I asked them directly."

The doors were supposed to open at seven, but it was more than half an hour after that before I arrived. Judging by the ease with which I found a parking space in the same block, the Tontine wasn't packing them in, although when I arrived, there was a reasonable crowd inside. Tables had been set up in the lobby and reception area, decked with wine, cheese, and finger food of every variety, all arranged in decorative displays. I caught a brief glimpse of a harried looking Wanda but lost her almost immediately in the crowd. I did glance up to find the painting of the Tontine dinner party back in its place, now showing three of the diners slumped over their plates. The alteration was very well done; it could almost have been a new painting entirely. I wondered whose work it was.

Michelle Bernstein was in the gallery that bore her name, standing beside a balding man about the same age whom I guessed must be Benjamin Fogle. I very much wanted to meet him, but the crowd was thick around them at the moment, and I wanted to look around first. I recognized the lieutenant governor and his wife. I'd done some business for him when he was still a legislator and he nodded amicably, turning immediately back to his conversation with a heavily bejeweled woman I didn't recognize. Probably a campaign contributor. A few of the other faces were familiar, but I couldn't put a name on all of them. I doubted any of them would know who I was.

Avery Carr hailed me eventually, put his arm around me and insisted that I try some of the white wine. "It's much better than it deserves to be, I think. I find it easier to put up with these things once I've had a glass or three."

I tried a glass and agreed that it was certainly palatable, though a bit sweet for my palate. "Thanks for inviting me by the way. I feel a bit out of place though. I probably know less about art than you do about the detective business."

"And you think these people know more than that?" He made an expansive gesture. "Nonsense. You make a living finding what lies behind pretenses and I doubt you've ever been in a room with so much pretense before in your entire life. Point to something and tell these people that it's art and they take out their checkbooks without a second thought. Left on their own they wouldn't know a Modigliani from an Al Capp."

I couldn't think of an appropriate answer to that so I made a noncommittal sound. Fortunately, he apologized and hustled off a moment later to greet some new arrivals.

Earl Garner was not attending, of course, but much to my surprise, Kristina Kwan was holding court, though in the central corridor rather than the gallery that bore her name. I caught her eye and I thought her face became suddenly and briefly guarded, but she turned away so quickly that it might have been my imagination. From there I entered the Trentano gallery and went straight to *Lumber Mill at Dusk*. I even crouched down long enough to count the blades of grass above the author's initials. Twenty-five. The same as appeared in the print, one less than in the plate shot in 1981 or earlier.

"Remarkable detail, isn't it?"

Michelle Bernstein, sans husband and admirers, had appeared behind me.

"Yes it is. Almost photographic. He was a talented man."

"This was one of his favorite paintings, but I never cared for it very much. It was dark and dreary even for him. But he labored over it longer than any of the others. Everything had to be just right. I thought he was going to have a stroke when it was damaged."

"Damaged?"

"Yes, about twenty years ago. While it was being moved in here, in fact. Someone got careless removing the crating and dropped a crowbar. There was a deep scratch right through Peter's signature. He was furious."

"It seems to have been repaired all right." I glanced down involuntarily.

"Peter insisted on taking care of it right away. He wasn't keeping a studio here by then so he used mine. Came in the next morning and spent the entire day on it. Some of the fabric was weakened so he had to be very careful not to tear it. There's still a weak spot, of course, but it doesn't show unless you look at the back of the canvas."

"I imagine he must have used a print to be certain he had all the details right."

She shook her head. "Peter had a remarkable facility for remembering details. He knew every inch of every one of his paintings, and particularly this one. He restored it from memory. It's quite remarkable. If you can find a good reproduction of the painting from before the accident and compare the two, you won't be able to find any differences."

I wasn't so sure of that, but my theory about forged paintings was on the verge of collapse. Trentano could easily have miscounted, or he might have decided consciously to eliminate a single strand of grass. For whatever reason, this discrepancy between the old reproduction and the new now seemed to have been resolved. I wasn't ready to jettison my theory but it was certainly in jeopardy, and with its demise would go another motive for the murder of Walter Spencer.

"Was that your husband I saw you with a while ago? The gentleman in the grayish green suit?"

She nodded. "He's off being charming at the moment." Her face twitched. "I didn't mean that to be catty. Ben's an investment counselor and this is an excellent place to find new clients."

"I hope I'll get to meet him."

"I'm sure you will." Someone I didn't know waved at her from the doorway and she excused herself. "Have to put on my distinguished artist face again."

Bernstein left me standing in the ruins of my hottest theory. I sighed, moved to a quiet corner and called Dusty on my cell. "Anytime you're ready," I said when she answered.

"I'm on my way. Anyone in particular I should be nice to?"

"Kwan is holding out on me, I'm sure, but I don't think she'll talk to you either. Bernstein's husband is here. You might be able to vamp him if you hint that you have a portfolio that needs attention. Stocks, not artwork. He's wearing a hideous greenish three piece suit and is losing his hair."

"I'll do my best."

I had just stepped back into the central corridor when I had my next surprise. Kristina Kwan was coming directly toward me. "Mr. Birch, I was hoping you'd be here. Could I talk to you for a moment or two?"

"Certainly." I glanced around uncertainly. There was considerable traffic going to and fro.

"Let's go upstairs," she suggested. "I'd rather not be overheard."

I followed her to the second floor. The door to Spencer's office was still open and I suggested we avail ourselves of his two chairs. I was trying to think of some way to gently prompt her into speaking, but she wasted no time. "I wondered if you'd been making any progress, tracking down Spencer's daughter I mean."

That was curious. She was apparently more interested in the missing daughter than the possibility of Spencer having been murdered. "Our inquiries are ongoing, Miss Kwan. And the results will be held in confidence, you understand, unless they prove relevant to the case at hand. But I will tell you that the identity of Spencer's daughter is not central to our investigation, although even if it was, I wouldn't be able to tell you what we'd learned."

"Of course, I didn't mean to pry." We both knew that wasn't true.

"Is there some reason why you're so interested?"

There was a brief hesitation, and I had the distinct impression she was trying to decide just how much to admit to me.

"It's just that if you did locate her, I thought I might take an interest in the girl. If Walter and I had stayed together, we might have had a child of our own. As it is, it's far too late to look forward to a family of my own."

I could tell by the way her eyes shifted away from me that she'd just told a half truth at best and I decided to take a chance and push back a little.

"You were married to Spencer at one time, I understand."

The briefest hint of wariness passed over her face. "Very briefly. It was a mistake. We were both young then and neither of us was ready for a long term commitment." She laughed. "I don't suppose we ever were ready for that matter."

"Wasn't that just about the time that Spencer's missing daughter was born?"

This time it was more than a hint. Kwan's voice became distinctly cool. "If you're asking me if Walter cheated on me, the answer is yes. But I certainly wouldn't have held a grudge for all these years." She had obviously decided that I thought Spencer's infidelity might provide a motive for murder. "Walter and I worked out our problems a long time ago and we remained friends despite the divorce."

"Did you also remain friends with Phyllis Reynolds?"

If I'd been expecting a strong reaction, I'd have been disappointed. Kwan regarded me calmly. "I suppose Avery told you the sordid details. Our circle was never very good about keeping secrets." She was wrong; they'd kept an awful lot of secrets and quite well too. "The answer is yes again. Phyllis and I had a terrible fight and didn't speak to each other for weeks, but a year later we were as close as we'd ever been."

"You all seem remarkably tolerant and even tempered."

"It isn't so much tolerance as blandness. It's no coincidence that Michelle was the only one of us to have a lasting personal relationship. Twice in her case, if you consider the time she spent with Paul."

"How did that end anyway?" The book had skirted the subject.

"Badly," Kwan replied bluntly. "I think Peter was terrified of the possibility of becoming domesticated and broke things off impulsively. He never seemed to understand why Michelle was so shattered."

"She seems to have recovered well."

"Artists are all egotists, Mr. Birch. We all believe that we're capable of creating objects which other people will find impressive or inspiring. It's a job prerequisite."

We were interrupted at that point by Avery Carr, who poked his head into the office. "Oh, it's you two. I thought we had some unauthorized strays up here."

"No one would dare, Avery," said Kwan casually. "They all know you run a tight ship. You have quite a good turnout, considering."

He shook his head. "Most of them came to be seen, not to buy. There's more business being conducted in the corridors than at the desk. Michelle's husband is handing out business cards right and left."

"You didn't really expect to sell anything tonight, did you?"

Carr shook his head. "Not really, no. But it never hurts to remind the leisure class that we're here. And some of the newcomers will want to buy something later on to establish their credentials with the establishment."

"Well, go back down and twist some more arms. Last quarter's results were disappointing."

Carr disappeared but I waited until he'd had time to get out of earshot before speaking. "He doesn't strike me as the arm twisting type."

Kwan laughed, possibly for the first time in my presence. "You'd be surprised. He's past his prime now, but he was quite the physical specimen in his time. I had to post bail for him more than once when he was younger." She immediately looked as though she regretted her words and started to stand up. "I should get back."

"Why was Carr in jail?" I made no move to get up.

She shook her head. "I shouldn't have said that. It's not my story to tell. I'm sorry."

I sighed. "I can find out my own way, Miss Kwan, but that means asking questions and stirring things up. It would be much more discreet if you just told me."

For a moment she appeared to be wrestling with her conscience. "All right, but it was years and years ago, Mr. Birch. Avery was a hard drinker then and sometimes he got belligerent. There were some fights and sometimes the police got involved. He was never found guilty of anything. If it wasn't self defense, he'd pay the other party off. But it's been almost thirty years since the last incident."

I waited but she didn't continue. "What changed?"

She pressed her lips tightly together and turned her head away. "He killed a man, with his fists. It was another bar fight, the last one. The other man was apparently very drunk, very belligerent, but Avery wasn't the kind to step aside to avoid a confrontation. They exchanged words, then blows, and the other man fell and hit his head. There were plenty of witnesses that it was self defense, but Avery blamed himself and he was never the same afterwards. He seemed to grow up overnight. That's all of it, Mr. Birch. I really need to go now."

I followed her downstairs, processing this new information. Avery Carr's early impetuosity was interesting, but even more intriguing was the fact that, despite her protestations, Kristina Kwan had deliberately set about making sure that I knew about it. She had feigned reluctance, but she was too much in control of herself to have let such an allegation slip out by accident. Was she trying to nudge me toward suspicion of Avery Carr, or away from suspicion of someone else?

Downstairs I made another quick circuit. Dusty had arrived and was deep in conversation with a man I didn't know. Wanda passed me and gave me an uncertain nod and the sketch of a smile, looking very harried and vaguely unhappy. Fogle was back with his wife and they were surrounded again; he was looking quite pleased with himself but she looked vaguely troubled. Kwan and Carr were talking to the lieutenant governor and his wife. Carr looked up and saw me, apparently made his excuses, and came deliberately toward me.

"Are you still finding all of this pretentious and boring, Mr. Birch."

"Not at all," I answered, a half truth. It was not at all boring. "Looks like a good turnout."

He half turned back toward the crowd. "Yes, though I could wish they were all here because of their love of the arts. I've had to answer almost as many questions about Walter's death as I did when the police were here. And they're not phrased as tactfully."

"I'm not surprised. People are fascinated with the morbid. I notice you've replaced the painting at the front entrance."

"The Tontine? Yes, I finished the alterations yesterday."

"Phyllis Reynolds did the original, didn't she?"

"Yes, she did. If any of us had more of a taste for the morbid than Peter it was Phyllis. She was obsessed with death. Her business card had a little sketch of the Grim Reaper working at an easel."

"The altered figure looks as though it belongs there."

"Yes, I've always had a talent for imitation, and Phyllis left us sketches of each figure as she envisioned them in the final version, presumably with all seven of us dead. Any form of artwork is a mix of imagination and craftsmanship, you realize. Successful artists also require a reasonable amount of luck. I'm a craftsman, Mr. Birch, who has enjoyed a good portion of luck despite a lack of imagination."

"I gather Earl Garner couldn't make it tonight."

"Couldn't, or more likely wouldn't. Earl has become increasingly withdrawn these past few years, and not just from the Tontine. Walter was the only one who stayed in regular touch with him, and now that Walter's gone..." His voice trailed off.

Benjamin Fogle emerged from the crowd, alone this time, headed in the direction of the rest rooms. It was too good a chance to miss. "I shouldn't keep you from your guests," I said as politely as possible. "We can talk another time if you'd like."

Carr took no apparent offense and made me promise to talk to him again before I left. I wondered if he, like Kwan, had something he wanted to tell me, directly or otherwise, or conversely if he was hoping to learn something from me.

Fogle was indeed using the facilities. I took my time washing my hands, giving him a chance to finish and catch up to me. I stepped back as he approached, tossed the paper towel into the trash. "Excuse me. Aren't you Benjamin Fogle? Michelle Bernstein's husband?"

He gave me a neutral, appraising look as he bent over the sink. "That's right. I'm afraid you have the advantage of me."

"Paul Birch. I met your wife a few days ago during the course of my work."

"Oh, you must be the private detective. Michelle mentioned that you'd been to the house. Something to do with old Spencer's suicide, wasn't it?"

"Something like that. I was hoping to have a word with you."

"I have an office in the city. I can give you a card and you can call for an appointment." Now that it was clear that I wasn't a prospective customer, his manner had become curt.

"I was hoping to avoid anything so formal. I just wanted to ask a few questions about your business dealings with Walter Spencer."

Suddenly nervous, Fogle glanced around. "I'm not sure that it would be prudent of me to talk about his affairs."

"I've been employed by his primary heir to look into those affairs, Mr. Fogle. And I'm also curious about your arrangement with Earl Garner."

That tipped the balance. Fogle switched from mildly hostile to reluctantly amenable, and visibly nervous. "Of course, we could deal with that informally, I suppose. I was just going to have a smoke. Would you care to join me?"

We stepped outside and walked to the corner, where a bench stood under a streetlight. I declined Fogle's offer of a cigarette and waited until he had taken a few puffs. "How did you get involved with Spencer and Garner?"

"Through Michelle, of course. Indirectly, anyway. She introduced us and Garner called almost two years ago now and asked for some investment advice. He wanted it for nothing, of course, and I did reduce my fees as a courtesy because of his friendship with my wife. He was anxious to make a lot of money quickly. I tried to talk him out of it, but he insisted on making risky investments. He was lucky at first, made quite a bit in a very short time as the market goes, but he got greedy, refused to take his profits, just reinvested them in even chancier places."

I doubted that he'd done so without encouragement from Fogle, but saw no point to pressing the issue. "And Spencer?"

"Garner brought him in shortly after his big coup. Spencer wasn't as aggressive, but he let Garner talk him into going along with his own plan. I resisted at first, but then I told myself, they're grown men, they've been warned. If they wanted to take unnecessary chances, it wasn't up to me to try to stop them."

No mention of the fact that Fogle had invested his own money alongside theirs, but I hadn't expected him to admit anything that wasn't absolutely necessary.

"Did you ever have reason to believe there was any tension between the two of them? After they began to suffer losses, I mean."

"I don't think I was ever in the same room with the two of them at the same time. In fact I only met Garner on one occasion. We conducted most of our business over the phone. They carped about each other a little. Nothing serious."

"Are you still handling Garner's investments?"

Fogle abruptly tossed his cigarette into the gutter. "No. We agreed to cut our losses and liquidate our holdings a few months ago." He didn't seem to notice that his choice of pronoun confirmed that he had been financially involved with Garner, not just acting as adviser. He got to his feet. "I have to get back. Michelle will be looking for me. I hope I've been helpful, Mr. Birch." He didn't sound that way.

"Very," I answered brightly, leaving him to wonder what I meant.

CHAPTER ELEVEN

Dusty passed me when I returned to the Tontine, her arm entwined with that of an elderly man who was looking quite pleased with himself. I didn't blame him. She winked at me but gave no other sign of recognition. I wasn't sure just how much more I could learn tonight and I was seriously considering leaving when Wanda Fredericks almost literally ran into me. I'm not sure she even recognized who I was. She backed off without looking at my face, mumbled an excuse, and hurried off. I was almost certain that she'd been crying.

Curious, I followed in her wake, saw her disappear up the staircase, still half running. It was none of my business, of course, but I make a living sticking my nose into other people's business. So I stepped over the rope and followed her. I made no effort to disguise my presence, but as I had noticed earlier, the steps were so heavily carpeted that I made very little noise.

Wanda was not in sight when I reached the second floor, presumably having disappeared into one of the offices. I took a tentative step forward, then began to have second thoughts. I probably would have gone back downstairs if I hadn't suddenly heard the sound of her sobbing.

She was, predictably, in Walter Spencer's office, sitting with her arms around her knees in the far corner, her head down, shoulders trembling as she cried. I hesitated in the doorway, trying to think of something to say. She must have sensed my presence, or possibly caught sight of my shadow, because her head came up and she brushed at her eyes.

"Oh, Mr. Birch. I didn't realize you were up here. I'll get out of your way." She scrambled quickly to her feet.

"You're not in my way, Wanda. I noticed you were upset and came to see if I could help."

She raised her hands slightly, then let them drop back to her sides. "I'm all right. Just an attack of the blues." A clearly insincere smile appeared and disappeared. "I got to thinking how much Walter... Mr. Spencer...would have enjoyed being here. He always liked talking to people."

"I gather the two of you were pretty close." I reminded myself that I had to be careful not to let slip anything I'd learned through Dusty.

"He was very good to me. Always polite and friendly, never condescending like some people." I had no doubt she meant Avery Carr. "He took the time to explain things. I can't believe he's gone, and I don't believe that he killed himself." Her voice rose toward the end, becoming almost challenging.

"The police concluded that it was suicide. Do you have any reason to think they're wrong?"

"I know that he'd had some disappointments recently." Her voice had lowered and she was obviously trying very hard to stay calm and collected. "And he was in a lot of pain. But he wouldn't have gone away without leaving some kind of explanation behind. He would have wanted us to know why he'd done it." She smiled, more genuinely this time. "He always liked to get the last word in."

"But why would someone else have killed him, Wanda? As far as I can tell, no one particularly disliked him."

She tossed her head and gave me a look that said I wasn't as smart as I thought I was. "He and Mr. Carr argued a lot, about the gallery. Mr. Carr is in charge, I suppose, but all of the partners are supposed to have a say. And they argued about other things too."

"What other things?"

She bit her lip. "I don't know exactly. But sometimes they'd go up to the second floor and close themselves in one of the offices and once I could hear them shouting all the way downstairs."

That was interesting, particularly since Carr had a history of violence, admittedly well in the past. "But you don't know what they were arguing about?"

"No," she admitted. "And Miss Kwan was furious with him too."

"I know that they were seeing each other and that she broke it off."

Wanda shook her head furiously. "That's not how it happened. He told her he didn't want to see her again, at least not until she told him some secret she was keeping." She shook her head, forestalling me. "No, I don't know what it was. I only heard part of the conversation and I went away before they noticed I was there."

"When was this?"

"A few weeks before...before he died."

"Where did this happen?"

Wanda looked around nervously, as though wondering if she'd said too much. "At his place. I used to bring his mail over sometimes when he wasn't feeling well enough to come into the city. Most of the time I'd just drop it through the mail slot, but I saw her car in the driveway and then I heard them in his office."

I'd been to the house, and if my memory was correct, the only way she could have eavesdropped on a conversation in Spencer's office was by going around through the side yard and up a short set of stairs to an elevated porch. Wanda couldn't possibly have overheard them by chance if she'd just been dropping off some mail.

Wanda seemed to have run out of steam for the moment. Her shoulders stumped and she swayed slightly. I thought she might faint and started to lift a hand to steady her, but she shied away. "Are you all right?"

"Yes, I'm fine."

She didn't look fine, but seemed steadier after a few seconds passed. "I should go back downstairs." Despite her words, she was obviously in no hurry to do so.

"Don't rush it. Wait until you're ready."

"They all hated him, you know. Ms. Bernstein was afraid he'd say something about how her husband cheated him and Mr. Garner was mad at him because he wouldn't loan him some money."

My ears twitched. "Earl Garner tried to borrow money from Spencer?"

She nodded enthusiastically. "He even came to the gallery once, but no one was supposed to know. Walter stayed after Mr. Carr went home and I didn't like leaving him alone so I stayed down in my office. There's always plenty of paperwork to be done. He told me he was expecting a visitor but he didn't say who, but when I let him in, I recognized him. I saw him at the board meeting last year."

"When was this?"

"Oh, months ago, just after Christmas I think."

"And they argued about money?"

"I guess. But they kept their voices down and I didn't hear anything. Mr. Garner stayed about an hour, then came down alone. He didn't say anything when I let him out, but I could tell that he was furious. And Walter came down later and told me to go home, that he'd lock up. He looked upset and I asked what was wrong and he said that Mr. Garner had wanted a big loan and that he'd had to turn him down."

An unlikely but provocative possibility occurred to me. "Did Spencer ever mention Earl Garner's brother?" Was it possible that it had been Carl and not Earl who had tried to wheedle money from Walter Spencer? And if so, wouldn't Spencer have seen through the impersonation? Or had the two former friends grown so apart that he could have been fooled?

But Wanda looked completely bewildered. "I don't know what you're talking about. I never even knew Mr. Garner had a brother."

I nodded. "Oh, he does. An identical twin named Carl. They're living together."

Wanda blinked and seemed to be staring right through me. "He never said anything about a brother." She wasn't talking to me either. Wanda had retreated into her own private space for the moment. My revelation seemed to bewilder her.

"Who didn't tell you about him, Wanda?"

My voice seemed to bring her back to the here and now. "What? Oh, I'm sorry, Mr. Birch. I was thinking about something else. I'm really sorry to have bothered you. Excuse me, I really have to get back. Mr. Carr won't be happy if he can't find me." And she brushed past me quickly, her expression troubled, leaving me wondering what it was that I had just missed.

Because I was sure I had missed something.

ᘰ

I followed her downstairs, a bit bemused. The evening had not been as productive as I'd hoped. My theory about art forgery had been blown out of the water, Fogle hadn't told me anything I hadn't already known, and my brief conversation with Wanda had left me with more questions than answers. If she was right, all of the partners had good reason to at least resent Walter Spencer, if not enough to kill him. But how much of what she said was objective and how much influenced by her obsession with the dead man?

Maybe Dusty had had better luck. I went to see if I could find her without making it obvious that I was looking for her.

The crowd seemed to have thinned a bit and I glanced at my watch, surprised to discover how much time had passed. Things would be winding up during the next half hour, at least according to the times listed on the invitation. I couldn't see any point in waiting until the bitter end and decided to slip out as soon as I'd found a way to let Dusty know I was leaving. I thought about calling her cell but I wasn't sure that was a good idea in such close proximity.

She was in the reception area, talking to Wanda, who seemed to have regained her composure. I eased myself over, ignoring Dusty, waited for a pause in their conversation. "Wanda, I'm heading out. I couldn't find your boss. Would you thank him again for inviting me?"

"Certainly, Mr. Birch, and thank you for coming."

"It was my pleasure." I nodded neutrally to Dusty and turned away.

I had walked less than a block when my cell phone buzzed. It was Dusty. "Meet me at the corner. The coffee shop." She disconnected before I could answer.

The Jolly Java was on the corner all right, but in the opposite direction, so I had to retrace my steps, slip through the increased flow of departing guests, and hoof it another block. The smell of brewing coffee was a welcome one though, and I ordered a cappuccino for myself and another for Dusty.

She arrived just as I found a tiny, none too steady table in one corner and settled into an uncomfortable plastic seat. Something else local must have just let out because a flood of young people arrived right on Dusty's heels, filling up the available seating and counter space.

Dusty glanced at the coffee I'd ordered and sat down opposite me. "Nice call." It was still hot but she drank a considerable portion before setting the cup aside and smacking her lips.

"What was so important it couldn't wait until we got home?" I glanced around. "We shouldn't be seen together, you know."

"Don't worry about it. You don't think any of that crowd would be caught dead in here, do you?"

I took a quick look around at the glitzy décor, and admitted to myself that she did have a point. And the coffee was good.

"First of all," she said, "the general opinion is that Spencer killed himself. Most of the people I talked to had no idea that there was an investigation under way."

"I don't suppose the partners would tell anyone they didn't have to. It's hardly the kind of publicity they're looking for."

"Did you get to meet Bernstein's husband? I tried twice but I guess I don't look prosperous enough."

"Briefly." I summarized our conversation. "He's apparently trying to conceal the fact that he was responsible for the losses."

"Not very successfully. A few people took his card tonight, but a few others were quietly cautioning them afterwards."

"I'm not surprised. Word tends to get around in situations like that."

The press of people increased, raising the noise level. Someone bumped into our table and nearly spilled our coffee, moved away without apologizing.

"Well, here's something less well known. Avery Carr once killed a man." She was so pleased with herself for having discovered this that I almost pretended I hadn't known. But we'd always made a point of being honest with each other and I wasn't about to break our bond now. "I heard the same thing earlier this evening. In a bar fight."

Dusty pouted. "You're taking all the fun out of this."

"I told you this isn't a fun job. Besides, that was a long time ago and it was self defense. People change a lot as they grow older. He seems pretty placid now."

"Maybe. But I just happened to overhear a Mrs. Feldstein recommending an anger management specialist to a Mrs. Vargas, whose husband is apparently prone to fits of uncontrolled rage. She mentioned that he'd done a marvelous job helping out Avery Carr."

I blinked. "When was this?"

Dusty shook her head. "She didn't say and I couldn't very well ask."

"I don't suppose you heard the specialist's name?"

She shook her head. "I only heard the tail end of the conversation."

I couldn't offhand think of any way to pursue that knowledge without going to a lot more effort than it was probably worth. Wanda might possibly know, if it had been since she'd come to the Tontine, but it would be awkward for either Dusty or I to ask her.

"Anything else?"

"Michelle Bernstein was none too pleased with her husband tonight."

"I'm not surprised. Did anything specific happen between them?"

"No, but you don't have to be an expert in body language when people are shouting at you, so to speak. They were barely civil to one another."

"Nothing from Wanda? She seemed quite upset." I recounted our encounter in Spencer's office.

"She was pretty distracted, but I've never seen her completely focused. It's like she's watching two television programs at once, and only catching bits and pieces of each one. I thought she might have been crying just before we left, but her face was so flushed from running around seeing to things that I couldn't be sure. We barely had a chance to talk, but she did say one thing that struck me as odd."

She hesitated, so I provided a prompt. "What was that?"

"I said that it was a shame that Earl Garner hadn't been able to attend. She gave me a real funny look and said that he could have come if he'd really wanted to, that he could be in two places at the same time if he wanted."

"Ah," I said. "My fault. She hadn't known about brother Carl until I mentioned him this evening. I think she felt badly treated because no one had ever bothered to tell her." I tried and failed to suppress a yawn. "Not even caffeine is going to keep me awake much longer. How about we finish this conversation at home?"

We finished our coffee and stood up and, just as I was trying to select the least congested escape route, I saw a thin young woman sitting on a stool at the counter that ran along the opposite wall. She was swiveled around in her seat, looking expressionlessly in our direction. Directly at us in fact. It was Wanda Fredericks.

"Oops!" I whispered. "The cat's out of the bag."

Dusty followed my eyes and made a startled sound. "What's she doing here? I thought she'd be cleaning up the mess for at least another hour."

"Apparently not." Wanda had turned away from us just as I met her eyes.

"Should we go over and say something?"

I thought about it, but I couldn't come up with anything plausible to repair the damage. "No. Let's just go. I think we've probably learned as much from Wanda as we're going to anyway." We left, weaving through the noisy but well behaved crowd. I felt a twinge of guilt about our deception. Wanda seemed to have enough troubles in her life without adding what she would almost certainly consider yet another betrayal of her trust, but it was done now and, after all, that was part of the job.

It had begun to cloud over and I wondered if the rain forecast for the next day was going to arrive early. "Where are you parked? I'll walk you to the car."

She was in the block behind the Tontine, so we rounded the nearest corner. It was an alley way, and not well lighted, the kind of place I usually avoid even in daylight, but it was a short distance and we made our way through it without incident.

"Right over there." Dusty pointed across the street. Her voice was troubled and I guessed that she was having the same misgivings about Wanda that I'd felt a moment earlier.

"She'll get over it," I said, immediately regretting what felt like a crass dismissal.

"I know. And we'd have had to tell her sooner or later. I don't like lying to people. I'm just sorry she found out the way she did. She's had a rough time. Did I tell you she was married for a while?"

I nodded.

"I think he abused her. She didn't say anything specific, but I could tell she was still afraid of him, even now. Apparently he got upset whenever she talked to another man, even casually. There was no actual physical abuse, at least none she admitted to, but he used to shout at her all the time and called her names. She was shaking when she told me about him."

Something stirred briefly in the back of my mind. "I wonder if he lives around here."

"I don't think so." She opened her car door. "They were someplace in western Connecticut. It was the farthest she'd ever been from where she grew up and she missed her father a lot. Her mother was already dead."

"She was close to her adopted parents then?"

Dusty nodded. "Her father at least. She mentioned him more than once." She slid behind the steering wheel and took her keys from her purse.

"I'll see you back at the house." I pushed the door closed.

I took the long way back to my car, processing the various tidbits of information I'd received during the course of the evening, shuffling them around to see if they fell into any new patterns. I would feel better when I reduced everything to writing; I can make much more sense of puzzles when I can look at the individual components. But I was already beginning to suspect that I was worse off now than when the evening began. The forgery angle seemed to be a dead end, and nothing else promising had appeared in its place.

If I'd been paying more attention, I might have noticed that I was being followed, but frankly I doubt it. Philip Marlowe might have eyes on the back of his head or a sixth sense for such things, but neither of those advantages had been included in my private detective kit. So when a voice called my name from the darkness, I was more than slightly startled.

"That really wasn't nice of you, Mr. Birch."

I recognized the voice and turned. She was standing in the shadows and I wouldn't have been able to recognize her if she hadn't spoken.

"Hello, Wanda," I said neutrally.

She stepped forward but it was still impossible to see her expression. "I guess she works for you. You asked her to make friends with me, to find out what I knew, didn't you?"

"No," I answered truthfully. "She had already met you. You know why I was hired, Wanda. It's part of my job to find out what people might say to someone else that they wouldn't say to me."

"I don't believe you," she said, her voice rising slightly. "If she was really my friend, she wouldn't have told you anything."

I sighed. "Whatever you might think about it, Wanda, Dusty does like you. She's told me so more than once. And neither of us thinks you've done anything wrong. We're just trying to find out what happened to Walter Spencer. You must feel the same way."

There was a short, uncomfortable silence, and when she spoke again, some of the anger was gone, replaced by uncertainty. "You could have just asked."

"Sometimes people get tense and forget things when they feel like they're being interrogated." And sometimes they hide things, but I didn't say that. "They're more likely to remember them when they're relaxed."

There was another pause. "Maybe you're right, Mr. Birch. But I still don't like it." And before I could say another word, she turned and stalked away.

What I'd said had been the truth, but I still felt like a cad all the way home.

Dusty met me at the door. She'd already swapped her dress for a fluffy pink bathrobe. "Coffee or brandy?" she asked. "Or a little of both?"

"The last sounds good." I described my encounter with Wanda while she was fixing us each a fortified coffee.

"I really feel bad about this," she said when I was done.

"You were the one who wanted to be an assistant private eye," I reminded her. "Most of my cases end up making someone feel bad. And strictly speaking, you never lied to Wanda, did you?"

She thought that over. "Not technically, no. Sins of omission and all that. But you're right. There's nothing I can do about it now. So what did we find out tonight that you haven't told me?"

I went over things again, in more detail this time, thinking out loud rather than talking to Dusty. And this time I retrieved my notebook first and copied down the highlights, even those that seemed irrelevant. When I was done, I sat staring at the pages, slowly realizing what I was going to have to do in the morning.

"I think we're wasting our time and our client's money, Dusty."

We were facing each other across the kitchen table. Dusty was leaning on her forearms, beginning to look sleepy. "You're giving up?" She sounded more resigned than surprised.

I shrugged. "Any of several people might have killed Walter Spencer and rigged it to look like a suicide. And there are certainly a number of things that seem consistent with that conclusion. But if that's the case, whoever is responsible did an excellent job at covering their tracks and it would take more resources than I have available to dig out the truth, if it's possible at all. People get away with murder all the time, whether we want to admit it or not. And it's still possible—even probable - that Spencer did commit suicide. He may have acted out of character in the process, but suicide itself is out of character. We know he owned the gun, we know he had the opportunity, and he certainly had a number of reasons to want to end his life."

She didn't argue with me, but I could tell she wasn't happy. "So what are you going to tell the niece?"

"I don't know," I said wearily. "I'll think about it in the morning."

It felt as though my head had barely hit the pillow when the phone began to ring, but it must have been an hour or so later, just after midnight. Dusty mumbled without waking up and rolled over so it was up to me to silence it. I managed to pick up the receiver without knocking over the lamp in the dark, but I'm not sure how intelligible my first few words were.

"Mr. Paul Birch?"

The voice was deep, masculine, official sounding. "Yes, that's me. What is it?"

"Sir, this is Sergeant Gainer of the Providence Police. I have your name listed as contact person in case of an emergency." He read off an address. "Are you the person I should be speaking to?"

"Yes, that's my office. What's the problem?"

"I don't have details, sir, but there are two officers on site and we need you to come down there as soon as possible."

I shook my head, hoping to rearrange my befogged wits into something resembling order. "All right, I'll be there in half an hour or less."

"Thank you, sir."

It took all of thirty minutes to get there despite the lack of traffic. There were two police cars in front of the building, both with their flashers blinking. I pulled up next to one and got out, and was immediately approached by a uniformed officer.

"I'm Paul Birch," I volunteered. "Your dispatcher called me."

The uniform stepped into the light and I recognized him. He'd been very cooperative when one of my clients had parked illegally a few weeks earlier, but I couldn't remember his name.

"I got here as fast as I could," I added. "What seems to be the problem?"

"We're not completely sure, Mr. Birch. Someone broke at least three of your windows but there's no sign of forced entry and they were all on the upper floor so they didn't trip your alarm system." All of our ground floor windows were alarmed, but we hadn't bothered with the second floor, an oversight I immediately resolved to correct. "If you'll turn off the alarms, we'll check things out for you, just in case."

At one time we used one of the national alarm companies, but they were so unreliable that I'd dropped them. I had my keys with me. I punched in the combination and opened the door, then stepped back as three of the four police officers went inside. "The lights for the second floor are at the foot of the stairs," I called.

They were perhaps too quick to have been entirely thorough, but unless someone had used a ladder to reach one of the broken windows, and then pulled it up behind them, there was no obvious way that anyone could have entered. They returned very quickly, looking more relaxed.

"It's all clear, Mr. Birch."

I made a quick survey of the office. Merrilee would not be happy, but other than a broken coffee cup and a lot of broken glass, there didn't seem to be any damage. It took another hour to answer the questions the police needed for their report, and to secure the building after they'd left. I dropped the storm windows on the three that were broken. It still hadn't started raining but I could hear thunder in the distance. I'd have Steve arrange for repairs in the morning.

The patrolmen had asked if I had any idea who might be responsible, but clearly they suspected kids and a prank. They might even have been right, but whenever I thought about it, the same image came to mind. It was Wanda Fredericks, standing on the sidewalk, lobbing rocks at my windows.

I wondered if I was right. Maybe I deserved it.

CHAPTER TWELVE

I had intended to officially take myself off the case the following morning, but when I called Kari Spencer's number I got her answering machine, and another try after lunch was no more successful. There was no answer at her uncle's house on either occasion. A bored police detective showed up right after that and I wasted more time taking him around the upper floor of the building where he collected the three rocks that had been thrown through the windows, which we'd carefully set aside. Two of the windows had already been replaced and two equally bored looking men were working on the third.

"We don't realistically have much chance of catching the individuals responsible, Mr. Birch, unless they're caught red handed doing the same thing and we can get them to confess."

I told him that I understood the difficulties, as indeed I did, but refrained from putting forward my own theory, that Wanda Fredericks was responsible. But I felt considerably less guilty about having misled her this morning.

Further efforts to reach Kari were forestalled by a completely unrelated emergency. I had hired Penny Worthington to do some clandestine surveillance for me. Penny is a human chameleon. She can change her appearance dramatically enough to fool her own family, and I've seen her as a bag lady, a debutante, and even a young boy. Sometimes she blends into the scenery so seamlessly that it's hard to tell she's there, other times she stands out so dramatically that no one seriously believes she could be anything other than what she appears to be.

I had asked Penny to keep an eye on a local businessman whose partners believed that he was preparing to loot the company of its liquid assets and do a bunk. I wasn't convinced that they were right, but he certainly had changed his life style rather dramatically in recent weeks, enough to make him worth watching. But Penny had taken a tumble down a staircase.

"Nothing's broken but I'll be hobbling for a while. I can still type so I'll email you everything I have, but you'll want to find a replacement. I think Victor Chan is available."

I didn't have a lot of confidence in Victor. He was a blowhard who thought he knew more than he actually did. His wife was even worse. But there weren't that many options open to me and I called him, brought him up to date, told him what I wanted. As long as he didn't decide that he knew better than I, it should all work out. By the time I had that taken care of and had reviewed Penny's email, the afternoon was pretty well shot and I completely forgot about Kari Spencer until I was already on the way home.

What the hell, I thought. I'm not billing her for any additional hours. It won't matter if I don't reach her for another day.

Dusty was subdued that evening. She insisted that she was having trouble with the novel, which was probably true, but I think the business with Wanda was at the root of the problem. I hadn't passed on my suspicions about the vandalism at my office, which might after all have been wrong, so Dusty didn't even have that mitigating factor working for her. We ate a quieter than usual evening meal and she disappeared into her office as soon as we'd finished cleaning up.

I took out my notes on the Spencer case and read through them again, one last pass I told myself, just to make sure I wasn't overlooking anything significant. Given unlimited resources and sufficient motivation, I could see a number of areas that could use a little illumination, but I had neither. This wasn't my kind of investigation. My areas of expertise were of limited use. I don't like failure any more than the next guy, but I wasn't even sure what constituted success in this case.

I scribbled a couple of comments and slid everything into a file folder. I'd take everything to the office tomorrow and put it in the master file, the file for closed cases. Not completed cases, but closed. We didn't have an awful lot of those, but it happened. Sometimes the truth is so well buried that it can't be unearthed, or it isn't worth the bother, or the client decides belatedly that ignorance is preferable. You'd be surprised how many times our findings are rejected, or even refused. People fear the worst but they don't always want to know what it is.

I turned off the lights and walked carefully to the stairs. There was a 40 watt bulb at the top that we switched on at night but the rest of the house was dark now. When I reached the landing, I saw that the door to Dusty's office was open and the lights were out. She must have gone to bed, relatively early for her. I was about to follow her example when I heard something outside.

Someone was on the patio.

I'm licensed to carry a handgun and I own one. It's very securely locked in my safe. In the office. I have no firearms at home. The only upstairs window that overlooks the patio was at one corner and the angle wasn't good. If I wanted to spy on my trespasser, I'd have to go back downstairs and use one of the ground floor windows.

I did so, moving as quickly as I could without making unnecessary noise. There were sliding glass doors at the back of the house that opened directly onto the patio, and an ordinary window from the pantry. I went to the latter first, eased the curtain open, and looked outside.

The sky was clear, the moon near to full, and there was a streetlight visible above the back hedge that shone down onto my property. The patio seemed to be completely empty except for the wicker furniture that was supposed to be there.

I was quite sure that I hadn't imagined the sound of human footsteps. I eased the curtain back and went to the sliding doors. These were curtained as well, but I could see more of the yard from that vantage point. A careful survey revealed no sign of an intruder. I felt a sudden rush of anger. Someone had invaded my privacy and I wasn't going to tolerate it. I went to the front room and retrieved a poker from the fireplace, a flashlight from the kitchen, then returned to the rear of the house.

The floodlights went on in a rush, and I unlocked the doors and slid them open. I stepped outside and swung the flashlight around, probing the few pockets of darkness that remained. Nothing seemed out of place and when I checked the gazebo, the padlock was still secure.

The world is a very different place at night. It's more than just an absence of light. The night sounds different, looks different, and feels different. Crickets were having a good time in the neighbor's yard, but it was very quiet where I stood, perhaps because my light had startled them, perhaps because they'd already taken alarm. I moved to the corner of the house and peered cautiously around into the side yard, using the flashlight to probe behind each of the ornamental shrubs. Then the other end of the house, around the hump of the garage and along the narrow passage between the far wall and the stockade fence the Hansens had put up to contain their dogs.

Then I walked around front, where the flashlight was superfluous. Streetlights bathed the area in a soft glow. A cat glared at me from across the street, but there was no other sign of life. If there had been a prowler, they'd either gone away or found a hiding place too clever for me. Could I have imagined the footsteps on the patio? I shook my head. I couldn't believe it was just my imagination, but there was nothing I could do about it now.

I went back to the house and made sure all of the doors and windows were locked before I went to bed. It took a long time to get to sleep.

Dusty was up before me the following morning, which happens so rarely that I went downstairs to check on her before taking a shower. She was sitting at the kitchen table, drinking coffee and reading the morning paper. Or at least pretending to read it.

"You're up early." I poured myself a cup.

"Guilty conscience," she answered without looking up.

"Wanda?"

She nodded, then sighed and sat back in her chair. "Maybe I should go talk to her. Apologize. She must feel terrible."

I thought about my broken windows and our mysterious late night visitor. "She probably feels angry, not sad. You've only known her for what? A week? It was hardly a betrayal by a long time friend. She'll get over it."

"I don't know. For Wanda that might have been a serious relationship. I don't think she really has any friends."

It was my turn to sigh. I sat down beside her instead of across from her, which was our usual arrangement, and touched her forearm. "She's a big girl. She isn't scarred for life. You were just doing your job, miss assistant private eye."

That got me a faint smile and her face brightened slightly. "So have you solved the case yet? I think Wanda might forgive us if we actually figured out who killed Spencer."

I shook my head. "No, and I don't think we're going to. I tried to call Kari Spencer yesterday to tell her I was suspending the investigation but she wasn't home."

Dusty looked distinctly unhappy. "You can't do that, Paul. You can't let a murderer go free."

"Murderers go free all the time. And we don't even know if Spencer was killed by someone else. The police think it's a suicide. Maybe they're right."

She made an unhappy sound. "All of the work we did can't be for nothing."

I gripped her forearm more tightly. "Dusty, a big part of my job involves proving that people's suspicions are wrong. If there are shortages in inventory, it isn't necessarily theft. Errors in accounting aren't necessarily embezzlement. A missing person hasn't necessarily been kidnapped."

Her shoulders slumped. "I know. But it just seems so unfair."

"Have some bacon and eggs. You'll feel better." I waited long enough to be sure her mood was perking up before retreating upstairs for my shower.

I had planned to try calling Kari Spencer again as soon as I arrived at the office, but things didn't go as I had planned. They often didn't. Tina had uncovered some interesting code hidden inside the proprietary accounting software of one of our clients and insisted that it had to have been an inside job. "There's no direct connection between the administrative computers and the ones operating the equipment, so no one could have hacked in from the outside." Eblis Manufacturing had been experiencing unpredictable failures in their automated assembly area, but an external audit had failed to turn up anything wrong.

"Why didn't Abe Henderson's people find it?" Henderson was one of the handful of programmers Tina admired and Eblis had hired him to review their software only a couple of months earlier. Our follow up was less public and we had been looking primarily for evidence of physical sabotage. Tina's second look at the programming was almost accidental; we'd been trying to identify vulnerabilities that could have been physically exploited while the software was running.

"Probably because it wasn't there at the time. Whoever inserted this module could easily have deleted it while Abe was on site and reinserted it after he was gone. I checked and there were no reports of incidents that month. The last was three days before Abe's team arrived and they didn't resume until almost a week after he was done."

"So it's someone in their I.T. department."

"Looks that way. Someone passed over for promotion, maybe, or with some other grudge against the company."

When I finally got to my own office and sat down, I looked at the phone and then away. I felt oddly reluctant to take that final step and end things. And after all, there was no rush. I could call later.

As if it had heard me, the damned thing buzzed. It was Tony Wilson.

"Elsie's typing up my report on Wanda Fredericks, but I thought you might want the highlights."

The last thing I wanted to think about right now was Wanda, but I'd asked for his help. "What have you got?"

"Wanda Fredericks, age 27, formerly Wanda Taylor. Adopted at the age of three months by Paul and Rachel Taylor of Braintree, Massachusetts."

Dusty had mentioned that Wanda had been adopted but it hadn't really registered. "Who handled the paperwork?"

There was a brief pause and an audible rustle of papers. "The Family Center in Brookline, Mass. I gave them a call just on general principles but you know how tight mouthed these people are. They wouldn't give me anything except the names and date and I already knew all of that."

"Okay, what else?"

"Lived in Braintree with her adoptive parents until she finished high school. Reportedly very close to her father, something of an outcast among her peers but nothing out of the ordinary. Her high school grades were okay and there was no disciplinary problem. One year of college before she dropped out. Worked a fair number of short term, low paying jobs. Married to Roger Fredericks, whom she met during the course of one of those jobs, for less than two years ending in divorce. She declined to ask for alimony. Moved back to the Providence area four years ago, same pattern. Miscellaneous office jobs. Worked for a temp agency for a year, then a chemical company for six months, then a nursing home and an adoption agency. The last was her longest time with a single employer, almost eighteen months. They fired her for sleeping on the job."

"That would be the Little Darlings agency in Woonsocket, wouldn't it?"

"Yeah, how'd you know?" Tony sounded surprised.

"I've met the lady," I told him, not wanting to have to explain Dusty's involvement. "How'd you get them to tell you why they terminated her?" Most companies are too worried about lawsuits to provide more than employment dates and job titles.

"I know one of the nurses up there. The same people run an assisted living center alongside the adoption agency. Nice symmetry. They get you coming and going."

"What about the ex-husband? Any contact with him since the divorce?"

"Not that I know of. You want me to look at him?"

"No, I don't think so. Is there more?"

"A little. She started working at the Tontine Art Gallery in Providence about two years ago and she's still there. Maybe she found her niche at last. Lives alone in a small apartment in a not very trendy part of town, keeps to herself, no evidence of a boyfriend. Neighbors hardly knew who she was."

"How about the parents?"

"Her adopted mother died six years ago, just before she moved to Providence. Lung cancer. Father passed away this past spring. I did a quick pass on them but they seem to have been typical middle class. She taught kindergarten for years and he was a mid-level supervisor for a chain of hardware stores."

"Any criminal record for Wanda?"

"She had some minor trouble in school but not even a parking ticket since then."

"What kind of trouble?"

"Truancy, mostly. A couple of fights. Nothing that stands out. Were you looking for something in particular?"

"No, not really. Just fishing, hoping something might jump out of the pond."

"What I've got here is a typical minnow, not a flying fish." He sounded apologetic.

"You can't find what isn't there. Thanks, Tony. Send over your report and your bill."

"Elsie will swing by at lunch time and drop them off."

I called home and had almost given up when Dusty picked up the phone. We had caller ID so she greeted me by name.

"I was thinking about coming home early this afternoon. Maybe we could go to a movie and dinner someplace."

"That sounds like fun." She sounded more animated than she had that morning, but I could tell that she was still troubled.

"It's a date then."

I had run out of excuses, so I dialed Kari Spencer's number next. There was still no answer, so I tried her uncle's number again. There was another series of rings and I was ready to abandon the effort when there was a click.

"Hello?" It was Kari.

"Miss Spencer? This is Paul Birch. I've been trying to get in touch with you."

"I've been staying with a friend."

I remembered my prowler and felt a tremor of alarm. "Has something happened?"

"No, nothing. But I was having trouble sleeping at my place. Every time a dog barked I'd wake up and I had the feeling sometimes that I was being watched. I kept imagining that someone was lurking in the shadows, watching my windows. It was my imagination, of course, but it felt so real that it was making me sick."

"Did you call the police and explain the situation?"

"No. I'd have felt foolish. And things have been fine since I've been staying with Julie. Have you made any progress?"

"Miss Spencer, I have some bad news for you." I had rehearsed the speech in my mind but it still sounded like what it was, an admission of failure. "I know this has to be very disappointing, but I really can't see any purpose in prolonging this any further. The only thing we've turned up is evidence that your uncle's financial situation was not as healthy as it once was. That strengthens the argument for suicide."

She was silent for a moment. "I appreciate your honesty, Mr. Birch. We have an accountant going through my uncle's investments and he's already broken the news to me about Uncle Walter's recent losses. Please don't worry. There's still a lot of money left. He was a lot wealthier than I realized. I could probably retire right now if I wanted to." She laughed nervously. "That's going to take some getting used to. Anyway, I can afford your services quite easily and I wish you wouldn't give up just yet."

I sighed and launched my prepared array of arguments. We went back and forth for several minutes and now I felt guilty about being unable to provide the closure she apparently needed, but I really felt it was in her best interests to let things alone and I stuck to my guns. Eventually, but reluctantly, she acknowledged my determination. "All right, Mr. Birch. Send me your bill and I'll see that it's taken care of. I do appreciate the work you've done."

I hung up with very mixed feelings. On the one hand, I'd had enough of the Spencer case, Wanda's hurt feelings, the lack of any real leads. On the other, I hated admitting defeat, and I liked Kari Spencer and felt badly about disappointing her. But business is business, after all, and there were better ways to spend my time. I had a prospective client coming in for a consultation the following morning and based on our preliminary conversation, his problem might evolve into a major investigation.

Steve's voice came through the intercom. "I have a call holding for you, Paul, on line 4."

I glanced down at the blinking light. "Who is it?"

"Michelle Bernstein."

Apparently even though I had dropped the case, the case had not dropped me.

"Good morning, Mrs. Bernstein. This is Paul Birch."

She returned my greeting quickly, running the syllables together in her haste. "I know this is presumptuous of me, Mr. Birch, but would it be possible for you to come out to my place this afternoon? My husband and I need to talk to you."

I groaned softly. "This really isn't a very good time. And I have to tell you that we've pretty much finished our investigation. I'll be writing up my final report for Miss Spencer in a day or two. And no, we've found nothing that casts doubt on the police report."

"We'd still like to see you." She sounded distinctly worried and I felt a twinge of curiosity. What could this be about? "We could come to your office if that's easier, but we'd prefer to keep this as discreet as possible."

I shook my head wearily. Apparently the Spencer case wasn't over quite yet. Bernstein wouldn't be this determined to talk to me if there wasn't a good reason. "All right, how about two o'clock?"

"That's fine." She sounded relieved, but still anxious. "We'll be expecting you."

I had lunch on the way. It had rained off and on during the morning but the sky was beginning to clear. There were two cars parked in the driveway. The Lincoln presumably belonged to Fogle. Bernstein must have been watching for me because the door opened before I touched the buzzer.

"Come right in, Mr. Birch. My husband will be with us in just a few minutes. He's on a conference call." I glanced around. What I could see of the house looked just as it had before, but Bernstein herself seemed very different. She was less composed, almost anxious. "Thank you for coming out here on such short notice. Let's go into my office."

I followed her into a small, orderly room one wall of which was lined with windows. There were bookcases filled with art books, a small roll top desk and matching chair, probably antiques, and an array of framed paintings and prints, including a small reproduction of Peter Trentano's *Lumber Mill at Dusk*. "Are any of these your work?" I asked, glancing around the room.

She shook her head. "Not in here."

I walked over to the Trentano, which seemed almost like an old acquaintance now. Almost involuntarily, I leaned closer and began counting the blades of the grass above the artist's signature.

"Benjamin is concerned that you might have gotten the wrong impression from what he said the other evening."

I struggled not to lose count, placed a mental bookmark on the thirteenth blade. "I don't think I understand."

"He's rather sensitive on business matters. It doesn't take much to get a bad reputation in the financial world, and even a hint of impropriety, right or wrong, can have devastating effects."

I counted twelve more blades of grass. "Are you suggesting that there was something improper in your husband's business dealings with Walter Spencer?" I asked as I counted.

"No, of course not. But sometimes investors take chances and it's not always clear to outsiders who was responsible for the decisions they made."

She was dancing around the subject, so I decided to remain silent and let her fidget and possibly say more than she intended. Besides, it gave me time to finish counting and, as expected, I found twenty-six blades of grass.

"This is an excellent reproduction," I said at last. "Much better than the other copies I've seen."

The change of subject seemed to disconcert Bernstein, but there was obvious relief to be on safer ground. "Yes it is. You'd be surprised how many prints are still taken from photographs that are decades old. Modern printing processes can't make up for a flawed negative. Paul never wanted his paintings disturbed and the lighting at the Tontine isn't what it could be, but we had them all re-shot about a year after he died. I have a full set."

I wanted to ask another question, but Benjamin Fogle chose that moment to join us. "Oh, there you are, Mr. Birch. Sorry to have kept you waiting but I had a couple of nervous investors on the phone.

Please sit down. Michelle, why don't you get us all something to drink?"

His tone to his wife was one I would never have dared use with Dusty, but she showed no obvious resentment. Perhaps she was inured to it. I asked for coffee and her husband said something about a brandy. "I don't know how much you know about investment counseling, Mr. Birch."

I actually knew quite a bit and numbered several of his colleagues among my clients, but I didn't say anything.

"Reputation is everything. Even the hint of wrongdoing can do irreparable damage."

"I can see that it's important that your clients feel confident about your integrity."

"Exactly!" He was sitting across from me and he leaned forward and put his hand on my knee, a familiarity I object to unless the hand belongs to Dusty. "And sometimes it's possible to over react when there's a possibility that your judgment has been at fault. My judgment, in this case."

"Are we talking about your investment work for Walter Spencer and Carl Garner?" I don't multi-task well. Keeping up my side of this conversation was interfering with my ability to process what I'd just learned from Bernstein.

"Yes, exactly. I may have led you to believe that my role was less prominent than it actually was in their case. I don't mean to say that I did anything unethical, and the ultimate decision was theirs in every instance, but I probably overstated things by implying that I hadn't developed the prospectus initially."

I made a giant leap of intuition at that point. The accountant dealing with the Spencer estate had recently told her about the massive investment losses her uncle had experienced during the past year, as she had just told me herself a few hours earlier. That almost certainly meant that someone had been in contact with Fogle, asking awkward questions, and there was almost certainly documentation proving that he had been more than simply a compliant agent. Fogel was engaged in damage control. As far as he knew, I was still actively investigating Spencer's death and any factors that might have contributed to it.

Bernstein returned with the drinks. The coffee was good. The brandy must have been as well, because Fogle made it disappear very quickly.

"I'm sure a man of your intelligence realizes how things like that work. And I can't honestly say that given the same information, I wouldn't have made the same recommendations again. There are no sure things in the market, Mr. Birch."

Fogle wanted reassurance and I disliked him enough that under normal circumstances I would have taken a good deal of pleasure from denying him that comfort, but there was a more pressing issue that I needed to concern myself with just at the moment. "I understand completely, Benjamin." He hadn't invited me to use his first name so I invited myself. "And I'm sure you wouldn't have put so much of your own portfolio in the same stock if you'd had any serious reservations."

Fogle's eyes moved swiftly to his wife, but I couldn't tell whether he was trying to decide if she'd told me more than she should have, or if he was concerned that I'd just told his wife more than she already knew.

"If it was possible to win every throw of the dice, they wouldn't call it gambling, Paul." His lips curled slightly when he said my name.

Bernstein's eyes moved back and forth between us and I was expecting her to fetch a ruler so we could compare measurements if we wanted to. It was obvious that she had picked up the subtext of the conversation.

I set down my half cup of coffee. "Unless there's something else, I really need to get back to the city."

Bernstein stood up. Fogle didn't. "Thank you again for coming on such short notice," she said, apparently meaning it. "I'll see you to the door."

She didn't say anything until we got there, but before I could get away, she spoke softly but firmly. "I apologize if my husband offended you. He's been very defensive lately, and sometimes it affects his manners."

"I'm sure that a job like his is hard on the nerves." Her as well as his, I suspected.

Bernstein nodded. "He had a spell of bad luck, and he's been trying too hard to make up the lost ground quickly."

"Then I hope things turn around for you soon." I put a very slight emphasis on "you", meaning it to be singular, but I was too preoccupied to play polite word games just now.

As I started for my car, my head was spinning with fresh possibilities.

CHAPTER THIRTEEN

My meeting with Bernstein and her husband had stirred the pot more dramatically than they could have guessed, and it occupied my thoughts so completely on the drive back that I ran a red light and was pulled over by a polite but censorious police officer who let me off with a written warning. I was more careful after that, meaning to sit down and think through the implications of what I'd discovered once I was back in the office. But that didn't work out either.

We had a small television set in the lobby, almost always turned off, but it was blaring when I arrived and Steve, Barry, and Tina were all watching it intently. I could see flashing lights on the screen.

"What happened? Did all of our clients drop us while I was gone?"

Barry shushed me and it was Steve who explained that someone had climbed out of a window of the Turk's Head building and was threatening to jump. The man's name sounded vaguely familiar, but Steve had to prompt me before I remembered. A few months back we'd uncovered evidence that Larry Holmes had been systematically diverting certain monies from his employer's cash flow. The aggregate had been fairly trivial and our client had elected to accept restitution and resignation in lieu of formal charges. I'm no psychologist, but it seemed evident to me that Holmes had been more interested in the thrill of stealing than in spending the money, and that he had deeper problems than petty theft.

And now he was out on a ledge.

He was still there when we closed up shop for the day, having accomplished very little during the afternoon. I turned on the radio to follow the story during the ride home and it had a happy ending, or at least not a tragic one, just as I was turning onto my street. Holmes was back inside and restrained for his own safety.

Dusty was in better spirits but still lacked some of her usual bounce. I considered talking out my latest discovery with her, but she announced that she was going to the main library for the evening. "I need to get my facts straight before I can write the last couple of chapters. I'll probably stop by Starbucks afterwards so don't get worried if I'm late."

I had forgotten to bring my working file back to the office, so it was still available. I took out the notebook, read through selected entries, then turned to a fresh page to record my most recent discoveries and suspicions. I had remembered to bring home my revolver just in case our night time visitor returned more aggressively.

Peter Trentano had originally painted *Lumber Mill at Dusk* sometime during the early 1970s. The earliest reproduction of which I was aware was the plate in the art book from 1981. Tina's enhancement had revealed that there were twenty-six blades of grass visible above the artist's signature, presumably the number Trentano had intended. The painting was transferred to the Tontine in 1986, during which transfer it was damaged. Trentano himself repaired it almost immediately. The painting presently displayed at the gallery only had twenty-five blades of grass, which variance may or may not have resulted from Trentano's reconstruction. The most recent print reflected the reduced number as well, which would be consistent with a flawed restoration.

But there was a problem in the timeline, a problem I hadn't been aware of until I saw the framed print in Michelle Bernstein's study. There were twenty-six blades of grass, consistent with the original version of the painting. That would have been fine for an older print, but Bernstein had told me that hers had been generated from a newer image, created around 1990, shortly after Peter Trentano's death. If she was right, there had been twenty-six blades of grass at the time, Trentano had not miscounted, and that led to some very interesting questions.

Had *Lumber Mill at Dusk* been altered again after Trentano's death? If so, for what reason? Or was there a more serious explanation? Had I been right earlier on? Could the entire painting be a forgery?

It was too soon to make accusations, but there were certainly a lot of new questions that needed to be asked. And cautiously. The theft of millions of dollars of artwork was certainly more than ample motive for murder. The torn off corner of the print in Spencer's office suggested that he'd noticed the same discrepancy. Had he been killed to prevent him from announcing his discovery? If so, whoever was responsible would certainly be capable of killing again, and for the same reason.

I was suddenly glad that Wanda had seen Dusty and I together, that Dusty had no reason ever to go back to the Tontine. I didn't want her within miles of the place until this was cleared up.

The house seemed oddly quiet with Dusty gone. It still surprised me how quickly I'd not only grown used to her presence, but actually counted on it. This wasn't the first serious relationship either of us had ever been in, but living together was a step up in both cases. I tidied a bit, read more than I usually did of the newspaper, tried unsuccessfully to find anything palatable on television that wasn't a re-run, and went for a walk that I had to cut short when it started to drizzle. I was soaked to the skin by the time I got home, stripped off my clothes and toweled dry, then decided to read in bed for a while.

I'd picked up a bestselling thriller that failed to live up to its reputation. Not only was it less than thrilling, but the author blithely ignored facts in order to advance his shakily constructed plot. I fell asleep while the granite-jawed hero was explaining the superior moral values of unfettered capitalism to the curvaceous but naïve nuclear physicist heroine, who also happened to be the country's top rated test pilot.

I am not a sound sleeper. I rarely dream, or at least I rarely remember my dreams when I waken, which probably means I don't get a lot of REM sleep or something. If the next door neighbors turn on the television at three in the morning, I wake up. If a dog barks in the yard, I wake up. If the refrigerator fan downstairs develops a murmur, I wake up. So when Dusty comes to bed late, I always wake up, except in those rare cases when she sleeps in her own room.

I didn't wake up until the first strands of pale light drifted in the window.

It was unusual to find her side of the bed empty, but not so rare that I took immediate alarm. If Dusty had come home very late, she might not have wanted to disturb me, and she knew she wouldn't be able to slip into bed without waking me. I shaved, showered, and dressed before leaving the room. Dusty's door was closed and I assumed she was there, went down to the kitchen and started the coffee.

It was when I went outside for the morning paper that I realized something was wrong. Dusty's car was missing.

The hairs on the back of my neck stood up and I began to sweat. I went back into the house and tossed the newspaper onto the couch, thinking furiously. Could she have been in an accident? I needed to call the police.

The answering machine was blinking. Three messages. The first was blank, the second a reminder that my physical was scheduled for the following week. The third was from Dusty, and the time stamp suggested that she'd called while I'd been out for my abortive walk the previous evening. She sounded excited.

"Paul, listen, I have to be quick because we're getting ready to go. I went to see Wanda, to apologize. She wasn't thrilled, but she says she understands why we had to do what we did, and she doesn't hold it against us. But there's more. She found something that she thinks might prove who killed Walter Spencer and she's going to take me to see it. But it's quite a drive and I may not be back until morning so don't worry if I'm not there when you get up. Gotta go. Love you."

I was simultaneously relieved, furious, and concerned. Dusty should not have gone anywhere near Wanda Fredericks again, particularly not without telling me. The fact that Dusty was an adult and that our relationship was informal didn't really occur to me at the time. It was a relief to know she wasn't lying on a slab in a morgue but it was unsettling not to know at least where she had gone. I tried calling her cell, but there was no answer.

Frustration always makes me hungry. I ate breakfast, all the time willing the phone to ring or the front door to open. Neither obliged.

The time came for me to leave for the office, but I didn't budge. Half an hour later I called and told Steve that I'd be in later in the day and arranged for him to delay or delegate a couple of things I'd scheduled. I wanted to be there when Dusty came home, not just to reassure myself that she was all right, but to yell at her for taking unnecessary chances.

I had barely hung up when the phone rang again, startling me. I figured it was Dusty belatedly bringing me up to date on her whereabouts, but the voice on the other end of the line was male.

"Paul Birch?"

"That's right. Who is this please?"

"It's Arthur Henderson."

My heart sank. I've known Senior Detective Arthur Henderson for a few years, more socially than professionally. His daughter had worked for me a couple of summers when she was in high school. He's probably the best detective the Providence Police have going for them, and his specialty was homicides. "Hello Arthur. Haven't talked to you in a while. How's Vicki?"

"She's fine. Paul, this is a business call, I'm afraid."

I felt light headed and sat down, the handset pressed uncomfortably close to my ear. My voice sounded unnatural. "What's happened?"

"I have a dead body with a connection to you." I licked my lips and found myself unable to speak. "It would be real helpful if you were to come over and talk to me about it."

I nodded, then realized Henderson couldn't see the gesture. "All right. Where do you want me?"

He gave an address. I didn't need to look it up. It was the Tontine Art Gallery.

I drove there in a daze, fortunately with exaggerated caution. There were flashing lights all along the block so I parked two streets over and walked back. I was challenged by a uniformed officer when I approached the front door, identified myself, and waited to be cleared. A plain clothes detective emerged from the building a few minutes later and introduced himself as Raymond Harris. I recognized the name. He'd been the investigating officer who signed off the report that Walter Spencer's death was a probable suicide.

"If you'll follow me, Mr. Birch."

Crime scene technicians were working in the lobby and reception area, on the staircase to the upper level, and I could hear more voices and rustling from the second floor. Harris brought me to the foot of the staircase and asked me to wait, then ascended out of sight. I felt sick.

Arthur Henderson's distinctive bass voice rumbled above my head. "Of course I want him up here. I wouldn't have called him over if I didn't want him up here."

Harris, showing no sign of embarrassment, descended half way and beckoned me up. As I reached him, he spoke in a low voice.

"Please try not to touch anything, Mr. Birch. The technicians haven't finished yet."

Henderson was waiting for me on the landing and we shook hands. Out of the corner of my eye I could tell that the activity was centered on Walter Spencer's office, but I couldn't bring myself to look directly. I was terrified of what I might see. I prepared myself to hear the worst, and when Henderson spoke, all the strength bled out of my legs and I nearly staggered.

But it was relief rather than grief. "We have a male victim, age about sixty. Multiple gunshot wounds to the head." My reaction must have shown in my face because he looked at me with sudden intensity. "Are you all right?"

"Yeah, fine." I roused myself. "Who is it?"

I was expecting to hear Avery Carr's name. Technically Henderson shouldn't have said anything, but Henderson closes a high percentage of his cases because he doesn't pay much attention to that kind of technicality, and he also knew me pretty well. And he also wanted my cooperation.

"He's been tentatively identified as Earl Garner. We're still trying to reach his next of kin."

"He has a brother. They lived together in New Hampshire."

Henderson's gaze sharpened. "A brother? That's news. You wouldn't by chance know where in New Hampshire."

I did. In fact, I knew the exact address, and he wrote it down when I repeated it. "I don't remember the phone number but you could call my office. It's on file."

Henderson ripped the page out of his notebook and gave it to a uniformed officer. "Take this to Ben and have him get in touch with the brother." He turned back to me. "Let's talk in here."

He led me to Avery Carr's office and gestured to the chair. I was still shaky and welcomed it.

"The manager here tells me you've been asking questions about the death of Walter Spencer a few months back."

I noticed that he hadn't referred to it as a suicide. "That's right. Spencer's niece wanted confirmation that the police investigation had reached the right conclusion. I didn't find anything significant to support her concerns."

"Ray did a pretty good job. He doesn't have much imagination, but he's thorough. I just read his report and it certainly must have seemed convincing at the time."

"But not anymore," I suggested.

Henderson gave just the faintest hint of a nod. He didn't like admitting that the police sometimes made mistakes. "We have a second victim, killed in more or less the same fashion, in exactly the same location. That's not a coincidence."

"Spencer was only shot once. You said multiple gunshots."

"The victim was shot four times, three of which would probably have been fatal. The fourth just grazed his forehead."

"Definitely not a suicide this time," I observed unnecessarily. "Can I see the crime scene?"

"Maybe. First, fill me in about your investigation."

The adversarial relationship between private investigators and the police that you see in movies and read about in books is pretty much fantasy. Oh, there are some shady operators in the business despised by the authorities and industry professionals alike, and similarly there are a few police officers who for one reason or another are antagonistic on general principles, but for the most part we stay on good terms and work constructively with each other when the need arises. Birch Investigations has uncovered quite a few cases of criminal activity and we've always notified the authorities or more commonly advised our employers to do so. Client confidentiality does not override our responsibility as citizens to uphold the law.

So I gave Henderson a brief but thorough summary of what I'd learned, leaving out only my suspicions about the forged Trentano painting. I still wasn't sure enough of my ground there to make it a part of the public record.

He listened, interrupting with an occasional question, made a few notes, and grunted uncommunicatively when I was done. "Still want to see the body?"

"No, but yes," I answered. "Who found him?"

"Avery Carr, the manager. He arrived this morning to find the front door unlocked and no one about. He apparently traipsed through most of the first floor before coming upstairs. Saw the body, froze in shock for a few seconds, then went back downstairs, locked the door, and called 911. At least, that's his story."

"What about Wanda? His assistant. She usually opens in the morning." My worries about Dusty came rushing back. Where was she?

"Miss Fredericks is missing. Her keys and jacket were found in the reception area downstairs. No sign of a struggle but no sign of the young lady either. We have people out looking for her car."

I swallowed. "Arthur, Dusty was with Wanda last night. I'm not sure where they went but she didn't come home." I pulled out my cell and called home, got the answering machine, and then tried Dusty's cell again. No luck. I shook my head.

"All right. Let's take a look at the body first. The techies should be about done."

I followed Henderson, wrinkling my nose at the distinctive coppery smell of blood. He raised an arm to stop me on the threshold but it wasn't necessary. I wasn't about to walk in there. There was a lot of blood. Garner had fallen out of his chair and was lying with his head twisted to one side in a massive pool of dried darkness. Very dried.

"This didn't happen this morning," I said.

"No, it didn't. Preliminary estimate is between eight and ten o'clock last night." Dusty's recorded phone message had been just after nine, possibly within minutes of the murder. Had she and Wanda been here, at the Tontine at the time? Where were they now? Were they still alive?"

I told Henderson about the call. He nodded slowly. "They may have left beforehand. There's no sign of a struggle, no blood except in here."

"Come on, Arthur. She might have left her jacket but she'd certainly have taken her keys with her."

As if on cue, a patrolman came upstairs a minute later to tell Henderson that they'd found Wanda's car, parked and locked, three blocks to the south. There was no sign of either woman.

Henderson saw the effect the news had on me. "We've sent someone out to the Fredericks girl's apartment to look around." He rubbed his chin. "How well do you know Avery Carr?"

I shrugged. "Casually. He was a potential suspect so I checked his history and talked to him a couple of times. He was cooperative enough."

"I'm going to talk to him again. Want to sit in?"

"Sure." What I really wanted to do was go out and find Dusty, but I wouldn't even know where to begin to look. Perhaps Carr could suggest a direction.

Someone had moved some chairs into the Phyllis Reynolds room and Carr was sitting there, looking pale and shaken, while another uniformed officer stood by to keep track of him. He glanced up when we entered the room, his mouth twitched nervously, and he got to his feet. "I see they've dragged you into this mess as well, Mr. Birch. I apologize for involving you, but it was impossible to answer their questions without mentioning your name."

"It's not a problem, Mr. Carr."

Carr and I both sat down but Henderson stayed on his feet, letting his eyes trail around the room as though he'd suddenly developed an interest in art. His eyes slowly moved back to examine the seated man with almost clinical neutrality. "Would you run through the sequence of events this morning for me one more time, Mr. Carr?"

Carr sighed wearily but didn't protest. "I arrived just before eight, about my usual time. I was surprised to find the door unlocked; Wanda is almost always here before me but she keeps the building secure until we open later in the morning. I thought perhaps she had forgotten so I went looking for her. I noticed her keys on the hook where she keeps them so I knew she was in, but she didn't answer when I called. Eventually I went upstairs."

"You looked in all of the rooms downstairs first?"

"Yes, except for the two studios in the back. I haven't unlocked mine in weeks and I keep the key to Michelle's in my wall safe. I wouldn't dream of going in uninvited unless it was an emergency. And Wanda doesn't have keys to either one, so it would have been pointless."

"You saw nothing unusual or out of place?"

"Other than the unlocked door, no, nothing."

"What happened when you went upstairs?"

"I saw the blood as soon as I reached the landing. It was quite a shock and I felt light headed and wondered if I was dreaming, reliving the past, you understand. But it passed in a few seconds. I walked halfway to the office door, but it was obvious even from that distance that he was dead, so I went back downstairs, secured the front door, and called you from the phone in reception."

"Did you go back upstairs at all?"

He shook his head. "Absolutely not. I stood at the front door and waited until the first police car arrived. I explained the situation and he asked me to wait outside while the building was secured."

"When was the last time you saw Earl Garner?"

"In the flesh? The last board meeting, several months ago. I can look up the date if you'd like."

"Have you had any communication with him since then?"

"We spoke on the phone a few times after Walter died. Nothing recently."

"Had he said anything to you about coming into the city?"

"No, not at all. I can't imagine why he was here."

Henderson rubbed his chin again. "You told me earlier that Garner had his own key to the building."

"That's right. All of the partners have keys."

"We have Mr. Garner's key chain, sir. None of the keys match the lock on the front door and there were no other keys in his possession. Can you explain how he could have come in?"

"No, I have no idea. Someone else must have let him in, I suppose."

"What time did you leave here last night?"

"Just after five. We closed early. Wanda had some personal business to attend to and I had a dentist's appointment at 5:30."

"Which of you left first?"

Carr shook his head. "We left at the same time. Wanda locked the door behind us. I'm quite sure of that."

"Do you have any idea what this personal business was?"

"She didn't say and I didn't ask. Wanda's not the most talented person in the world but she does put in a lot of hours without complaint and I didn't begrudge her a short day if she needed it."

Henderson glanced at me and I cleared my throat. "Had Wanda been acting strangely the last day or two?"

Carr snorted. "That girl acted strangely from the day I hired her. If I hadn't been doing a favor for a friend, I would have replaced her a long time ago. Oh, she's earnest and hard working and apparently honest enough, but she's moody, takes criticism badly, and she's constantly flitting from one place to another. She makes the customers nervous. She makes me nervous."

"But did anything in her behavior change just recently?" I persisted.

"Well, she took Walter's death very badly. He flattered her constantly and I think she was infatuated with him. She's been insisting all along that he would never have killed himself."

"You seemed to have doubts yourself a short time ago."

"I was surprised that he had done it, but I didn't doubt that he took his own life." He glared at Henderson challengingly. "Despite what has happened since, I have not changed my opinion."

We were straying from the subject. "If she thought Spencer was murdered, maybe she tried to do a little detective work herself."

"I couldn't say. I never paid that much attention to what the girl did unless it was job related."

I sat back, frustrated. This wasn't going anywhere and I was frankly more worried about Dusty than interested in the clashes of personality at the Tontine.

Henderson let the silence stretch a few seconds before speaking. "When I asked you about Mr. Garner's next of kin, why didn't you mention that he had a brother?"

Carr stared at him as though he'd sprouted wings and a halo. Then he started to laugh. It was a genuine laugh, but tinged with a hint of hysteria and it went on for just a bit too long to be entirely natural.

"What did I say that was so funny, Mr. Carr?" Henderson did not sound amused.

"Earl Garner's brother," he said, his voice still not completely under control. "I assume you mean Carl."

Henderson glanced at me and I nodded. "I believe you told me that he had no living relatives."

"Yes I did. Who told you about Carl?" He glanced at me and read it in my face. "Was it you, Birch? Have you actually met Carl?"

I shook my head. "I haven't had the pleasure."

Carr laughed again, but this time it was clearly forced, and he cut it short. "I'm sorry, gentlemen, but you really have no idea how funny this is. You see, there is no Carl Garner. Earl was an only child. Carl is an elaborate practical joke."

CHAPTER FOURTEEN

Several years ago I read *Magic* by William Goldman, the story of a mentally disturbed ventriloquist who is driven to murder. I was several chapters into the book before I realized that the narrator was the ventriloquist's dummy, and that revelation made such a drastic change in the interpretation of everything that had gone before that I turned back to the first page and started over, the familiar words now transformed into an entirely new experience.

That's how I felt when Avery Carr told us that there was no real Carl Garner.

"It started as a simple joke about twenty years ago. Earl was invited to speak at the commencement of some small arts college out in the Midwest. It was the first time he'd ever been recognized so publicly and he made quite a big deal of it. A few days before he was to speak, a package arrived with copies of the program they'd printed. Someone had gotten his name wrong and it was Carl, not Earl, in every instance. He was royally pissed at the time, but later he found it funny. After that, whenever he screwed up, he blamed Carl. If he was late for a speaking engagement, it was because his brother had taken the car keys. If he forgot to return a call, it was because Carl didn't pass the message on."

Carr's light tone faded. "For reasons I never completely understood, Earl became more reclusive as the years passed, and he drank more. Carl was around a lot more and his pranks and shortcomings became more serious."

"Are you saying that Garner had some kind of split personality?" asked Henderson.

Carr shook his head. "Not at all. He knew there was no such person as Carl. Sometimes I think the bad brother was more real to the rest of us than it was to him. But he went to elaborate extremes to keep the illusion alive. He said he found it useful to have different personalities in order to deal with different kinds of people."

"So he lied to me when he said he didn't know that I was coming up to see him in New Hampshire," I said quietly.

"Oh, I'm quite sure of that. Earl didn't think of it as lying, exactly. He shaped Carl to be his meaner, earthier side. Carl drank,

Earl didn't. So when he was drinking, it was Carl doing it. Twisted logic, I suppose, but it worked for him. It didn't really hurt anyone, and it spared him a lot of embarrassment."

My head was spinning, but one fact emerged from the confusion. If Carl Garner didn't exist, than he couldn't have provided an alibi while his brother was elsewhere, or vice versa. Which meant that Earl had not murdered Walter Spencer, using either persona, although given what had happened last night, I'd pretty much decided that already. So the suspect list was down by one, or technically two. But did that bring the solution any closer, or did it just muddy the waters?

Henderson asked a few more questions without eliciting anything useful. When he turned to go, I stood up and followed. We walked outside, where he glanced over at the small crowd of camera crews and reporters distastefully. "Arthur," I said urgently. "Wherever Wanda Fredericks is, Dusty is probably with her."

"Seems likely."

"She's important to me, Arthur."

"I know that. I'll watch out for her if I can." He asked for a few details, including her license plate and a description of her car and I gave him everything he asked for.

"I know it's too early for a missing persons report…" I started.

"She's not a missing person. She's a potential material witness. I'll get the word out."

"Thanks. Do you need me anymore?"

"Not right now. Want to give me your cell phone number?"

I did, and I did, and then I went back to my car. But I had to wander around for a while because I'd forgotten where I'd left it.

There was no doubt in my mind that wherever Wanda had gone, there too was Dusty, and presumably not voluntarily. It occurred to me that Dusty's car might also be parked near the Tontine and I spent almost an hour driving up and down the streets, and cruising a couple of nearby strip mall parking lots before concluding that I wasn't going to find it. I wasn't sure if that was good news or bad.

I drove to the office and gave everyone a decidedly abbreviated account. Predictably they offered to help if they could, but no one could suggest anything actually useful. I felt a twinge of completely irrational irritation, recognized it for what it was, and decided that I was not fit to deal with regular business. Fortunately the new client I was supposed to have met with during the afternoon had been forced to reschedule. I spent a couple of hours in my office, then decided I wasn't accomplishing anything and that I might as well go home.

Before I left, I opened the safe, dug out the box that held my revolver, and put it in my briefcase along with a box of ammunition. On the way out I asked if Tony Wilson's full report had ever shown up and Steve retrieved it. That went into the briefcase as well. I'd read it as soon as I got home.

The zombie portion of my mind must have taken over because I found myself parking in my driveway with absolutely no recollection of the drive home or any portion of it. I looked around hopefully, but Dusty's car hadn't appeared while I was gone. The house seemed emptier than usual, but that was no doubt my imagination.

I put my briefcase on the kitchen table, poured myself a brandy, and took out the gun. It hadn't been used for months and it had been locked away from the dust, but I cleaned it anyway, then loaded it and set it aside.

Tony Wilson's report was thorough, as always, filled with small details he hadn't mentioned on the telephone, none of which altered the picture of Wanda which I had now formed in my mind. I went through it a second time just to be sure I hadn't missed anything. It kept my mind occupied. When I was done, I opened the Spencer file and turned to a blank page.

There were lots of unanswered questions, but only five of them seemed important and I listed them.

Who wrote the anonymous notes to Walter Spencer about his niece?

How and why did Walter Spencer die?

Assuming that one or more of the PeterTrentano paintings was a forgery, who was responsible?

Who killed Earl Garner, and had he been drawn to the Tontine or had he come on his own, perhaps to confront the murderer?

Where was Wanda Fredericks and, most importantly to me, where was Dusty?

I was pretty certain that I knew the answer to the first question. Wanda had to be the anonymous correspondent. I could guess at her motives. The father to whom she was strongly attached had recently died. Walter Spencer was an available and willing substitute to whom she transferred her affection. It was possible that he'd confided in her about his belief that Kari was actually his daughter, not his niece. Threatened by the possibility that she wasn't the apple of his eye, she had tried to nudge him away from Kari. Wanda had worked at an adoption agency, but not the one through which Kari had been placed. Was it possible that the agencies shared some records? Could Wanda have known something about Kari's real parents?

I turned back to the appropriate page in Wilson's report. Wanda had left Little Darlings two months before starting at the Tontine. I frowned. Carr had said something about hiring her as a favor to someone. Could it have been Spencer? Wanda might have found his name in the agency's records and fixated on him, contrived to meet him and convince him to recommend her for the job at the Tontine. I made a note to talk to Avery Carr about the circumstances surrounding her employment.

The second question was more difficult. I suppose it was possible to cast Wanda as the villain here as well. Spencer might have rejected her for some reason. Perhaps he figured out who was sending him the letters and confronted her about them. But Wanda had as good an alibi as I'd ever heard of. In a mystery novel, she would have been the primary suspect simply because it was so good. But unless she had a twin sister considerably more substantial than Earl Garner's phantasmal brother, there was no possible way she could have been responsible for Walter Spencer's death.

Nor could Wanda be the guilty party implied in question three. The forged painting was the most compelling motive I'd come up with, and there seemed to be only a handful of people who could have pulled it off. Carr, Bernstein, Kwan, Garner, and Spencer, or some combination among them. Kwan probably shouldn't be on the list; she lacked the appropriate skill set but she might have had a partner. I was pretty sure that Spencer had recently discovered the truth, which would have provided a very good reason for someone to want him out of the picture, no pun intended. Garner and Kwan both hoped to close the gallery and liquidate the assets, which would certainly have resulted in exposure of the fraud. That made them unlikely suspects, although I couldn't rule them out. There hadn't been any serious chance that their wishes would prevail until Spencer began to waver, and then Spencer was dead and the status quo remained unchanged. But Bernstein and Carr seemed more likely candidates. I needed to think that through some more.

The last two questions were so intertwined that it was impossible to consider them separately. Dusty had tracked down Wanda and the two of them, for reasons unknown, had gone to the Tontine. They had probably arrived at the building either shortly before or shortly after Carl Garner had died and, I could only assume, had been confronted by the killer and abducted, also for reasons unknown. But if that was the case, why weren't the two of them lying dead in the gallery? What purpose could be served by abducting them or, I acknowledged reluctantly, of hiding their bodies?

I pushed the notebook away and went to the phone, dialed the Tontine. A recorded message told me that the gallery would be closed indefinitely. No explanation was provided.

I searched through the Spencer file until I found what I wanted, the business card Avery Carr had given me. There were three phone numbers listed, one of which I'd just tried. The second was probably a private line to his office. I let it ring but if he had an answering machine, it never picked up. A machine did respond to my third call, but half way through the recorded message there was a click and Avery Carr was on the line.

"Mr. Carr, this is Paul Birch. We need to have a conversation. Are you still with the police?"

He sounded incredibly weary. "No, I'm at home. I'm very tired, Mr. Birch."

"I'm sorry to disturb you," I said insincerely. "But there are two more lives at stake, Mr. Carr. I'd like to come over and see you."

Carr was silent for so long that I wasn't sure he was going to answer at all, but at last I heard him clear his throat. "All right, Mr. Birch. I'll be here. Do you have the address?"

"Yes."

It took me a while to locate the shoulder holster. Somehow it had managed to find a home in my sock drawer, pushed way in the back. I spent some time adjusting it without finding a comfortable position, and I felt rather melodramatic when it was finally in place, badly concealed by a sports coat. But I felt a lot better knowing it was there.

Avery Carr's house was not what I would have expected. It was on the east side of Providence, only a few minutes' drive from the Tontine, and almost invisible from the street, surrounded by an ivy covered brick wall too high to look over. The driveway was guarded by wrought iron gates, currently open, and even when I pulled inside, I couldn't immediately see the house, which was hidden behind a wall of hedges and ornamental shrubs. One section had been cut in the shapes of four crouching men staring at some featureless objects on the ground in front of them. Dice?

I parked next to the mini-topiary and followed a flagstone path to the front door. It was getting dark and either Carr had turned on the lights or he had a sensor or timer that did it for him. I rang the doorbell, which was not audible outside, and shifted my feel restlessly while I waited. Perhaps thirty seconds passed before I heard a rustling and the door opened.

"Come in, Mr. Birch. Can I offer you a drink?"

Carr was wearing slacks and a turtleneck and looked tired and worried. He led me into a living area larger than some homes. At the far end there was a real fireplace, currently cold but obviously well used. We had to descend three steps to reach the center of the room, an oval shaped inset area large enough to accommodate two good sized couches, two matching loveseats, and two reclining chairs, plus a scattering of small tables. The walls were, predictably, almost completely covered with framed paintings and photographs. I thought I recognized Michelle Bernstein's style in a small still life. I didn't see Peter Trentano's distinctive hand in any of them.

I really wasn't in the mood for another drink, but I've noticed that some people aren't really at ease until they've provided one, so I asked for a brandy and soda. I walked around the room while he was fixing it at a good sized wet bar in one corner. "Quite a collection of art you have here. Are they all original?"

"Oh yes. I could never see any point to displaying prints, actually." He turned and brought me my drink. His own glass had been topped up with some dark, amber liquid. "You seemed quite anxious to talk to me, Mr. Birch. Suppose we sit down and get this business over with."

Carr dropped onto one of the recliners with an air of immense weariness. I took a seat facing him on one of the loveseats, pretending to taste my drink. "You said something earlier about hiring Wanda Fredericks as a personal favor to someone. May I ask who?"

There was a flicker of change in Carr's expression and I was almost certain that it was relief. He'd expected something else, obviously. Well, I didn't plan to disappoint him. But I wanted to clear up some loose ends first, while he was still inclined to be cooperative.

"Certainly. It's no secret. Michelle Kwan called me one day and said she was trying to do a favor for an old friend and would I be willing to give this friend's daughter a job. It seemed a reasonable enough request and, as I think I've already told you, Wanda proved to be a mixed blessing. Difficult at times, but a very hard worker. She's very bright, as a matter of fact, but she doesn't take direction well."

Carr went on about her abilities for a little longer but I didn't pay attention. A possibility had suddenly arisen in my mind. Was the old friend Kwan mentioned actually Phyllis Reynolds? Could Wanda Fredericks have been Spencer's real daughter? But no, that wouldn't work. The baby had been placed with the Little Darlings agency in Lincoln, and Wanda had been adopted in Massachusetts.

I recovered myself just as Carr was saying that he had wanted to replace Wanda with someone more outgoing for some time. "Then why didn't you?"

He sighed. "It was Walter, of course. He became very fond of her. She'd sit and listen to him reminisce for hours on end and Walter really enjoyed having an attentive audience. I don't mean to imply that she was using him, Mr. Birch. She was genuinely interested and he was understandably flattered. I might have insisted despite that, but Walter began to waver about his opposition to closing the Tontine, and to be entirely honest, I kept her on in order to influence his decision."

"How seriously was he considering changing his vote?"

Carr took a very long drink. "Walter lost a very large amount of money, in an investment scheme. It was money he had earmarked for a scholarship program with a local college. He was very upset by the loss, and that's why he began to talk about closing the gallery. It was obvious that he didn't want to do it. He thought we might be able to compromise, liquidate some of the assets and still remain open. It wouldn't have worked."

"He wanted to sell the Trentano paintings."

Carr glanced quickly in my direction, clearly surprised that I'd guessed. "Yes, not all of them, of course, but enough that his share would make up for his losses."

"But your bylaws don't allow it."

"No, they don't. Nor does Peterl's will. None of the paintings can be sold unless the Tontine closes permanently. Walter always had difficulty accepting that he had to abide by society's laws, and he'd become worse about it as he'd grown older. I think he believed for a while that I was making things up just to thwart him."

"And you didn't want the Tontine to close."

"No, of course not. It's been my life for too many years." His reply was glib, a canned response. It might have been true once, but Avery Carr's loyalty to the Tontine was no longer a love affair. It was a marriage of necessity.

"And in any case, you wouldn't have wanted to sell the Trentano paintings even if the bylaws would have allowed it."

He blinked and sat slightly forward. "I'm not sure what you mean, Mr. Birch."

I shifted position slightly, so that I could reach my shoulder holster in a hurry if I needed to. "How many of them are forgeries, Mr. Carr?"

This is the point where writers say time seemed to freeze. That's not exactly true. I could hear the mantle clock's ticking quite clearly, and the pop as an air pocket escaped the ice in my drink. Avery Carr's face darkened slightly, his eyes narrowed, and he uncrossed, then recrossed his legs.

"What makes you suggest such an outrageous thing, Mr. Birch?" His voice was hollow, shaken, and I knew that he was guilty.

"You slipped up on *Lumber Mill at Dusk*. There's a discrepancy." I explained about the variations in the grass.

He listened attentively and nodded when I was done. "It would be that one that tripped me up. I always hated that particular piece, frankly. That's why I saved it for the last."

"The last? Then the others…?"

He nodded. "Every one of them. I spent about a year on each. That's the only reason why I still have a studio at the Tontine, you see. I never did understand why Paul was so successful. His paintings are invariably dreary and his execution was slapdash. That's why he was so prolific. It's also why he's so easy to imitate."

"And copy," I added.

"And copy," he agreed.

"You must have known you'd get caught eventually," I said.

Some of the animation returned to his face. "Oh? Why is that? The paintings never left the Tontine and they've already been studied to death. If someone was to physically analyze the paint and canvas, they'd catch on readily enough, but the brushwork is indistinguishable from the original." He sounded quite proud of himself. "But I did hurry through that last, I'm afraid. I wanted to be done with it. As long as the Tontine remained open, I was safe. If I was the last surviving partner, then it wouldn't matter, and if I wasn't, then I'd be dead and gone and wouldn't have to listen to the recriminations."

"But if Spencer had changed his vote, you'd have been exposed?"

"Yes, but he didn't need to change his vote. I'd already agreed to loan him what he needed for his damned scholarship." Carr's anger came and went in a flash. "But I may have overplayed my hand, made him suspicious."

"How did you dispose of the originals?"

"Oh, I sold them, of course. To private collectors. You'd be surprised how often it happens. But I wouldn't want you to think I did it for the money. Or at least not just for the money."

"Why else then?"

"Petty revenge. My partners never thought much of me, artistically that is. They elected me as chairman to give me something to do. So I did something else, something they weren't expecting. Are you going to tell the police?"

"I don't know," I answered truthfully. Legally I was obligated to, of course, but right now I had more important, personal things to worry about. Like Dusty. I was suddenly acutely aware that not only was I alone in the room with a man who might have cold bloodedly murdered his lifelong friend, but that no one even knew that I'd intended to come here. Fine thing, Mr. Private Eye. You fell right into the kind of situation that always strikes you as unrealistic when you see it in a movie. "Walter Spencer figured out the truth, didn't he?"

Carr nodded. "I don't know how he tumbled to it. He asked me to stay late one night, said he had something important to tell me. I thought he'd probably decided to shift his vote and wanted to break it to me personally, and I spent most of the afternoon organizing my arguments. But that's not what he wanted to talk about."

"Did he threaten to expose you?"

"Not directly. He was rather dazed by the discovery, and saddened. It was the first time I felt any regret for what I'd done. Walter wasn't as good a friend as he could have been, but he was one of the few I have. I hadn't intended to hurt him."

That sounded like an attempt to ameliorate his guilt, and I wasn't buying it. "So you killed him to protect yourself."

Carr looked quite honestly appalled, as if the idea had never occurred to him. "Of course not! This happened almost a week before his death. Walter wasn't going to call the police. He would have acted on his own, told the other partners perhaps. The end result would have been the same. I asked him to give me a chance to buy back the originals. I still have all the money I received. More, in fact. I've been living off the interest income for more than ten years now. There was no chance of that happening, of course. I didn't even know who had ended up with some of them. But it bought me some time to think, to get my affairs in order, to prepare myself for exposure and disgrace. I told Walter that he owed me that much and he agreed."

"His death was rather convenient for you, wasn't it?"

His eyes dropped and his voice became more subdued. "I suppose I'm responsible for his death, at least in large part, but I didn't kill him. I may be a thief but I'm not a murderer. I was quite as shocked by it as everyone else."

I tried to decide if he was lying to me. His story wasn't completely implausible, and it tallied with other things I'd learned about Walter Spencer and his aversion for law enforcement. "If you didn't kill him, then someone else did."

"Obviously."

"Do you know who killed Spencer?"

"Yes, I do. Walter Spencer committed suicide. I told you that a long time ago. He was in pain, he'd been disillusioned about the identity of his daughter, his financial difficulties were far from extreme, but they were substantial, and he was no longer able to participate in his favorite pastime, the creation of artwork. Add to that my betrayal and you have the final straw. He had a gun, the despair became too great, and he killed himself."

"It might have happened that way, but you're guessing just as much as I am and either of us could be wrong."

Carr shook his head. "No, Mr. Birch. I know something that you don't. Walter Spencer left a suicide note."

CHAPTER FIFTEEN

"The police didn't find a suicide note." The words came out before I had a chance to think about what I was going to say. I realized then that there were several possible explanations, the likeliest of which was that Carr had removed it before the police arrived.

"Nevertheless, there was one. When I heard that woman screaming and rushed upstairs, I was sickened by what I saw, but I have to admit feeling a sense of relief as well. If Spencer was dead, perhaps my secret had died with him. I stood at the office door, staring down at the thing that used to be a friend of mine, and I felt exhilarated for a moment, as though I'd been given a fresh lease on life. But then I saw the notebook lying open on the desk, inscribed with Walter's distinctive, labored care. He had gone on for several pages, justifying what he was doing, railing against the establishment which, he believed, leeched all of the artist's integrity in favorite of popularity. Some of it was angry, some of it maudlin, and much of it disjointed. I didn't have time to read all this on the spot, obviously, but I was afraid that somewhere in his last speech, Walter had revealed my own crime."

"So you made off with it."

"Yes. Locked it in my wall safe until things had settled down. I took it home with me that night and read it through."

"And had he exposed you?"

"No, and yes. He hadn't said anything explicit about the forgeries, but he had mentioned an unspecified betrayal by a long and valued friend as part of the reason he could no longer endure life."

"May I see it?"

Carr shook his head. "I'm afraid not. I destroyed it." He glanced toward the fireplace. "I toyed with the idea of turning it over to the police, telling them that I'd found it somewhere or that it had been mailed to me. But in the end I didn't care to take the chance. I detest television, but I've seen enough to know that police today can determine a great deal more from physical evidence than they were capable of in the past."

He might have been lying to me, but he sounded so plausible and unrehearsed that I believed him.

"Spencer might have committed suicide, but Earl Garner didn't."

"No, of course not. He wasn't the type anyway. Earl often rubbed people the wrong way, but he was a recluse and had few opportunities to make enemies. I can't imagine why anyone would hate him that much."

Nor could I. But obviously he'd managed.

"Do you have any idea why Garner came to the Tontine last night?"

"Not the faintest. I haven't spoken to him in ages."

"How about Wanda? Why would she have gone back later in the evening?"

"I couldn't say. She did stop by after hours from time to time to catch up on her work. I believe I mentioned that she was a hard worker. Of course, had she gone about things in a more organized manner, she could have avoided the necessity, but she was on salary so it didn't matter financially."

"You trusted her alone in the gallery?"

"Oh yes. She was reliable and Kristina had vouched for her. She didn't strike me as sophisticated enough to steal anything valuable. At least not successfully."

I floundered around for something else to ask, but Carr didn't appear to know anything else useful. There was always the possibility that he was a consummate actor, that Dusty and Wanda were lying dead in the basement right under our feet. He hadn't panicked when he learned that I knew of his theft. He remained confident, even friendly. Of course there are plenty of confident, friendly psychopaths in the world.

But I couldn't cast him as the chief villain. It just felt wrong. I finished my drink and stood up.

He followed suit and we walked to the door without speaking. There he paused. "About my indiscretion, if you're planning to notify the police this evening, I'd like to make a few calls to old friends first. I may not have another opportunity."

It was what I should have done, but I had my own agenda now. "You can call them another time," I said quietly. "But don't wait too long."

"Thank you, Mr. Birch." He opened the door. "At least I'll be spared the effort required to alter Phyllis' dreadful painting again. Whether or not you reveal my secret is only of passing interest to me. The Tontine will never reopen after this latest tragedy. Michelle has already called to tell me that she thinks it's time to lay the dinosaur to rest, and Kristina has been of that opinion for some time. You might speed the process a little, but in the long run you won't affect the outcome."

I didn't answer. I just walked to my car.

I drove to the nearest strip mall, found the quietest corner, and parked, letting things percolate in my mind. I now had plausible answers to my first three questions. Wanda had written the anonymous notes, Walter Spencer had killed himself, and Avery Carr was responsible for the art forgeries. I still needed to know who had killed Earl Garner and where Wanda and Dusty had been taken.

Something else occurred to me as I sat there. The police and I had both assumed that Garner had been targeted for death and the two women had stumbled into it and been abducted. But what if it was the other way around? What if someone had lured Wanda to the Tontine in order to kill or kidnap her? Garner might have showed up unexpectedly, only to be eliminated as a potentially dangerous witness. Where exactly Dusty fit into this scenario I wasn't quite sure, but I couldn't rule out the hypothesis. While working at the Tontine, Wanda might have uncovered something, something even worse than the art forgeries. Possibly she was in possession of knowledge so dangerous that it justified murder in someone's mind.

Kristina Kwan had recommended her to Carr. Just how had that come about?

I took out my cell phone, consulted my notes, and tried Kwan's office. No answer, and I didn't have her home number. But I knew someone who did. I called Carr and he answered promptly, but his voice was slurred. I told him what I wanted and he reeled it off without looking it up.

"Thanks."

I dialed the new number and Kwan picked up on the fourth ring. "I assume you've heard about what happened at the Tontine."

"Of course. The police have already been here to see me." There was a wary tone in her voice, and a hint of hostility.

"Avery Carr tells me that he hired Wanda Fredericks on your recommendation."

A lengthy pause. "To the best of my recollection, that is correct. He'd been looking for someone reliable, and I thought she would fit in well. Avery is a bit of a bully. He always has been. Wanda has been an outsider most of her life and has a thick skin. I thought the chemistry might work out. It hasn't been an unqualified success, but she's lasted longer than most of his previous assistants."

"May I ask how you met Wanda in the first place?" There was such a long silence this time that I thought we'd been disconnected. "Miss Kwan? Are you there?"

"I'm sorry, Mr. Birch." She didn't sound sorry. "I was trying to remember just exactly how our paths crossed. I believe we first met at a charity event for an adoption agency. My company supports a number of them locally."

"Little Darlings? Up in Woonsocket?"

"It might have been. She had occasion to do me a favor and I asked about her. She was very highly thought of by her superiors."

"They fired her for sleeping on the job."

"I know that. She told me about it when she came to see me. Non-profits don't pay their hourly help very well and she'd been working a second job and it was just too much for her."

"She initiated the contact then?"

"That's right. I believe she sent me her resume and I asked her to come in. I didn't really have anything that was appropriate for her, but I felt sorry for her."

"Carr says you told him she was the daughter of an old friend."

"Avery's memory isn't always accurate."

That sounded like an evasion but I didn't press the point. "You know that she's missing."

"So I understand."

"Did she ever say anything to you that suggested she might have enemies?"

"I believe there was an ex-husband, but I don't remember the details."

"Have you spoken to her recently?"

"We've run into one another at the gallery of course, but we never had more than a casual conversation. Why the sudden interest, Mr. Birch?"

"It's possible that Wanda is playing a bigger part in everything that's been happening than we think."

Kwan laughed, but it sounded artificial. "I find it difficult to cast her in the role of femme fatale. She's so self effacing that it's irritating."

"It may be that she saw or heard something that she shouldn't have and that she's been snatched for that reason. One of my people is apparently with her, you know."

"Oh? No, I hadn't heard that. But if you have someone with her, then why don't you know where she is?"

"I have reason to believe that both of them are being held against their will. If so, time becomes a major factor."

"Yes, I understand that. There are a couple of people I could call and ask about her. People who might tell me things they wouldn't say otherwise. I donate a lot of money to Little Darlings, for one thing. It might take me a while, an hour at least. Where can I reach you if I have any luck?"

"I'm on my way home right now, but I have a stop to make on the way. I should be there in just over an hour. Let me give you my phone number." I gave her the one for my cell as well.

ç

I had the address of Wanda Fredericks's apartment. It was only a few minutes away, a respectable but declining neighborhood of aging apartment buildings and small businesses. Although the police had almost certainly swept the area, I drove around almost at random on the off chance that Dusty's car might have been there. It was possible that she'd met Wanda here and that they'd driven to the Tontine together. But I had no luck and it was starting to get dark anyway.

I was reluctant to go home to an empty house, so I parked the car and walked to Wanda's apartment building.

It's ridiculously easy to bypass the security system at most of these places. Wanda lived on the third floor so I picked a name at random from the sixth and buzzed the apartment.

"Yes?"

"UPS. I have a package for Reynolds."

"All right." And the door buzzed. It wasn't even a challenge. I took the stairs to the third floor and found Wanda's door without difficulty. The police had probably been here as well, but they hadn't put up crime scene tape and they were long gone by now.

Opening a lock with a credit card isn't as easy as it looks on television, but if the lock is old enough, it can be done. If there had been activity in the corridor I wouldn't have chanced it, but I never saw a soul during the five minutes or so it took for me to find the right angle. There were no security cameras. The door popped open and I went inside.

I turned the lights on and glanced around. It was barely large enough to qualify as a studio apartment. The kitchen wasn't much bigger than the bathroom, the bedroom was tiny, and the main living area could have comfortably accommodated a group of as many as six people, so long as none of them were overweight. It was neat and orderly, not difficult because there was a minimum of furniture. There were a half dozen prints on the wall, matted but not framed, and they were all by Walter Spencer. There was a bare minimum of dishes and pans in the kitchen, and almost no food in the cupboards. The tiny refrigerator had milk, butter, a head of lettuce, and some thawed chicken breasts.

The bedroom closet was tiny, but still large enough to hold Wanda's complete wardrobe. The dresser drawers weren't even full. The quilt on the bed was the kind a child would have, cartoon animals in a variety of poses, and I had the feeling that it was quite old, possibly from her childhood. The big surprise was the overstuffed scrapbook on the night table. It was crammed with articles from newspapers and magazines, flyers and promotional materials, even a few pages excised from books. All of them dealt with the career of Walter Spencer. I upgraded my opinion of her relationship from infatuation to obsession. I thumbed through it idly, then closed it.

There was a photo album, smaller, in the drawer of the night table. This one was filled with photographs, most of them of a thin, obviously shy young girl pretending to smile at the camera. Even in the oldest of these I could see Wanda Fredericks, or Wanda Taylor as she was then. In most of the pictures she was alone, obviously posed, and equally obviously not enjoying herself. Others featured a rotund woman and a tall, heavy set man with a long beard, dark in some pictures, almost white in others. These, presumably, were the Taylors. The few in which Wanda looked comfortable were those where she was standing or sitting with her adopted father. Most of them had a common setting; the same house—or portions thereof—appeared in the background of a surprisingly large number of the pictures. Apparently the Taylors hadn't traveled a lot.

I replaced the album and sat back on the bed, wondering what I was doing here. If there'd been anything to suggest who might have abducted her or why, the police would have taken it. I was wasting my time. But I needed to do something and this was the only thing that had occurred to me. I have rarely felt more helpless.

After a last look around, I doused the lights and left, locking the door behind me.

There were no messages on my answering machine when I got home, and Kristina Kwan never called. I tried her home number after another hour, and left a terse message on her answering machine. I went through all of my notes on the Spencer case again, and then re-read Tony Wilson's report on Wanda. Then I made a new list. I know. I do that a lot. A list helps me to organize my thoughts, to turn abstracts into concrete objects.

This was a list of potential kidnappers. Right at the top was Avery Carr. He had a powerful motive and there had been plenty of time for him to waylay the two women, dispose of them in some fashion, and return to his normal life. I couldn't see him in the role, but that didn't mean he wasn't guilty. After all, my detective instinct had been ambivalent about whether or not it thought Walter Spencer had committed suicide, so we know how unreliable my intuition is.

Next came Kristina Kwan. Motive unknown, but I suspected her relationship with Wanda was less casual than she implied. I didn't know if she had an alibi for the time in question, but I doubted it. She lived alone and had been in the area. Michelle Bernstein and Benjamin Fogle followed, working either individually or as a team. Fogle's financial adventures might have been even less savory than they appeared. And last, of course, was the outsider, a complete unknown, a player I hadn't even considered. Wanda's ex-husband,

Walter Spencer's missing daughter if she had not in fact died as a child, a long time enemy of Earl Garner, any of these could qualify.

I thought about calling Henderson but stopped myself. If he'd learned anything, he would have called me right away. It would serve no purpose to bother him unnecessarily. I closed the notebook and pushed it away from me. My head was spinning and my stomach felt as though someone had cupped it in their hands and squeezed. I decided to take a shower.

As I passed through the front room, I paused to look out the window, imagining Dusty's car appearing at the corner and turning toward the house. We live in a quiet neighborhood, on a street that doesn't lead anywhere. There's not much traffic and the local kids play street hockey on our block because there are so few interruptions. I glanced around and almost backed away, but then I noticed something unusual.

Bob Olsen lives two houses down on the opposite side of the street. Bob's a nice guy who restores vintage cars as a hobby. He retired a couple of years ago, right after his wife died, and since then he's done a lot of traveling, going to the places Marie always wanted to see as a kind of posthumous courtesy. This week he was in Tokyo and he wasn't due back for another couple of days.

So why was there a van parked in front of his house?

It was none of my business and I turned away, was halfway up the stairs before I paused, remembering the prowler I'd sensed a few nights back. Was someone watching the house? The van was ideally situated if it was keeping my place under surveillance, or at least as ideally as was possible in an area where there was really no cover. Was I getting paranoid?

I had to know, obviously. I had shed my shoes, so I padded back downstairs and put them back on, peered out the window again. Nothing had changed.

If I opened the front door, I'd be immediately visible if anyone was looking that way, so I went to the back of the house, exited through the sliding doors. I was already wearing dark clothing, so I blended into the shadows as I made my way across the backyard and eased myself through Mrs. Cabral's lilacs. There was a television playing rather loudly in the living room; Maria was hard of hearing. It would certainly cover any small noises I might make.

I moved to her front yard, using her shrine to the Virgin Mary as cover, and crouched there to examine my objective. The van was still in place, interior lights out. There was a short break in the canned laughter from behind me, long enough that I heard the faint hum of an engine. It was the van.

If I'd been in a movie, I'd have crept forward behind a series of unlikely objects until I was close enough to race up to the door and confront the driver. Or maybe a passing truck would have ambled by, taking long enough for me to cross the front yard and reach the street, ready for the final sprint. Unfortunately, this wasn't a movie. I could have tried crawling the rest of the way, but I probably would have been spotted anyway, and it certainly wouldn't have left me in a position to jump up and see who was watching my house. So I stepped boldly out of cover and started walking forward determinedly but without running, hoping whoever was inside would dismiss me as a neighbor.

It didn't work. The engine roared and the van pulled away, accelerating down the street. I ran out onto the pavement, trying to read the license plate, but someone had either broken or unscrewed the tiny light bulb that illuminated it. And then it reached the corner and was gone.

I stood there for a while, even after it was out of sight, trying to figure just what it was that I had gotten myself into.

The phone was ringing when I finally got back to the house. It was Kristina Kwan, calling to tell me that she hadn't found out anything useful. "I thought she might have stayed in touch with some of the people she worked with, but apparently they haven't seen or heard from her since the day she left."

"How about relatives or family friends?"

"I've just finished talking with a few of her high school friends. They still get together occasionally, but they haven't seen Wanda for several months now. They didn't know anything helpful."

I couldn't help wondering how Kwan could be so familiar with Wanda's social life, or why she was expending so much effort on it now. So I asked. "Why are you taking such an intense interest in this, Miss Kwan? What does the girl mean to you?"

"I feel responsible for her. She wouldn't have been working at the Tontine if I hadn't talked Avery into giving her the job. And I had similar problems fitting in when I was younger, at least until I met Phyllis and the others. I suppose I identify with her." This time it sounded like the truth.

I closed my eyes. My head was starting to pound. "Well, I haven't had any luck either, and I'm fresh out of ideas at the moment." Since she had sounded sincere this time I let a hint of warmth creep into my voice. "Thanks for your help, Miss Kwan. If I find anything out I'll let you know."

CHAPTER SIXTEEN

As you might expect, I did not have a restful night. I kept waking up and rolling over, half expecting Dusty to be lying next to me, but of course she wasn't. Darla got disgusted and went downstairs to sleep on the couch. I'm an early riser but I usually wait at least until the sun is peeping over the horizon. It was pitch dark when I shaved and showered the following morning. The darkness suited my mood.

I dressed casually. The office would run fine without me for a day or two. I heard a car pause outside and the plop of the newspaper landing in my driveway. When I went to retrieve it, I looked up and down the street. No sign of the mysterious van from the previous evening. I hadn't expected it to be there. If I was under professional surveillance, they would have switched vehicles at a minimum. But there were no strange cars on the street, and it was too early for service vehicles.

I glanced at the story about the murder but it told me nothing I didn't know. I paged quickly through the other pages, then stopped when I reached the real estate section. Something seemed to click in my mind but I couldn't bring the thought to the surface. Frustrated, I threw the paper into the recycling bin. Breakfast was probably a good idea, but I had no appetite. I stood and was halfway out of the kitchen when I paused and glanced back to the discarded newspaper.

Why had I been reading real estate ads of all things? And suddenly I knew what my subconscious was trying to tell me.

I almost ran through the house, found Tony's report, and flipped it open, running my finger down the pages until I found what I was looking for. Wanda's adopted parents had lived in Braintree and the father had only died less than a year ago. Even if he'd had a valid will, it would have taken at least six months to wind up the estate, probably longer. It was entirely possible that the property had not yet been sold. I could find out by making a few phone calls, of course, but it was less than an hour away. It would be just as quick to drive up and take a look, and that course would also satisfy my need to do something..

Google provided detailed directions. I gathered up all of my paperwork and strapped on my shoulder holster, covering it not entirely adequately with a windbreaker.

Ten minutes from the house, my cell phone buzzed. I needed gas anyway so I pulled into a self service place before answering. It was Kristina Kwan. "What gets you up so early?" I asked.

"I have some business to attend to this morning and I wanted you to know that I wouldn't be at the house. You have my cell number?"

"Yes I do."

"You're on the move fairly early yourself, Mr. Birch."

"And how would you know that, Miss Kwan?"

"I tried your home phone first and got your answering machine."

I should have realized that. Some detective I was. "Did Wanda ever talk to you about her parents?"

"I knew she was adopted, if that's what you're asking."

"Her father died fairly recently. Do you know if the estate has been resolved?"

"She never mentioned it to me. Is there a reason why this is relevant?"

It was my turn to be hesitant. I wasn't sure how much I should tell Kwan. She seemed to honestly wish to help, but I suspected her motives. On the other hand, I was grasping for straws and Dusty's life might be at stake. "I don't know, but I think Wanda might be the key to this. She was very close to Walter Spencer, emotionally that is, and she was probably abducted by Earl Garner's killer. Why wasn't she just killed on the spot?"

Kwan made a noncommittal sound. "It could all be coincidence."

"Maybe. But I wonder if there is something in her background that explains what's going on. Something from her childhood. I'm going to take a look at the place she grew up in."

"That's a long way to go just to look at an empty house."

"Well, I may do more than just look." My tank was full and I replaced the hose. "I have to go."

"Good luck, Mr. Birch." It was a minute or two later that I wondered why Kwan had mentioned an empty house.

The drive seemed to take much longer than usual, although my watch said otherwise. I got off the highway and followed a series of lefts and rights into what passed for a rural neighborhood this close to Boston. There was a shortage of street signs in the area and even with my Google printout I had some difficulty, but eventually I was moving slowly past a row of older residences, trying to read the numbers. Number 268 was hard to miss, however. The house itself wasn't particularly impressive, and the fair sized yard had gone completely wild. The grass hadn't been cut in months, probably not since the previous fall, and the foundation shrubs needed pruning. Several small flower gardens, wrapped around trees or abutting the house, had been overwhelmed by weeds. There was no For Sale sign.

The house was fairly large and had an attached two car garage. It was set well back from the road and looked lifeless. Curtains were drawn across all of the windows except for one on the second floor. There was a scattering of trash blown into the hedges. A squirrel ran across the roof of the house as I pulled into the driveway, which was otherwise empty.

Technically, I suppose I was trespassing, but I was beyond the point where I cared about that. I got out of the car and walked to the front door, intending to ring the doorbell, but I had second thoughts and turned away. The side yard was at least as unkempt as the front, but the back was worse. Mr. Taylor must have cut back on his efforts to keep the place up even before he had died. Parts of it were pretty near impassible.

There were no windows on the garage so I was unable to look inside, but one of the rear windows on the house proper was not completely curtained. I found a cinder block and stood on it so that I could peer over the sill. It was a kitchen, neat and orderly, with an old gas stove sitting incongruously beside a modern refrigerator with an ice maker in the door. There was no movement or sign of recent occupation.

I finished a complete circuit of the house and returned to the front door. There was no doubt in my mind that no one was living here, that no one had since Wanda's adopted father had died. Either the estate was still tied up in probate, or maybe Wanda just hadn't gotten around to disposing of it. I assumed she was the only heir, although that might not be true. I made a mental note to check into that. What if there was someone else who stood to gain if Wanda was out of the picture? What if she knew the location of some unsuspected but valuable commodity that had belonged to her parents? I decided I'd been watching too many melodramatic movies and told myself to stick to the facts, and only the most probable conjectures.

It would take more than a credit card to get me past the front door lock, I realized, and realized as well that I was seriously considering another break in. The licensing board would be very unhappy with me if this ever got out.

There was a door on the side of the garage, but it was even less promising, so tightly fit into its frame that it might have been nailed there. The windows were all available, of course, but oddly I was more averse to vandalism than I was to housebreaking. Fortunately, there was another alternative.

At the rear of the house, just to one side of a very small patio, there was a bulkhead door that led down into the basement. It was of fairly recent vintage, reinforced metal all around, and I could not have battered my way through it with a sledgehammer. Most people padlock bulkhead doors, but this one was tied shut with a piece of heavy wire. It wasn't as casual as it might seem. It took me at least ten minutes to undo the wire, which was corroded in spots, and unravel it from the door handles.

The house was probably empty and there were no neighbors close enough to be alarmed by a little noise, but I opened one half of the bulkhead door with exaggerated caution, easing it down to its resting place. The hinges could have used some lubrication, but they weren't nearly as corroded as the wire had been. A short flight of wooden steps led down to another door, a conventional one, unpainted and featureless.

I half expected to be thwarted by another lock, but this one was secured by a simple hook and eye, on the outside. When I eased it open, I found a sliding bolt on the inside, but it had not been engaged and in fact was rusted in place. There wasn't much light; the slit windows around the foundation were mostly covered by plants, intentionally or otherwise, and it took a few seconds for my eyes to adjust. The smell was strong but not unfamiliar—musty and dusty. I stepped into the clear and eased the door closed behind me, wishing I'd had the foresight to bring the flashlight from the glove compartment in my car.

The contents of the basement were pretty much what you'd expect. There was an oil furnace and tank in one corner, which made me wonder why there was a gas stove above, and a washer and dryer opposite, with a long, bare table that was probably used for sorting and folding laundry. The basement was unfinished and, as with most of these older houses, the floor and walls were uneven, and the exposed rafters of the ceiling were draped with curtains of dust. A very large insect, probably a centipede, dashed out of sight, and I could see at least three large spider webs from where I was standing.

Conveniently there was a broom only a few paces away, leaning against one wall, and I grabbed it and used it to clear the space ahead of me. Thick, sticky ropes of dust gathered around it quickly, until it looked more like a club than a broom. I found an overhead light, a bare bulb with a pull chain, but it clicked without lighting when I pulled it. Either there was no power or the bulb was shot.

There was a work bench with a bright red tool box on a shelf, other tools arranged on pegboard to either side. Two snow shovels and a leaf blower stood in a wooden bin, beyond which was a potting bench and more tools, hoes, rakes, and such, all intended for garden work. The stairs to the first floor were at the opposite end of the basement, hidden at first behind the oversized furnace, revealed as I made my way forward. At one point I thought I heard movement from above my head and I froze, but it wasn't repeated and it might have been normal settling noises. Or possibly the squirrel I had seen earlier had found its way inside.

There were some cardboard boxes piled on a platform of cinder blocks near one wall and I paused to glance at them. Household records in the first, check registers, bank statements, utility bills. The second held part of a set of dishes, not very good quality. They'd obviously been packed away for years, not just a few months.

I reached the foot of the staircase, which was snug up against one wall. On the wall opposite was a modern circuit breaker box above two meters, gas and water. I opened the box but I still couldn't tell whether or not the power was on. A pair of earwigs ran along the top of the box and disappeared. I've had a thing about earwigs ever since the kids I played with as a child told me that they crawled inside your ears in order to lay eggs in your brain. I shivered and turned toward the steps.

Somehow it hadn't felt like illegal entry while I was in the basement, but upstairs was a different story. People had lived there. They might be dead now and past caring but I was still intruding on their privacy. It felt bad. But if there was any chance that something in this house could help find Dusty, it outweighed any rumblings from my conscience. I started up.

Only one of the steps creaked, and that one just faintly. I reached the top of the stairs, half expecting to find the door latched, but it swung free when I nudged it. I found myself looking into the kitchen, though from a different angle than before. Although it was neatly laid out with everything in its place, there was a perceptible feeling of neglect even before I noticed the thin layer of dust that covered everything. Presumably no one had lived here since Mr. Taylor's death, and it was quite possible that the kitchen hadn't been used since well before then.

I brushed aside a cobweb and set foot on the ground floor.

There was a clock on the opposite wall, but it had stopped at 11:16. Probably ran on batteries. I noticed a smoke alarm on another wall. There was a light switch beside the basement door and I flicked it up. No change upstairs or down, but it still didn't mean the power wasn't on. The stove was too old to have an inset LED clock. I put my hand on the refrigerator door. No vibration, and the metal was room temperature. Not operating, but still not conclusive.

Beyond the kitchen was what was obviously a pantry. I could see shelves full of canned goods, and another shelf that held less frequently used kitchen equipment—a fancy looking coffee maker, a collection of colanders, a food processor. There was only one other way out of the kitchen, a doorless arch beyond which a very short corridor was visible. Moving with slightly more confidence, I started in that direction.

There were pictures on the walls there, framed photographs. I recognized Wanda Fredericks and her parents. There were also a few in which Wanda posed with a heavy set man about her own age, including a conventional wedding picture. This must be Fredericks, the ex-husband. I peered at the pictures closely for a few seconds, memorizing his face. He seemed fairly bland, even bored. Wanda didn't look thrilled in any of them either, not even the wedding shot. She looked distracted, uncertain, and intimidated. I wondered if I would have interpreted the images the same way if I hadn't already met her and formed my opinions of her personality.

The corridor ended abruptly. There was a dining room to my right. White sheets had been spread covering the tables and what I assumed was a pile of chairs. There was a half exposed sideboard beyond; the sheet seemed to have come loose and slipped down. A large, glass fronted cabinet stood just beyond that, filled with crystal—goblets, wine glasses, dishes, salt and pepper shakers, condiment sets, and so forth. A beam of sunlight had found a chink in the curtain and fell across the front of the case, providing a spotlight effect.

There appeared to be a living area to my left, but it was hidden behind an enormous oversized potted plant whose leaves were curled and blackened where they hadn't disintegrated into dust. I took another step and froze, because that was far enough to let me see an overstuffed chair that had been just out of my line of sight. Dusty was sitting there, reclining with her head back and eyes closed. Her bound wrists were just visible at the small of her back and she had been efficiently gagged. I couldn't tell if she was breathing or not because of the gloom but there was no sign of blood or any other injury.

I had hoped to find some clue about what was going on, but I had never expected to find Dusty here. My suspicion that something in Wanda's past was at the heart of Earl Garner's murder seemed to have been confirmed. My instincts told me to rush over to her and find out if she was all right, but fortunately my brain forestalled my emotions. I needed to know what the situation was before I exposed myself.

Crouching, I touched the shoulder holster to reassure myself that I was still armed. I considered drawing my weapon, but for the moment I preferred to have my hands free. Then, ever so slowly, I moved my head to peer around the desiccated plant and examine the rest of the room. Some of the furniture was covered, some was not. There was another overstuffed chair, a match to the first, but it was turned partially away from me. Not so far that I couldn't recognize the occupant. It was Wanda Fredericks. All I could see was one shoulder, one lower leg, and part of her face in profile, but it was enough for me to positively identify her. From what I could see her position was almost a mirror image of Dusty's.

So who else was in the house, and where were they? I still hadn't heard anything to betray the presence of another, but obviously there had to be someone here. The kidnapper certainly wouldn't go off and leave his two captives so loosely bound. Unless, I thought with a shiver, they were both dead already. Wanda was just as immobile as Dusty.

I edged further around the corner. Another archway, no door, led into a second hall. I could just make out the shape of what I thought must be the front door. There was also another staircase, this one leading to the second floor. I looked for a connecting door to the garage, but if one existed it should have opened into the kitchen or pantry and I hadn't noticed it. Although I still wanted to enter the room and determine Dusty's condition, I throttled the impulse for a bit longer. The kidnapper would certainly be familiar with the lay of the house by now. If it came to a fight, I wanted to reduce that advantage as much as possible. Slowly, deliberately, I let my eyes trail around the room.

There was a fireplace, but it was a false front, probably superimposed over a real one no longer in use. In addition to the two chairs, there was an ornate Victorian style couch, a small glass topped desk, two end tables and three floor lamps. There were more potted plants scattered about, all of which had succumbed to the same fate as their big brother. The floor was carpeted but heavily worn; even in the gloom I could pick out the traffic lines. No photographs on the walls but I could see a framed embroidery beyond the couch, although I couldn't make out the words.

Just then there was a sigh and I froze. It was Dusty. Her head moved slightly and she shifted her hips, then settled back. She hadn't opened her eyes, but she was breathing and apparently not seriously injured. I felt both exhilarated and frightened, the first because she alive, the second because it was my responsibility now to make certain that she remained that way.

I took my weapon out of the holster. It felt odd in my hand. I hadn't fired it in almost a year. There just didn't seem to be time lately to go to the practice range. And I'd never carried it on a job. Frankly, I didn't like firearms. It always seemed to me that the opportunity for accidental mischief outweighed any security they provided, at least in my case. Your mileage may vary. But I have to admit that I felt better having it available right at that moment. Someone had already killed Earl Garner. I wasn't planning to be the next victim.

I stood erect and edged around the corner, weapon raised. More of the far corridor, actually just a rectangular hall, came into view, enough to convince me that no one was standing there. If the kidnapper was in the house, he had to be on the second floor. Or she. Moving crab fashion, I sidled over to Dusty's chair, crouched and touched her on the shoulder.

She moaned and moved a little, but didn't open her eyes. I nudged her a little harder with the same result. Dusty was harder to awaken than I was, but not this hard. I guessed that she'd been drugged. If the two women were knocked out with tranquilizers or something similar, it would explain why their captor was so willing to leave them unsupervised.

I didn't want to expose myself to anyone standing on or descending the stairs, so I retreated to a wall and worked my way around behind the seat where Wanda lay slumped to one side, partially curled into a fetal position. I couldn't see her face, but her shoulders moved a little and I could tell that she too was alive. She was more likely to be hysterical than Dusty if I managed to rouse her, and that was the last thing I needed right now, so I left her alone, concentrating all of my attention on the hall.

Slowly the entire staircase came into view except for the very top steps. No one stood there, waiting to ambush me, and the front hall was empty except for a coat rack, a small table, and a framed mirror on one wall. I relaxed slightly, but I wasn't looking forward to going upstairs, however necessary it might be. Even with his captives drugged and tied, I couldn't imagine any plausible scenario in which their abductor would just leave them alone in the house.

There was no help for it, I realized. I was going to climb the steps. I had no idea of the floor plan up there, and for that matter, what if I was wrong in assuming that a single individual was involved? What if there were two of them, or even more? Then, belatedly, a possible solution suggested itself. I stepped back and fumbled inside my pocket until I found my cell phone.

I turned away from the stairs to reduce the chances of being audible above, and as I did so, Wanda rolled over slightly, her face turned in my direction. And she opened her eyes.

Frantic, I made a quick shushing motion, almost dropping my cell phone in the process, hoping she wouldn't shout or speak or do anything to give us away. Her eyes widened and her mouth opened and I thought all was lost, but then she nodded to indicate she understood. I felt a sudden rush of relief, showed her both the pistol and the cell phone, hoping to reassure her.

"It's all right," she said in a normal speaking tone, shockingly loud under the circumstances. "There's no one else here."

Wanda seemed confident that she was right, but I had no idea how long she'd been unconscious, or how much of her wits remained unscrambled. Her voice must have carried to the second floor, but there had been no response, not a whisper of sound. Apparently she was right. I relaxed a little, but not completely.

"All right. Let's get you untied." There was an end table right beside her chair and I was about to put down the cell phone and my weapon to free my hands. Wanda promptly sat up and that's when I noticed that her hands weren't bound.

They were, in fact, holding a quite serviceable revolver in a two handed grip and she was pointing it directly at me.

CHAPTER SEVENTEEN

I could lie and pretend it all came to me in a flash, but it didn't. I probably looked pretty stupid, frozen where I was with my mouth open. For a second I thought she must be hysterical, that she was confusing me with the kidnapper, but I'm not entirely stupid, and I knew before she said another word that there was no such person. Or more correctly speaking, the kidnapper was at the moment pointing a gun at me.

"Put your gun down on the table, move away and keep your hands raised." Wanda stood up, the weapon looking disproportionately large. She had both hands firmly wrapped around it and they didn't appear to be shaking.

"It was you who killed Earl Garner!" I should have kept my mouth shut, I suppose, but my brain was churning along, processing all of this new input, and some of it inevitably spilled over into my speech centers. "But why?" I laid down my weapon and backed away.

Wanda glanced down at the end table, opened the drawer, and pushed my weapon inside smoothly and efficiently. "Come around this way." She gestured to her left. "And move slowly. I don't want to shoot you, Mr. Birch, but I will if I have to."

Since I didn't want her to shoot me either, I was cheered a little. Taking very small, deliberate steps, I edged around, keeping my distance. "What is this all about, Wanda? Why did you do it?"

"Go and sit on the sofa." There was a tremble in her voice which I thought might be fear, but it was anger. "He deserved to die!" She almost shouted it. "He killed Walter!"

I reached the couch and turned, but I didn't sit. "Earl Garner didn't kill Walter Spencer," I said slowly. "It was a suicide after all. I'm sorry."

"You're lying!" This time it really was a shout and I involuntarily took a step backward. She drew a deep breath and made a visible effort to regain control of herself. "Now sit down and keep your hands where I can see them."

I did as I was told. "What did you do to Dusty?"

Wanda looked momentarily pained. "I gave her some of my sleeping pills. She's all right." There was a hint of defensiveness, which I hoped to exploit.

"Do you want to tell me what happened, Wanda?" I decided to keep using her name as much as possible, figuring that the more personal I made this, the less likely she was to do something I'd regret.

"He killed Walter so I killed him. What else is there to say?" There was a brittle laugh at the end that made me uncomfortable.

I forced myself to relax slightly and kept my voice conversational and, I hoped, reassuring. "Why do you think that Garner killed Walter?"

She stepped forward and rested her hip against the arm of the recliner, but her expression was fierce and unhappy. "I thought he was the one right away, but I didn't see how he could have done it."

"What made you think that? The two of them were friends."

Wanda shook her head furiously. "Like Dusty and I were friends?" We both glanced over to where Dusty lay unmoving in the other chair. "She lied to me, Mr. Birch. Everyone lied to me except Walter. He was like a second father." Her eyes sparkled and she half turned away, wiped her face with the back of one arm. The muzzle of her weapon never moved away from me, however, and I stayed where I was.

"Dusty was only doing her job, Wanda. We were trying to find out what happened to Walter and we didn't know who we could trust. Neither of us meant to hurt you. We just wanted the truth."

"Well, I know the truth now. I figured it out before you did, didn't I?" She sounded mildly pleased with herself, but the obvious unhappiness in her face spoiled the effect.

"All right," I said with a calmness I didn't feel. "Explain it to me. Why do you think Garner killed him?"

She edged around to the front of the chair, and seated herself. "They used to fight all the time, you know. On the phone. I couldn't hear what Mr. Garner was saying, but Walter would get very upset and shout at him. And once I heard him say something like 'I have a gun now and I'm not afraid to use it'. I could tell something was bothering him, that he was worried, but I couldn't think of any reason why anyone would hurt him."

I felt a wave of dismay. If I was right, if Wanda had sent Spencer the anonymous notes, then it was Wanda that had so upset him, not Earl Garner. How could I bring myself to tell her that? And if I did, if I could make her believe it, would I just trigger an even more irrational act? But I didn't believe that Spencer had bought a gun just because of the notes. Avery Carr had a history of violence and Spencer was about to confront him about the art forgeries. Perhaps the anonymous notes were just an excuse, to explain his need for a gun when he consulted Garner. Maybe it was actually meant to be an insurance policy in case the interview went badly. It was another question to which I would probably never find a satisfying answer.

"But Garner had an alibi, Wanda. He was on the telephone from his place in New Hampshire when Walter was killed. He couldn't have been in two places at once."

Her mouth twitched into a triumphant smile and she leaned forward toward me. "I couldn't figure that out either, Mr. Birch. That's why I didn't do anything right away. I thought he must have hired someone to do it for him, but I couldn't be sure that it happened that way and I didn't know how to find out the truth. I was thinking about going to see him, to make him tell me how he did it, but then you started asking questions and I decided to wait a little longer and see if you could figure out what really happened. But you didn't, did you?" She didn't wait for me to answer. "But I did. You helped me find the truth but I was the first to realize what really happened. I might never have figured it out on my own."

I didn't know what she was talking about and my confusion must have been obvious because she shook her head impatiently. "His brother, remember? I never knew he had a twin brother until you mentioned it. So his brother was the one on the telephone while he went and killed Walter. It was so simple once I knew that."

My head started to hurt. I probably should have remained silent, but I blurted out the truth before I could think it through. "Earl Garner didn't have a twin brother, Wanda. It was a hoax. He fooled me into believing it for a while, but it isn't true. He couldn't have killed Spencer. He didn't do it."

The gun wavered and her face went through some interesting transformations. Then she steadied down and her voice became audibly unfriendly. "You're lying to me again, Mr. Birch. Everyone lies to me. No one believes I'm smart enough to see the truth. You think I'm stupid!"

I shook my head. "I don't think you're stupid, Wanda." It was the truth, but my shaking voice probably didn't carry much conviction.

"Don't patronize me."

That hadn't been my intention, but there was no ready answer. It was probably a good idea to keep her engaged, not let the conversation lapse, but in retrospect I probably would have chosen a different conversational gambit than my next if I'd had time to think it through. "So what's next, Wanda? What are you going to do with us?"

She looked distinctly unhappy and there was a hint of a whine in her voice when she answered. "You shouldn't have come here. The two of you are always sticking your noses in when you're not wanted."

"I came here because I thought you might be in trouble and I wanted to help."

Wanda wasn't mollified. "You don't care about me! You care about her! That's why you came. You were both spying on me."

I needed to redirect the conversation. "How did Dusty get involved anyway?"

"She came to the gallery. I was just cleaning things up and getting ready to go and she came knocking at the door. I'd have hidden and waited until she was gone, but I know she saw me. So I let her in."

"Was she there when Garner arrived?"

"Of course not!" She sounded as though that was a profoundly stupid suggestion to make. "That would have spoiled everything. He was already dead. I made sure of that. I would have just sent her away but she knew I was there. She'd have told people and they'd have known I killed him."

"How did you get Garner to come to the Tontine anyway? I thought he never came to the city."

She smiled this time, remembering. "Oh, I was clever about that. I called and told him that Walter had given me something to hold for him, something that I was supposed to give to Mr. Garner after he was gone. He wanted to know what it was but I told him that the package was sealed and I didn't know what was inside and that Walter had made me promise to hand it to him myself." She laughed, but it sounded forced. "I told him that Walter said it was worth a lot of money that the government didn't know about."

Given Garner's recent financial difficulties, that would have been the perfect bait. "Didn't he tell you that he hadn't killed Spencer?"

"He started to, but I knew it was just going to be another lie. So I shot him. My daddy taught me how to shoot this, you know." She wagged the heavy revolver. "He always kept it by his bed, in case of burglars."

"The police are looking for you. They'll come here eventually."

"I know that." She suddenly sounded much younger. "I told you, I'm not stupid. I'll be gone by then."

"Gone where, Wanda?"

"I don't know!" Her eyes sparkled with tears. "Some place. I haven't figured out where just yet."

I decided not to push in that direction any more. "Was it you who broke the windows at my office?"

She nodded. "I was so furious with you. And her." She glanced quickly toward Dusty's inert form and back. "I had to do something. But I shouldn't have. It was childish. I'm sorry about that."

"It's over and done with. And you came to my house afterwards, didn't you? During the night."

A look of puzzlement clouded her face for a moment. "No, I don't even know where you live."

Well, I couldn't expect to have all the mysteries solved in a single conversation. That reminded me of another whose solution needed confirmation. "Did you send notes to Spencer about his niece, Kari?"

"That bitch! He did so much for her and she hardly even came to see him. He told me she was his daughter but I knew that she wasn't. He needed to understand that but I was afraid he'd be mad at me if I just told him how I knew."

"How did you know? Was it when you were working at the adoption agency in Woonsocket?"

She nodded.

"But Kari's adoption was through the Lincoln Child Services agency."

Wanda smiled. "No it wasn't. It was supposed to be but they had a bad fire and all the pending adoptions were temporarily transferred to Little Darlings."

That only partly explained it. "But why would you have read her file. You'd never heard of Walter or Kari Spencer."

"No, but Miss Kwan had been nice to me and when I saw her name while I was scanning the old records into the new computerized system, I got curious and read the file."

"Kristina Kwan? She put a child up for adoption at Lincoln?"

But Wanda shook her head furiously. "I don't know who the mother was. But Miss Kwan handled the arrangements for this specific adoption herself. The agencies aren't supposed to make exceptions, but they do sometimes, particularly for people who make big contributions, like Miss Kwan does."

"Kristina Kwan was involved in Kari's adoption?" But Kari's blood type was wrong. She couldn't be Walter Spencer's child by Phyllis Reynolds. Was it possible that Walter hadn't actually fathered the child? My head was spinning.

"That's right," she nodded.

"Did Kari's mother, Walter's sister, know who the real mother was?"

"I don't know. Miss Kwan might have told her, I suppose, if she knew. The records said she was a foundling, parents unknown."

I was still searching for something to say when Wanda stood up, showing signs of increasing agitation. "I'm sorry, Mr. Birch, but I can't just let you go. You're going to have to stay here until I figure out what to do next, and I can't just let you walk around."

Wanda wasn't the only one feeling a hint of panic just then. "Wanda, I know you don't want to hurt anyone. Let's just sit and talk this through."

She shook her head. "No more talking. I can't trust anything you say anyway. I can't tie you up while you're awake so you're going to have to take some sleeping pills."

The idea of being unconscious and at Wanda's dubious mercy didn't appeal to me. She was acting like a trapped animal, desperate and capable of anything. "I'm not your enemy, Wanda. I want to help you."

"No one else can help me now. I have to help myself. Daddy used to tell me that, and he was right. Now I want you to go over to the table there in the corner. There's a bottle in the little drawer in the middle. They're just sleeping pills. They won't hurt you. You're going to take some of them and then you're going to lie face down on the couch until you go to sleep. If you don't do exactly what I tell you to, if you try to get away, I'll shoot you, Mr. Birch. I don't want to do that, but I will if I have to. Now stand up, very slowly, and keep your hands where I can see them."

"Wanda..."

"No more talking. Just do it!"

But the talking wasn't over quite yet. Another voice broke the sudden silence, startling both of us.

"That's enough, Wanda. It's time to put an end to this." Wanda let out a short cry and turned toward the sound, and if I hadn't been so completely taken unawares myself, I might have leaped forward and wrestled the weapon out of her hand. But by the time that possibility occurred to me, she'd recovered enough to retreat, her eyes shifting rapidly back and forth between me and the new arrival.

Kristina Kwan had stepped out from behind the dead plant. She had obviously followed me in through the bulkhead door.

"Put the gun down, Wanda." Kwan sounded and appeared completely confident that she'd be obeyed, but I noticed that she kept her distance.

"No! What are you doing here? Why can't you all just leave me alone?" I didn't like the brittle hysteria audible in Wanda's voice. What little self control remained to her was eroding quickly.

"Put the gun down before you hurt someone." Kwan's voice was low, soothing. "We can straighten all of this out."

Wanda shook her head. "No, it's too late for that. Walter's dead. They're both dead. I had to do it for him. He was like a new father to me."

Kwan sighed and looked momentarily uncertain, or perhaps just weary. "He was more than that, Wanda. He really was your father."

It was a thought that had occurred to me as well, but I'd dismissed it as improbable. Spencer's daughter had been placed through Lincoln, via Little Darlings, and Wanda was adopted out of state. How was it possible? Was Kwan bluffing? It didn't sound like a bluff. It sounded like a reluctant admission.

Wanda wasn't buying it easily either. "How could that be? His daughter died. I know, I saw the file."

Kwan looked distinctly unhappy. "The infant who died was not Walter's daughter. I bribed one of the clerks to make a few alterations to the official record to help cover the tracks. Phyllis was my friend, but she was afraid that Walter would one day decide to track down his daughter, so she enlisted my aid in creating an elaborate lie.

There was a falter in Wanda's voice. "Then Kari must be his daughter after all, not me."

"No," Kwan answered immediately. "Phyllis took you to Boston and made arrangements there. I was the only other person who knew the truth. She made me promise never to tell Walter. She wouldn't have told me except that she needed my help laying the false trail in Lincoln. After she died, I tried to find you, but it took years and by then you were married. I kept an eye on you but it looked as though you'd made a life for yourself. After the divorce, when you were working for the temp agency, I asked for you specifically. It wasn't an accident that you ended up filling in for my receptionist."

"You were very nice to me," Wanda said softly. "I wanted to stay."

"That might have been best, but I was afraid I might slip and say something I shouldn't. You reminded me of your mother sometimes. When I heard that the agency in Lincoln was looking for clerical help, it seemed to be the perfect solution. It never occurred to me that you might have access to those old files, or that they'd mean anything to you."

"I saw your name." Wanda's voice was very low now and the hand holding the weapon had dropped a bit. "I was curious. I started asking questions and Mrs. Hopper told me that I had violated my confidentiality agreement and she fired me. They made something up because they didn't want people to know they hadn't secured their records. But I didn't talk to anyone outside the agency! She just didn't like me! "

"Hopper told me you'd been caught sleeping at work." Kwan sounded confused for the first time.

"She didn't want anyone to know what I'd been doing, so she made up that story and told me it'd be easier for me to get another job than if we told the truth. And then you got me the job at the Tontine and I met Walter and so I didn't care anymore." Her face fell. "I was happy there, Miss Kwan, even if Mr. Carr wasn't very nice to me."

"And you knew that Kari Spencer wasn't the daughter Walter was looking for and you decided to tell him." It was the first time I had spoken for a while, and the words came out almost of their own volition.

"I couldn't let him go on believing a lie, could I? She didn't care about him at all."

"That's not true," said Kwan. "They weren't as close as they'd been when she was younger. She had her own life to live. And she did love him. Kari was the one who hired Mr. Birch, remember? She wanted to know if someone had killed her uncle just as much as you did."

Wanda shook her head and the gun hand came back up. "No, she didn't love him the way I did. She couldn't have. You're just trying to confuse me, both of you. I don't want to listen to any more of this!"

"So what are you going to do, Wanda? Kill all three of us?" I grimaced, wishing that Kwan hadn't put that particular possibility into words.

Wanda glanced around. "There's plenty of sleeping pills. I'll tie you both up and then go."

"Go where, Wanda? The police are already looking for you. They'll come here sooner or later. There's no place left to hide."

"Things will be much easier if you turn yourself in," I added. "The police will understand why you did what you thought needed to be done. They'll know that you're sorry."

I was trying to be reasonable, but I should have known that reason is of little use when confronted by hysteria. And Wanda was rapidly losing her composure now.

"But I'm not sorry! I'm glad that he's dead! He killed Walter! He killed my father!" Her grip on her weapon tightened and her voice dropped. "I'm sorry you came here, Miss Kwan. I really am. Now please go over and stand beside Mr. Birch." She gestured with the gun, now holding it two handed again.

Kwan sighed but made no effort to comply. Wanda shifted position and took a step backward, away from us. "I mean it! Don't make me shoot you! I don't want to hurt any of you but I will if you don't do what I say!"

For a second or two, I thought Kwan would refuse. Her face was twisted with anguish now and her hands were tightly clenched. I wondered if I'd have time to reach Wanda if she turned and fired at Kwan, or would she be able to bring the gun back to bear on me first? If the way had been clear, I thought I could probably have reached her in time, but there was a coffee table between us. I'd have to hurdle it or go around.

But Kwan finally nodded and started to her left, moving in my general direction but not directly, as though she wanted to delay reaching me for as long as possible. I didn't realize why at first, but then I noticed that Wanda had moved again, was now facing us with her back to the chair where Dusty lay asleep.

Except that the chair was empty now.

Somehow, despite the ropes around her ankles and wrists, Dusty had managed to lever herself upright. She was precariously balanced on her feet now, about four paces behind Wanda. I almost opened my mouth to warn her back, but the last thing I wanted to do right now was startle Wanda. Frozen in an agonizing moment of indecision, I blurted out the first thing that occurred to me.

"Are you sure it was Earl Garner? What if it was Avery Carr who killed Walter? He had a much better motive." I might be putting Carr's life at risk, but I decided he could fend for himself. "Did you know that he stole some of the artwork from the Tontine and replaced it with forgeries?"

I heard a hiss of surprise from Kwan. Wanda was less easily convinced. "You're just trying to confuse me again. It won't work, Mr. Birch."

"I'm telling you the truth, Wanda. He admitted it to me yesterday. The Trentano paintings are all fakes. He also admitted that Walter had found out what he'd done. That was why Walter bought a handgun. He was going to confront Carr and he was afraid of what might happen."

She shook her head. "Mr. Carr wouldn't do something like that. He's devoted to the gallery." But she sounded uncertain, so I pressed my advantage.

"If you're right, if Spencer didn't kill himself, then it might have been Carr who did it. Or maybe it was someone else entirely." I glanced toward Kwan, whose eyes were focused beyond Wanda's shoulder, to where Dusty had managed to move only a few inches from where she'd started, shifting her feet in slow, tiny arcs, trying not to make any noise.

A board creaked, whether under Dusty's weight or elsewhere I couldn't tell, but it was loud enough that Wanda started to turn her head.

Kwan spoke up immediately. "Walter wouldn't want you to do this, Wanda. He would have been very disappointed in you. He had his faults, but he was a kind man, a good man. I loved him too, you know. Even after we got divorced, I still loved him. And I'll miss him now that he's gone. All we have is our memories of him now, and I'll have to live with the knowledge that I couldn't help him. Won't you let me help you?"

I could tell that the words had reached Wanda on some level, and once again the muzzle of her revolver dipped. And just then, Dusty lost her balance, began to topple, and tried desperately to turn it into a purposeful lunge. Wanda whipped her head around and her body started to follow, swinging the gun, and I knew I couldn't wait any longer. I took two steps and jumped, my trailing foot catching the corner of the coffee table. It partially deflected me, but I caught her right arm with both of my hands and jerked it down.

There was the single sharp crack of a gunshot and then a rattle as the revolver skittered across the floor.

CHAPTER EIGHTEEN

Wanda tried to squirm away from me but I threw my left arm over her shoulders, holding her down, and after a minute or two she stopped struggling, collapsed into sobs. I glanced around, saw Dusty awkwardly trying to sit up while Kwan retrieved the handgun and deliberately emptied the cartridges onto the floor.

"Do you need any help, Mr. Birch?" Her voice was shaking.

"No, I don't think so." I loosened my grip and got up onto my knees, but Wanda was obviously spent. I wouldn't have been surprised to find that she was more relieved than disheartened. It was over now, and she didn't have to make any more unpleasant choices. Most of her choices from this point on would be made for her.

Kwan untied Dusty, who was still rather groggy, but whose spirits seemed good as she sat on the floor, rubbing her wrists and ankles to restore the circulation. "Is she all right?" She nodded toward my prisoner, who had now curled up on the floor in a near fetal position.

"I hope so." I glanced up at Kwan. "We need to call the police."

"I know." She reached into her pocket and took out a cell phone. "What should I tell them?"

The truth? Well, a version of it anyway. I felt no animosity toward Wanda. Dusty was okay and that was all I cared about. "Tell them that we found her here, that she confessed to killing Earl Garner, and that she needs medical attention."

"And what about this?" She held up the revolver.

"It's the same gun that killed Garner. It's evidence. We can say she surrendered it to us."

For the first time since I'd known her, Kwan looked vulnerable and humbled. "Thank you, Mr. Birch."

Dusty retreated to the recliner and sat with her head back, still obviously under the influence of the sleeping pills, and Kwan walked around and sat down on the couch. Her eyes came to rest on Wanda's recumbent form and remained there. Beneath me, Wanda seemed to have fallen asleep. I sat on the floor beside her, one hand across her shoulders, until we heard the sirens.

As they were pulling into the driveway, Kwan turned toward me. "That business about Avery and the stolen paintings? Was any of that true?"

"Every word," I said.

She gave a little laugh. "We've all made such messes of our lives." And she moved off to a corner and didn't speak again until the flashing lights began to light up the neighborhood.

In real life, sometimes a few of the loose ends stay loose, and this was no exception. I never did find out who was prowling around my house the night after Wanda broke my office windows. A prospective burglar, a neighborhood kid, my imagination? The mysterious van had been driven by one of Kristina Kwan's employees. She knew that I was looking for Wanda and wanted to know if I actually found her, so she'd sent one of her security guards to keep an eye on me. Obviously surveillance was not his strong point. I don't think she'd completely thought the situation through at that point, but she must have realized that damage control was no longer enough. Wanda was in serious trouble this time, and it wasn't going to go away.

Had she known that Wanda had killed Earl Garner? On some level she almost certainly did, although she might not have admitted it to herself. She was probably still hoping that some alternative solution would suggest itself. Perhaps Wanda had acted in self defense, or shot him in the mistaken belief that he was a prowler. She was too intelligent a woman to accept either scenario for long.

I was also spared the necessity of deciding whether or not to expose Avery Carr. The day after Wanda's arrest, he quietly disappeared, taking with him the vast bulk of his personal wealth. He left behind a lengthy description of his illicit activities, ostensibly in the form of a confession, but I've been told informally that it read more like a prolonged boast. The discovery that the Tontine's assets were rather less than a third of what they should have been did not sit well with Benjamin Fogle. He was interviewed more than once, inveighing against the perfidy of Avery Carr and the incompetence of the authorities, who had yet to track him down. A month later, he was arrested for assaulting his wife, who refused to press charges but did take out a restraining order and file for divorce.

Wanda's lawyers haven't announced their strategy yet, and there are rumors that they will enter a plea of incompetence. Wanda is a troubled, bruised personality who might have led a reasonably normal life if circumstances had not conspired to make her perceive a great wrong where none existed.

The biggest surprise for me came a week following the events in Braintree. Kristina Kwan called my office and asked if I could lunch with her. By then I was involved with a new project but my curiosity was roused and I agreed. We met at a quiet, pricey place on the East Side where I'd eaten once before, but they obviously knew Kwan by sight and took us directly to a secluded table.

After some banal small talk, we placed our orders and Kwan came right to the point. "There's a question you've wanted to ask me for a while, isn't there, Mr. Birch?"

I thought I knew what she was referring to. "I assume you watched over Wanda out of loyalty to Phyllis Reynolds."

"Yes, and not closely enough, obviously. But that's not the question I had in mind."

"It's none of my business," I said quietly.

"But you'd still like to know who Kari's real mother is." She was smiling slightly, sure of herself.

I had to concede the point. "Of course I would."

"Well, since I told Kari herself last night, I don't think the secret needs to be kept any more. Kari is my daughter, Mr. Birch, and her father was Walter Spencer."

I had half expected the first part, but the rest caught me by surprise. My first reaction was disbelief, but then I remembered that her relationship to Walter had been ruled out by a blood test, not DNA. If Kwan was the mother, the results would have been entirely different. I must have looked as startled as I felt because she laughed at me. "You should feel flattered. You're only the third person to know the truth."

"But how is that possible?" I tried to remember the timing of events, but it was all a fog.

"When Phyllis got pregnant and Walter admitted being the father, I was understandably furious. I threw him out of the apartment and didn't speak to him for almost a year, by which time we were no longer married. But partway through the proceedings, I discovered that I was pregnant. I thought about getting rid of the child, but it was much more difficult in those days, and I had moral qualms, so despite my aversion to the role of mother, I let the pregnancy proceed. Kari was in fact born two days before the divorce was final."

"But how did you keep the others from finding out?"

"I went to Italy for several months, supposedly to mope about Walter's infidelity. When I returned, I quietly arranged a meeting with Walter's sister. She was unable to have a child of her own but she'd been putting off applying through an agency because she was aware of the length and complexity of the process. And it might have revealed her husband's gambling problems. I told her that I knew of an undocumented child who could be processed through the system rapidly. It didn't take much to persuade her; we were friends. Of course, I convinced her not to tell Walter of my involvement because of our recent estrangement. As far as I know, she never did."

I shook my head. "Then Wanda was wrong and Spencer was right. Kari really was his daughter."

Kwan sat back and sipped at her martini. "Yes, they both were. They're half sisters."

"So why are you coming clean after all of these years?"

She dropped her eyes and her voice grew sad. "I've realized how potentially dangerous secrets like that really are. If Wanda had known the truth from the outset, none of this would have happened."

"You're not responsible for what she did."

"No, but I'm partly responsible for what she is. I can never forget that."

"How did Kari react?"

Her face fell slightly. "She's not overjoyed. I've tried to influence her a few times in the past, and I'm afraid she decided I was a meddlesome and unfaithful friend of her uncle. It will take a while to gain her trust, but I intend to make the effort."

We talked some more, but the important things had already been said.

Dusty and I reached our second anniversary together and we're as comfortable with each other as we were at the start. Even Darla has finally accepted her, although she still sleeps on my side of the bed. I take this all as a very good sign. Her spy thriller didn't do well enough to justify a sequel, so the dining room table has remained just a dining room table since then, but she's working on the plot for what she tells me will be a "really over the top" horror novel, so I come home each day wondering what scene of carnage might be waiting for me.

But as long as it's make believe, dead bodies don't bother me.